Praise For Donna Andrews
And Her Meg Langslow Mysteries

COCKATIELS AT SEVEN

"Suspense, laughter and a whole passel of good clean fun."
—Publishers Weekly

"More fun than seven cocktails—and a lot safer, too."
—Richmond Times-Dispatch

"The plot, in true 'You Can't Take It With You' fashion, involves plenty of snakes, as well as the titular cockatiels and assorted exotic birds. The author has a fine sense of pacing and a droll...sense of humor. This is character-driven fiction, and Andrews maintains the action within the confines and sensibilities of her town-and-gown setting." *—The State* (Columbia, SC)

THE PENGUIN WHO KNEW TOO MUCH

"Deliciously daffy."
—Publishers Weekly (starred review)

"Andrews always leavens the mayhem with laughs. So march yourself down to the bookstore or library and check out *The Penguin Who Knew Too Much*."
—Richmond Times-Dispatch

"Andrews' eighth Meg-centric mystery moves along like the best beach reads." *—Entertainment Weekly*

MORE...

"The level-headed, unflappable Meg takes it all in stride…This eighth cozy in the series makes the most of humorous situations, zany relatives, and lovable characters."   —*Booklist*

NO NEST FOR THE WICKET

"Fun, lively, charming."   —*Publishers Weekly*

"Andrews strikes just the right balance between comedy and suspense to keep the reader laughing and on the edge of one's seat…Fans of this series will no doubt enjoy this installment, while new readers…will be headed to the bookstore for the earlier books."
                          —*Romantic Times BOOKreviews* (4 stars)

"Any day when I start reading about Meg is cause for delight. Ending the book makes me yearn for more than one per year. Hint."   —*Deadly Pleasures*

"As usual, Andrews is a reliable source for those who like their murder with plenty of mayhem." —*Kirkus Reviews*

"Andrews's talent for the lovably loony makes this series a winner; to miss it would be a cardinal sin."
                                —*Richmond Times-Dispatch*

OWLS WELL THAT ENDS WELL

"A loony, utterly delightful affair."   —*Booklist*

"It's a hoot...a supporting cast of endearingly eccentric characters, perfectly pitched dialogue and a fine sense of humor make this a treat." —*Publishers Weekly*

"Death by yard sale epitomizes the 'everyday people' humor that Andrews does so well...for readers who prefer their mysteries light...Andrews may be the next best thing to Janet Evanovich."
　　　　　　　　　　　　　　　　—*Rocky Mountain News*

"Andrews delivers another wonderfully comic story....This is a fun read, as are all the books in the series. Andrews playfully creates laughable, wacky scenes that are the backdrop for her criminally devious plot. Settle back, dear reader, and enjoy another visit to Meg's anything-but-ordinary world."
　　　　　　　　　　　　—*Romantic Times* (starred review)

WE'LL ALWAYS HAVE PARROTS

"Laughter, more laughter, we need laughter, so Donna Andrews is giving us *We'll Always Have Parrots*...to help us survive February." —*Washington Times*

"Perfectly showcases Donna Andrews' gift for deadpan comedy." —*Denver Post*

"Always heavy on the humor, Andrews' most recent Meg Langslow outing is her most over-the-top adventure to date." —*Booklist*

"I can't say enough good things about this series, and this entry in it." —*Deadly Pleasures*

"Hilarious...another winner...keeps you turning pages." —*Mystery Lovers News*

CROUCHING BUZZARD, LEAPING LOON

"If you long for more 'fun' mysteries, à la Janet Evanovich, you'll love Donna Andrews's Meg Langslow series." —*Charlotte Observer*

"There's a smile on every page and at least one chuckle per chapter." —*Publishers Weekly*

"This may be the funniest installment of Andrews' wonderfully wacky series yet. It takes a deft hand to make slapstick or physical comedy appealing, yet Andrews masterfully manages it (the climax will have you in stitches.)" —*Romantic Times*

REVENGE OF THE WROUGHT-IRON FLAMINGOS

"At the top of the list. . . a fearless protagonist, remarkable supporting characters, lively action and a keen wit." —*Library Journal*

"What a light-hearted gem of a juggling act. . . with her trademark witty dialogue and fine sense of the ridiculous, Andrews keeps all her balls in the air with skill and verve." —*Publishers Weekly*

MURDER WITH PUFFINS

"Muddy trails, old secrets, and plenty of homespun humor." —*St. Petersburg Times*

"The well-realized island atmosphere, the puffin lore, and the ubiquitous birders only add to the fun." —*Denver Post*

MURDER WITH PEACOCKS

"The first novel is so clever, funny, and original that lots of wannabe authors will throw up their hands in envy and get jobs in a coffee shop." —*Contra Costa Times*

"Loquacious dialogue, persistent humor...a fun, breezy read." —*Library Journal*

"Half Jane Austen, half battery acid...will leave you helpless with heartless laughter ... Andrews combines murder and madcap hilarity with a cast of eccentric oddballs in a small Southern town." —*Kirkus Reviews*

"Andrews's debut provides plenty of laughs for readers who like their mysteries on the cozy side." —*Publishers Weekly*

St. Martin's Paperbacks Titles by
DONNA ANDREWS

Cockatiels
at Seven

Donna Andrews

St. Martin's Paperbacks

This is a work of fiction. All of the characters, organizations, and events portrayed in this novel are either products of the author's imagination or are used fictitiously.

COCKATIELS AT SEVEN

Copyright © 2008 by Donna Andrews.
Excerpt from *Swan for the Money* copyright © 2009 by Donna Andrews.

For information address St. Martin's Press, 175 Fifth Avenue, New York, NY 10010.

Library of Congress Catalog Card Number 2008013626

ISBN: 0-312-37716-9
EAN: 978-0-312-37716-8

Printed in the United States of America

Minotaur hardcover edition / July 2008
St. Martin's Paperbacks edition / July 2009

St. Martin's Paperbacks are published by St. Martin's Press, 175 Fifth Avenue, New York, NY 10010.

10 9 8 7 6 5 4 3 2 1

Acknowledgments

Authors are apt to compare their books to children—and like children, books often require a small village's worth of people to bring them into existence. I'd like to thank . . .

All the folks at St. Martin's Minotaur, who publish the book to begin with, and then work diligently to get it into readers' hands. I owe a debt of gratitude to Andrew Martin, Pete Wolverton, Hector DeJean, Lauren Manzella, Toni Plummer, and especially my editor, Ruth Cavin, who plucked Meg's first adventure out of the entries to that year's Malice Domestic/St. Martin's Press Best First Traditional Mystery contest and said "Yes!"

My agent, Ellen Geiger, and the staff of the Frances Goldin Literary Agency, who take care of the business side of things so I can focus on the writing; to the staff at Curtis-Brown, especially Dave Barbor, who helps make Meg international.

My name twin, Donna Andrews of Maryland, who graciously offered to help with the proofing.

My writing group, the Rector Lane Irregulars, for many evenings of critique, cheerleading, and friendship: Carla Coupe, Ellen Crosby, Laura Durham, Peggy

Hanson, Val Patterson, Noreen Wald, and Sandi Wilson. And the other friends who read drafts, listen to me brainstorm, and generally provide moral support: Kathy Deligianis, Suzanne Frisbee, David Niemi, Dina Willner, and all the Teabuds.

The friends who let me borrow their canine friends: Barb Goffman for Scout, Suzanne Frisbee for Paris and Julie, and Tracey Young and Bill Sommers for the inimitable Spike.

My family, for being not nearly as much like Meg's family as most people think. And especially my nephews, Aidan Jay Andrews and Liam Stuart Andrews, who helped inspire Timmy and even let me borrow Kiki.

One

"Meg, are you busy?" Dad asked.

I didn't turn around. The iron rod heating in my forge was approaching white hot, which meant it was the perfect temperature for working. So instead of answering, I gripped the rod with my tongs, pulled it out, slapped it onto the anvil with a satisfying clang, and began hammering one end into a point. Okay, I confess, I showboated a bit, just to emphasize how very busy I was. I worked faster than I normally would, with just a little flourish as I turned the rod, left, right, left, right, over and over, shaping the point. Then I moved an inch and a half back and began shaping and narrowing another area.

When I'd done as much as I could without heating the metal again, I plunged the rod abruptly into the water bucket, sending up a cloud of faintly acrid steam. I closed my eyes as I breathed in the familiar, strangely soothing odor. Or maybe it wasn't the odor I found soothing. When you're feeling annoyed, whacking things with a two-pound hammer works infinitely better than counting to ten.

"Yeah," I said. "I'm busy." I turned to see both Dad

and Dr. Blake standing in the doorway of the barn where I'd set up my smithy. Technically, I was allowed to call Dr. Blake "Grandpa" now that the DNA tests had proved he was Dad's long-lost father, but that would take some getting used to, so for the moment I went to great lengths not to call him anything at all.

I pulled the iron rod out of the bucket, held it up and sighted along the shaft. The end I'd been working on had now taken on a shape like a rough spear point. I smiled at the smooth, flat surfaces, with just enough faint dimpling to prove that they had been hammered on a forge rather than poured in some factory. Nice work, if I did say so myself. And a good start on having a productive Monday morning.

"That's not finished, is it?" Dr. Blake asked.

My mellow mood evaporated.

"No, of course not," I said.

"What is it?" he asked. "Some kind of primitive boar spear?"

"A towel rod. This is only step one of a five- or six-step process. When it's finished, it will look like this."

I strode over to the section of the barn where I stored completed work and picked up a towel rod made of a single iron bar hammered into a graceful curve with a curling leaf on each end.

"The part that looks like a spear point is what I'm going to turn into the leaf on this end," I said.

"Oh, I understand," Blake said, in a falsely hearty tone that suggested he didn't understand at all.

"She sold a pair of those to the governor!" Dad said.

"Lieutenant governor, actually," I said. "And it was his wife doing the shopping."

"Nice," Blake said. I suppressed a sigh. I could tell he was trying, but since my work had nothing to do with zoology or the preservation of endangered species, his own particular obsessions, he was having a hard time.

"Still," Blake went on. "Think of all the time you could save if you could find a way to automate some of those steps. You could make ten times as many iron doodads in the same time. And more cheaply, I expect."

"That's not the point," I said. "It's handmade. It's not like every cookie-cutter towel bar you can buy down at the hardware store. Every one is unique."

"Unique, handmade—I suppose they're nice, but look how labor-intensive this is."

"Yes," I said. "It's labor-intensive. Like taking care of the animals down at your zoo. Think of all the time you could save if you just freeze-dried and stuffed them all. No need for feedings several times a day, cleaning the cages, hauling them to and from the vet—just dust them off every few weeks. You could probably take care of ten times as many animals with the same staff. And more cheaply."

"That's not the point," Blake said.

"So you're busy, then?" Dad asked—probably to change the subject and keep the peace. Blake was frowning at me. Did he disapprove of my sarcasm? Surely he didn't think I was serious about taxidermying the zoo's inhabitants?

"Very busy," I said. "The cupboard is nearly bare." I

swept my arm in a dramatic half circle to indicate how very large the storage end of the barn was, and then fixed my gaze on the pitifully small pile of finished metalwork in one corner.

"Oh, dear," Dad said, shaking his head in sympathy.

"And I'm scheduled to do that really big craft show over the Labor Day weekend," I said. "Only three weeks away. What with all the distractions I've had this summer, I haven't had nearly as much time to work as I thought I would."

"Hmph!" Blake snorted. "Does young Michael know you consider your wedding and honeymoon distractions?"

I ignored him.

"We won't bother you, then," Dad said. "But can we use your shed?"

"Which one?" I asked. "And for what?" The three-acre property Michael and I had bought contained not only an enormous Victorian house and a two-story barn but also a bumper crop of small sheds and outbuildings in various states of disintegration.

"Any one you're not using," Dad said. "Don't you want us to tell you about our project?"

He sounded eager. I suspected the tale would be an interminable one.

"Later," I said. "Pick a shed as far from the house as possible." If both Dad and Dr. Blake were involved, they almost certainly wanted the shed for some project related to birds or animals from the small local zoo that Blake had recently bought. "Downwind, if that's likely to be a problem. And I'm not doing any midnight feedings."

"Oh, of course not," Dad said. "Thanks!"

Blake nodded his thanks and dashed off without speaking. Dad lingered.

"Something else?" I asked.

"He doesn't mean to be insulting," Dad said.

"No, but he manages it quite brilliantly."

"It would help if you'd show an interest in some of his projects," Dad said.

"There's a difference between showing an interest and letting him take over my life," I said. "Like those orphaned wolverine cubs he tried to foist off on me."

"Wolverines are really quite sweet at that age."

"And require feeding every hour with an eyedropper," I said. "No thanks. I'm letting you use one of the sheds—try to convince him that's a sign of profound interest in whatever you two are doing."

Dad shook his head and followed Dr. Blake.

I picked up the iron rod and stuck it back in the forge.

It had barely begun to redden when my brother Rob ambled into the forge holding a leash.

"Hey, Meg," he said. "Mind if I borrow Spike?"

"I don't mind if you take him off our hands permanently," I said. Technically Spike, an eight-and-a-half-pound furball with delusions of Rottweilerhood, belonged to my mother-in-law, but Michael and I had had custody ever since her allergist recommended a trial separation. We'd grown used to having him around, but I still cherished the forlorn hope that someone else would grow profoundly attached to Spike and insist on adopting him. So far, Rob was the only possible candidate, and Rob wasn't responsible enough to be trusted with a pet rock.

"No, I just want him for the afternoon." Rob strolled over to the indoor pen where Spike usually snoozed while I worked, and climbed over the fence.

"Just don't let anything happen to him or Michael's mother will kill you," I said, turning back to my forge.

"No problem." I heard the small scuffle as he cornered Spike and a muffled ouch as he failed to avoid getting bitten. I was pulling the hot iron rod out by the time he led Spike through the gate. He stopped to watch.

I didn't rush it this time, because I was performing the slightly more complicated job of spreading the point at the end of the rod and working it into a rough leaf shape. Sometimes it took me two heatings to finish the transformation, but I was in good form today. I finished the leaf, plunged it into the water bucket, and drew it out to examine.

"That's so cool," Rob said.

"Thanks," I said. I sloshed a dipper full of water over the rod, to cool the parts that had been above the water line. My good mood was returning.

"I could never do that in a million years. I think you're so lucky to have a creative outlet."

I frowned slightly. Rob didn't usually lay it on this thick unless he had an ulterior motive.

"Something else you wanted?" I asked.

"No—what do you mean?"

From the expression of utter innocence on his face, I deduced that Rob did, indeed, want something, but had decided now was not the right time to ask me.

Just then Spike lunged toward the forge, barking

wildly. He hated all large mechanical objects, but seemed to feel a particular antipathy for my forge. Perhaps the faint roaring noise it made sounded like growling to him. We'd built his holding pen after the third time he'd nearly flambéed himself while trying to attack the forge.

"Go find something his own size for Spike to pick on," I said. As Rob and Spike sauntered out, I thrust the rod back into the forge for the third time. Should I start heating another rod or two? It was more efficient to have several pieces going at once, working on one while the others were in various stages of heating. No, I decided I'd rather work up to a good rhythm before I started to multitask. After all, I had all day. Michael was at the college, attending more of the interminable faculty meetings that filled the weeks before Labor Day and everyone else who wanted me for anything would just have to take "I'm busy" for an answer.

I pulled the rod out, picked up the cross peen hammer, and began the next—and nearly final—step of leafmaking: the precise strokes that flattened the iron and gave the impression of the veining that ran through the leaf. Again, I managed the job in a single heating— I was definitely in good form today. I held up the leaf and was nodding with satisfaction when—

"Oh, Meg! Thank God you're here! I need your help!"

I jumped and accidentally hit the leaf with my hammer. The metal was in that awkward stage, still hot enough to cause third degree burns, but not hot enough to be flexible. The leaf cracked off and dropped to the ground, landing on a few leaves and bits of straw that sizzled when it touched them. I grabbed the dipper and doused the area before looking up at my newest inter-rupter.

I saw a petite, plump woman with short, blond hair in a pixie cut, wearing jeans and a pale blue t-shirt with a faded Caerphilly College logo. She looked vaguely fa-miliar, but it took me several embarrassingly long mo-ments of gaping and peering to come up with a name.

"Karen?" I said finally. "I didn't recognize you with the new haircut." The last time I'd seen her, she could sit down on the end of her long, thick, wavy blond mane. The fact that she'd gained a good thirty pounds since our last meeting didn't help with recognition either.

"Oh, I know," she said, ruffling the hair with a sheepish look. "Ever since I had Timmy, I just couldn't seem to find the time to take care of it."

I nodded. Odds were Timmy was also the reason for the thirty pounds, not that I was going to mention it. Just because I was currently winning the diet battle didn't mean I couldn't understand someone who was having a harder time.

"And then when Jasper ran out on us, I decided the hell with it. I'm going to make things easier for me, and never mind what some man thinks of my hair."

"Right," I said, nodding. Jasper had run out on Karen and baby Timmy? Had I forgotten that, or had it been longer than I remembered since I'd seen Karen?

Apparently I didn't do a very good job of concealing my surprise.

"I'll tell you all about it later," she said. "But right now—could you do me a big favor?"

"Sure," I said. "If I can."

"Could you take care of Timmy? Just for a little while? I need to do something without him along. And my day care lady had to go out of town yesterday because of a death in the family and there just isn't anyone else I can trust. Don't worry; he won't be any trouble; he's a little angel. Wait; I'll show you."

She dashed out the door and then returned, pushing a large stroller. A blond toddler was asleep in it. His mouth was stained with chocolate and he was clutching a small green blanket and a ratty black stuffed toy.

"Isn't he adorable?" She smoothed a lock of his hair that hadn't been out of place.

Yes, he was adorable. Of course, he was also fast asleep. Even Spike looked adorable while asleep. And it must have been longer than I thought since I'd last seen Karen. Timmy was much bigger than I expected. At least two years old. Maybe three if he was small for his age. My youngest nephew was twelve now, but I remembered what he and his siblings had been like at that age. Angelic wouldn't exactly be the word I'd choose to describe them.

"I know it's an imposition," Karen said. I looked up to find her staring at my face with an expression of desperation, almost panic. "There just isn't anyone else I can trust. Meg, please, take care of Timmy for me."

"Of course," I said. "But what's going on, anyway? You seem—"

"Timmy, honey!" Karen said. I glanced down to see that Timmy had awakened.

"You remember Aunt Meg, don't you, Timmy?" Karen cooed.

I didn't think it likely, myself, and Timmy didn't

waste much time trying to place me. His bright little eyes were already busily exploring the surroundings and he was squirming as if the rest of him couldn't wait to follow.

I glanced around and felt a sharp twinge of protective anxiety about my workspace. "Let's go up to the house," I said. "This really isn't the best place to turn a kid loose."

"Good idea," Karen said. The protectiveness on her face was aimed at Timmy, but at least we saw eye to eye about the fact that Timmy and my blacksmithing tools were not a match made in heaven.

"Let me shut things down here and I'll join you," I said. As Karen wheeled Timmy out, I turned off the gas to my forge and looked from it to my still depleted stock of merchandise.

"Just for a little while," I said, echoing Karen's words. I allowed myself to feel a moment of resentment that something was interrupting me just as I was finally settling down to do some real work.

But a shriek from outside broke into my moment of self pity, and I rushed out to see what was wrong.

Two

"Don't worry," Dad was saying. "It's perfectly safe."

Karen wasn't still shrieking, but she was clutching Timmy with a fierce grip and staring at Dr. Blake, who had a six-foot green snake draped over his shoulders. Timmy, now released from the stroller, was staring at the snake with rapt attention. For that matter, so was Karen, but she didn't look nearly as happy as Timmy did.

"It's an Emerald Tree Boa," Dad said. "They're not poisonous. They grab their prey and swallow it alive."

Karen clutched Timmy a little harder.

"Don't worry," Dr. Blake said. "She rarely eats anything larger than a squirrel. And she ate only two days ago. She's still busy digesting that meal."

"And she lives at the zoo," I said. "Why is she digesting over here instead of in her own pen, and how quickly will she be going home to digest in peace and quiet? You know how Mother feels about having snakes around the house."

"She's having a very difficult shed," Dad said. "We need to help her through it, so we brought her over here to keep an eye on while we're working."

"Of course, if you suffer from ophidiphobia," Blake said. "That's—"

"I know—fear of snakes," I said. "No, I have no problem with reptiles, but if you value your tree boa, I'd keep a good grip on her. Because I bet Timmy would love to play with a snake—"

"'nake!" Timmy echoed.

"—and do you have any idea how rough toddlers are on things?"

"No, Timmy," Karen said. "Ouch-ouch-ouch! No snake!"

"Want 'nake!" Timmy muttered, a little rebelliously. In fact, I saw him take a deep breath, as if he had a lot more to say on the subject and didn't plan to let anyone interrupt him. Fortunately, Dad and Dr. Blake swung into action and provided a distraction.

Dad picked up a large cotton sack, dampened it with a watering can, and held it open so Dr. Blake could insert the snake. The snake writhed quite dramatically, so it took several tries before they finally got her into the sack.

"What's that you're putting her in?" I asked.

"Snake bag," Dr. Blake said, as he tied the top of the bag. "The moisture will help loosen the skin, and as she writhes around in the bag, the friction of the coarse material will help rub it off."

The snake was still thrashing about quite energetically inside the bag, which bulged and flowed like a giant brown canvas amoeba.

"What if she gets out of the bag?" Karen asked.

"Don't worry—we'll put her in a safe place."

Dad had finished tying a double knot at the mouth of

the bag, and Dr. Blake took hold of the other end and helped him carry it to the safe place—our newly completed and as-yet empty hot tub.

"Michael and I were planning on using that," I protested. "He's having a long day of meetings and he'll need to relax when he gets home."

For that matter, I had been looking forward to a good soak to ease the sore muscles I'd planned on having after a day of hard work. And while it didn't look as if I would be getting much blacksmithing done, I still might end up with the sore muscles, depending on what kinds of trouble I had to haul Timmy out of.

"If the boa's still here when Michael gets home, you could always move him to one of your bathtubs," Blake said, over his shoulder. He was striding off, already focused on his next project.

"I hope you weren't planning to bring a bunch of snakes over here," I told Dad. "Because Karen was going to leave Timmy here with me for a little while, and I don't think she'd feel all that comfortable if the place is going to be swarming with snakes."

Of course, while I wasn't fond of snakes, I would feel more philosophical about their presence if they made Karen change her mind about entrusting little Timmy to my care.

"Oh, no," he said. "No other snakes; and we'll only have this one here for a few hours. And don't you worry," he added, turning to Karen. "I'll make sure Dr. Blake doesn't bring over any dangerous animals."

"Or birds or reptiles?" I asked.

"No dangerous creatures at all," Dad said. "Timmy, would you like to meet the llamas?"

He held out his hand. After inspecting him for a few moments, Timmy decided that Dad was okay. He threw his green blanket over his shoulder like a serape and toddled off, with one hand in Dad's and the other clutching the stuffed animal. Which I'd decided was probably a cat.

"He'll be fine with Dad for a few minutes," I said. "Now what is going on with—"

"That's great!" Karen exclaimed. She turned and began walking briskly—almost running—toward the front of the house. I jogged along, trying to keep up. "As soon as I get back, I'll tell you all about what I've been doing for—my goodness, it must be a year or two since we've really had a chance to talk!"

She reached the opening in the hedge and stopped for a moment, looking slightly nervous. Then she stuck her head out and gazed in both directions before venturing out from behind the hedge. Her reluctance to leave the shelter of the shrubbery let me catch up with her.

"Look, is there anything particular I should know? About taking care of Timmy, or—"

"Of course," she said, digging into her suitcase-sized purse and pulling out a thick wad of paper. "I almost forgot to give you this. It's got everything you should need—meals, nap schedules, his pediatrician's name and number—just in case of emergencies."

I took the papers and blinked with surprise. Timmy came with a fatter instruction manual than most appliances. And did she keep this care and feeding guide around all the time in case of emergencies? It wasn't the sort of thing you dashed off in five minutes. If she had done it especially for me, then dropping by without notice to entrust me with Timmy wasn't exactly a sudden, last minute decision.

"I left everything you should need in your front hall," she said. "And you can call if you have any questions. My cell number's there. Oh, Meg, you can't imagine how grateful I am!"

She gave me a quick hug, climbed into a battered sedan so old it probably qualified as a classic car, and drove off at least ten miles per hour above the speed limit.

"Now that was odd," I said, to no one in particular. "What was she so worried about?"

I scanned the landscape. Since we lived fifteen miles outside the tiny college town of Caerphilly, Virginia, there weren't generally a lot of pedestrians on hand to observe our guests' comings and goings. Nor did our road see a lot of cars. We were sandwiched in between Seth Early's sheep farm, across the road from our house, and the farm Mother and Dad had recently bought, which surrounded us on the other three sides. If you kept driving beyond our house, you'd pass three or four other farms, a small ramshackle motel that had been converted into furnished apartments, and a largely empty offsite storage establishment before the road dead-ended a few miles away at Caerphilly Creek. Not exactly a landscape that made most people nervous.

I was turning to go back to the house—or more likely, back to the pasture, to make sure Timmy was enjoying playtime with the llamas—when my cell phone rang. It was Michael.

"I'm sure you will be shocked to know that this year's incoming freshmen have no memory of a life without cell phones and personal computers."

"And they have no idea that Paul McCartney was in a band before Wings," I said.

"You're behind the times. These days they have no idea McCartney was ever in a band at all." He was trying to sound cheerful, but his voice had that slightly frayed quality it usually had when he'd been spending too much time in small rooms with his fellow faculty members.

"Take heart," I said. "Won't being tenured give you the freedom to play hooky from a lot of these summer indoctrination sessions next year?"

"But that's next year. And it's assuming I get tenure—".

"Which you said was looking good."

"But it won't happen till spring. It doesn't help much when you're immersed in the minutiae of academia. But speaking of immersing, I can't tell you how much I'm looking forward to relaxing in the hot tub this evening."

Dad had said the boa constrictor would only be there for a few hours. What were the odds she'd still be there when Michael got home? Should I mention the possibility?

And for that matter, would Timmy still be around? What exactly did Karen mean by "just a little while?"

"Meg? Is something wrong?"

"No," I said. "Remember how disappointed you were that all my nieces and nephews were visiting their Australian grandparents this summer? How you said summer wasn't really summer without having some kids around to help you enjoy it?"

"Meg! Are you trying to break the news that you're—"

"No," I said. "But knowing how you feel about kids, I thought you'd be pleased that at the moment we have a loaner child. A two-year-old, or thereabouts. He might still be around by the time you get home."

"That's great!" he said. "Wait till you see how much fun the farm is for a toddler!"

"If Timmy's still around, you probably won't have much time to loll in the hot tub this evening," I went on. "So I suppose it's okay that Dad and Dr. Blake are storing a boa constrictor in it at the moment."

As I'd expected, there was a brief pause before Michael answered.

"Obviously you're having a much more interesting day than I am," he said. "With all that going on, dare I hope that you might arrange to have some kind of emergency this afternoon? Something that would urgently require my presence?"

"I could plan on it if you like."

"Two o'clock would be ideal. That's when they start our diversity training session."

"I'll see if I can work up a good case of ophidipho-bia by two," I said. "That's—"

"Fear of snakes, I know," Michael said. "Later, then. Love you."

I was a little distracted as I hung up. I had spotted someone lurking in the bushes at the edge of Seth Early's sheep pasture—not in itself alarming, since Mr. Early often lurked there himself. I wasn't quite sure if he was lying in wait to capture the thieves he believed were just waiting for the opportunity to steal his sheep, or to catch a glimpse of my cousin, Rose Noire, with whom he was smitten. I paused a moment to wave when he popped over the hedge again, and then spotted an unfamiliar figure running away.

Definitely not Seth Early, who was tall and lanky and almost always encased in denim. This lurker was short and stocky and wore a dark blue or navy track suit with a white stripe down the pants seam. Not the best choice for doing surveillance, since the white gleam of the stripe let me track his progress as he scuttled along behind the hedge and then disappeared over a small hill.

How odd. I opened my cell phone up again and called Mr. Early. Who was his usual taciturn self.

"Yeah," he said, by way of a greeting.

"Hi, this is Meg Langslow," I said. "I just wanted you to know that some guy was lurking in your pasture. He seemed more interested in watching our house than your sheep, and he ran away when he realized I'd spotted him, but I thought you'd like to know."

"Thanks," Mr. Early said, with a hint of genuine warmth in his tone. "I'll check the perimeter. Let me know if you spot him again."

"Roger," I said. "And let us know if you learn anything."

"Right."

I felt a little guilty—I didn't really think the intruder had designs on the Early sheep. But it never hurt to be careful, and Mr. Early seemed to enjoy checking the perimeter. His bark was worse than his bite, especially since Chief Burke had forbidden him to carry around his shotgun, so he wasn't any danger to innocent passersby. And odds were the man I'd seen was innocent—a shy birdwatcher, or a motorist whose bladder couldn't last till the next service station.

But just in case he was watching our house . . . what if it was Jasper, or someone he had hired to do surveillance on Karen? Karen really hadn't told me much about her marital status. Was she divorced, or merely separated, and was there some kind of child custody battle? I knew from talking to my cousin Horace, who worked for the sheriff's office in my hometown, how nasty custody battles could get.

I pulled out Timmy's instruction manual and dialed Karen's cell phone number.

No answer. I left a message. No answer on her home phone, so I left another message there.

Odd. If I'd just entrusted my toddler to a friend I hadn't seen for a couple of years—a friend who had little experience taking care of small children—I'd have the cell phone not only on but actually in my hand, so I could answer before the end of the first ring. Or was that just me? Me worrying not only about taking care of Timmy, but also about the whole angst-ridden subject of Michael and I starting our own family. Not something most people begin worrying about within a few months of getting married, when they're still getting used to wedded life, but since Michael and I were both well along in our thirties, we knew we didn't have unlimited time to dawdle. But were we really ready? Specifically, was I really ready?

Not something I had time to think of right now. I

shoved the cell phone back into my pocket and set out for the llama pasture, making plans as I went.

According to Timmy's instruction manual, he was supposed to have lunch at eleven. No chance of getting back to work in my forge for the time being, but I might get a few other things done if I could enlist Dad and Dr. Blake to give Timmy some zoology lessons until lunch. After lunch he was supposed to nap for a couple of hours, and surely Karen would be back by the time he woke up.

Three

"Auntie Meg! Look at meeeee!"

I smiled and waved to indicate that yes, I was looking, then glanced at my watch. Past two. Six hours and
still counting. Timmy raced off to do another lap
around the yard, the bunch of balloons trailing behind
him. He wasn't anywhere near the pool. The Emerald
Tree Boa was still in the hot tub. All the Band-Aids I'd
put on Timmy's boo-boos, real or imaginary, were still
in place, though the oldest ones were getting pretty
filthy. Timmy had stopped asking every five minutes
when Mommy was coming back, though that didn't
mean he wasn't still wondering. I had Kiki, the stuffed
cat, at my side, so the next time Timmy realized he
wasn't holding his beloved feline, I could probably pop
her into his hands before he got too worked up. Kiki
was also wearing Band-Aids on two of her paws,
though to me her boo-boos looked more like dirt and
stains than injuries. How would Timmy react if I suggested putting Kiki through the washer? Probably not
something I wanted to find out.

I glanced down at the stack of childcare manuals
my cousin, Rose Noire, had dropped off after lunch as

her contribution to Timmy's welfare. Perhaps after Karen had taken Timmy back I'd actually have time to read one.

But Michael would be home any time now. I leaned back in the lawn chair and reached for my cell phone.

"Isn't he cute?"

Even though I'd been expecting him, I started at Michael's voice. He planted a kiss on the top of my head and slumped into the adjacent lawn chair.

"Thank God you're home," I said.

"Is something wrong?" he asked, looking startled.

"Not at the moment," I said. "It's been at least an hour since we had to haul any more dangerous objects into the barn."

"Dangerous objects?"

"Anything Timmy could hurt himself with, or anything we care about enough that we'd want to hurt him if he broke it. The barn is pretty full of dangerous objects. We may have to expand to one of the sheds."

"You sound a little frazzled," he said. "Have you been taking care of Timmy all by yourself?"

"No, Dad and Rob have been helping. But he wore them out. They both went off to rest while I was trying to get him to nap, and never came back. And everyone else is avoiding us, because they're afraid if they come near me, I'll make them haul more stuff into the barn. Or change a diaper."

"He's still in diapers? Isn't he a little old for that?"

"How should I know?" I said. "I'm not exactly sure when kids usually get toilet trained, and even if I was, I don't actually know how old Timmy is. I'm guessing two, two-and-a-half. Could be older if he's short for his age."

"Why don't you ask his mother—Kate, is it?"

"Karen. Walker—you know, my friend who works in the college financial administration office? I'd love to. She's not answering her phone. Hasn't been answering it all day. That's the real problem."

"When's she due back?"

"That's why I've been calling. She said 'just for a little while.' It's been over six hours. That's almost a whole working day. Under the circumstances, do you think six hours qualifies as 'just for a little while?' "

Michael made a sympathetic noise. At least I think it was a sympathetic noise. Maybe it was a whimper of dismay at learning that the woman he hoped to make the mother of his children wasn't quite the natural at child care as he would have liked.

"And you should see the mountain of stuff she left with him," I went on. "A dozen changes of clothes. A carton of over 100 diapers. Two sets of pajamas. A folding crib. A car seat. A whole bag full of books. What if 'just for a little while' means just for a year or two while she runs off to Bali to find herself like Rose Noire did a couple of years ago?"

"Don't worry," Michael said. "I'm sure 'just for a little while' doesn't really mean overnight—she probably just brought the pajamas in case whatever she's doing took a little longer than planned. The way you bring an umbrella even if there's only a slight chance of rain. Just what is she doing, by the way?"

"She didn't say. And it didn't seem important for 'just a little while,' but after six hours, I want to know."

I hit the speed-dial button I'd assigned to Karen's cell phone and put it on speaker. Michael and I both stared at the phone as it rang unanswered twelve times before the phone company's generic answering message kicked in.

"Chase me, Auntie Meg! Chase me!" Timmy shrieked, and began running around our lawn chairs.

"Not again," I muttered. I began levering myself out of the chair.

"Relax; I'll chase him for a while," Michael said.

"Timmy, Michael's going to chase you," I said.

Timmy took off. Clearly, a track and field scholarship was a strong possibility for him in another fourteen or fifteen years. Maybe even cross-country. And Michael was much more enthusiastic about chasing than I was, and did a better job at it.

Of course, he'd only been here five minutes. Give it time.

I leaned back and closed my eyes.

My cell phone rang. Not Karen, alas. But a useful call, nevertheless. Dad, reporting in on a sleuthing mission I'd assigned him.

"No sign of her in any of the nearby hospitals," he said. "And Sammy hasn't heard anything useful, either." Since Sammy was in the Caerphilly County police force, with access to all the local scoop about accidents and arrests, this was useful news. At least Karen probably hadn't gone straight from our road to a hospital, jail, or morgue.

"Thanks," I said. "Let me know if you hear anything."

"I'll keep my ears open. Bye." He was probably already doing more than keeping his ears open. He was probably badgering all sorts of people for information.

Mother and Dad had only recently bought the farm next door—partly to save it from development and partly so he and Mother could have a pied-à-terre near any grandchildren Michael and I might produce. And they weren't there full time—Mother liked to refer to it as their summer place, though I suspected they'd find an excuse to visit any time of the year that something interesting was going on here. But already, Dad was more securely plugged into the local grapevine than Michael and I ever would be. So if there was anything to be learned about Karen's whereabouts, Dad would find it, and if there wasn't—well, at least people would be keeping an eye out for her.

"Horsie-horsie! Horsie-horsie!"

I glanced up to see that Michael was giving Timmy a piggyback ride. Timmy had worn out five human steeds so far this afternoon—me, Dad, Rob, and two cousins unlucky enough to drop by for a visit. I wondered how long Michael would last.

Four

Michael either enjoyed Timmy's company or pretended to, freeing me to clean up some of the chaos our little visitor had created in the house and start thinking about dinner. A good ten seconds of thought convinced me that with Timmy underfoot and the thermometer hovering near ninety, cooking was not a sensible option. I placed a carryout order for pizza and Greek salad at Luigi's, our favorite local restaurant, and convinced Rob to pick up the food. Actually, it didn't take much convincing, partly because Rob had never met a pizza he didn't adore, and partly because he suspected he'd get drafted to help with Timmy if he didn't make the pizza run.

As usual, I ordered enough food to feed at least twice as many people as I was expecting. Not surprisingly, Mother, Dad, Rose Noire, and Dr. Blake appeared shortly after Rob and the food arrived—though they claimed to be less interested in the food than in taking advantage of the wide-screen TV Dad had given us for Christmas and the satellite system that had been Rob's housewarming gift.

"My new special is on *Animal Planet* tonight," Dr.

Blake announced. "The latest one in the 'Animals at Risk' series."

"Oh, those are the shows where you rescue different animals that are being tortured or exploited, aren't they?" Rose Noire asked. "I'm not even sure you should be showing that kind of violence. Especially not to impressionable minds," she added, nodding toward Timmy.

I closed my eyes and sighed, hoping she and Dr. Blake wouldn't start another of their arguments. For two people who both loved animals as much as they did, they could certainly find a remarkable number of animal-related issues to disagree about.

But to my relief, instead of staying to argue, Rose Noire volunteered to take Timmy off our hands while the rest of us ate. Of course, everyone else went running outside as soon as they heard the ghastly moans coming from the backyard.

"Relax," I called after them. "Rose Noire is trying to teach him to meditate."

"To meditate?" Michael said, pausing in the doorway. "That horrible noise is meditating?"

"She's chanting 'om,'" I explained. "That's Timmy's version of om."

He went to look anyway, and then came trooping back sheepishly with the others when he discovered that no one was being tortured. Well, perhaps Rose Noire was, but she was gritting her teeth and enduring it.

Everyone else still flinched when a particularly heart-rending groan resounded from the yard. I found myself wondering if I'd discovered an important truth normally revealed only to actual parents: that you can find even the most horrible racket soothing if it's far enough away and demonstrates that the child responsible is still perfectly healthy.

Still, I wasn't sorry when Dad and Dr. Blake offered to take a turn amusing Timmy after dinner. And I felt positively mellow when Mother took Rob and Rose Noire off to do the dishes.

"Meg has had a difficult day," Mother said.

I leaned back, poured myself another glass of wine, and savored being alone with Michael for the first time all day.

"You did have a difficult day," he said. "I'm sorry."

"Not your fault," I said. "Not even Timmy's fault. Karen, now—when she finally turns up, I have a bone to pick with her."

"What if she doesn't turn up until sometime tomorrow?"

"We've already taken that possibility into account," I said. "Remember, the mountain of equipment she left included a portable crib. I set it up in the bedroom next to ours at naptime. We hauled the rest of his stuff up there for the time being—it was in the way down here in the hall."

"So he'll be fine tonight," Michael said. "But tomorrow?"

My stomach suddenly tightened, and I pushed my glass away. What if she didn't turn up tomorrow? What if she never turned up at all? What if she had dumped Timmy on us before disappearing as completely as Amelia Earhart and Jimmy Hoffa? The mountain of equipment had also included a bag containing a Timmy-sized snowsuit and two matched knitted hat and mitten sets.

"I'll manage tomorrow," I said. "I just hope everyone who helped with Timmy today doesn't get wise and disappear."

"Maybe your mother could help."

"Mother? Are you crazy?" I had to chuckle at the idea, and my stomach unclenched a bit. I tried another sip of wine.

"Well, she's done it before, hasn't she?" Michael said. "I know it's been quite a while since she's taken care of a toddler—"

"Meaning quite a while since I was a toddler? Gee, thanks."

"Actually I was only thinking about the ten years or so since your nieces and nephews were toddlers."

"Good save. But no, Mother was never a hands-on grandmother. For that matter, she was never a hands-on mother. She doesn't do childcare—she delegates."

"You mean you had nannies?"

"No, but we always had two or three needy relatives living with us. Aunts or cousins who were going through what the family euphemistically calls 'a bad patch.' A messy divorce, a complicated bankruptcy, something like that. They did the diapers and midnight feedings and potty training—anything messy or strenuous."

Considering the look on Michael's face, I decided not to tell him about Cousin Alice, the relative who had spent the most time taking care of me during my first three or four years. Even though it was justifiable homicide and she'd served her time, I sensed he wouldn't react well.

"So your mother didn't actually do anything?" he asked.

"She was an early adopter of the 'it takes a village'

approach to child-rearing. With Mother in the all-important role of lady of the manor. She supervised."

"That's it?"

"If you're wondering, I don't think it's ideal, and it's not how I'd approach parenthood, but it worked pretty well. Pam and Rob and I didn't turn out too warped, did we? Well, Pam and I, at least. And you can probably put down Rob's eccentricities as much to heredity as environment."

"It's . . . different," he said. "And it does rather explain a few things."

"Such as?"

"Well, it explains why you're not bothered by Rob moving in."

"Moving in where? Here? You're joking, right?"

"He hasn't formally moved in—no mail forwarding or anything. But he has started leaving a bunch of his stuff in one of the bedrooms on the third floor."

"You're serious. How long has this been going on?"

"Couple of weeks. It wasn't till this week he brought over the sleeping bag. He probably doesn't realize anyone noticed."

I closed my eyes and counted to ten. I knew Rob wasn't happy at the run-down apartment building where he'd been living, and several times I'd suggested that I'd gladly help him look for a better place. If he'd gotten fed up with the Whispering Pines, why couldn't Rob just come out and ask if he could stay with us while he found new quarters? Since the house was several times larger than we could possibly need, his chances of guilt-tripping us into saying yes were probably near a hundred percent.

Unless his plan was just to move in and skip hunting for a new place altogether. Also a possibility. Why did everyone in my family have to sneak around and make things dramatic and complicated and—

"I'll talk to him," I said.

"I'm not saying it's a problem or anything, Rob being here," Michael said. "I just didn't want it to come as a big shock if you found out yourself."

"Good; so you won't mind if I don't kick him out immediately. He might come in handy with Timmy."

"He might come in handy generally," Michael said. And then, as if deciding he'd veered too close to the all-important subject of starting a family of our own, he chuckled and added, "If only to have someone willing to take care of Spike when we need a break."

Just then Rob came strolling in holding Timmy at arm's length.

"Knee Pompey," Timmy said. At least that's what it sounded like—I had no idea what he actually meant, though from his expression, Timmy clearly thought he was imparting critical information.

"He's starting to smell really bad," Rob said. "Here, take a whiff."

"I don't need to take a whiff," I said, holding out my hands to keep Rob from shoving Timmy's diapered bottom under my nose. "I can tell from here that he needs a new diaper."

"A diaper?" Rob repeated. He managed to give the impression that this was a new vocabulary word whose meaning he didn't quite comprehend.

I closed my eyes and took a deep breath before realizing that the calming effect of deep breathing wasn't nearly as effective downwind of a poopy diaper. I wasn't too fond of the diaper routine myself, and would really rather not do it right now, when we were about to cut the chocolate cake Dad had brought over. But some-one had to do it.

"There's a whole box of them up in his room," Mi-chael said. I opened my eyes to see that he had stood up and, wineglass in hand, was leading the way toward the stairs. "I'll show you how to do it so you'll know for next time."

Rob blinked a couple of times, then obediently fol-lowed Michael upstairs.

"I knew there was a reason I married him," I mur-mured as I listened to the diaper-changing lesson in progress upstairs and nibbled my cake.

I pulled out Timmy's instruction manual and checked my watch. It was seven-thirty. His normal bedtime was supposed to be eight. And surely, given the amount of exercise he'd had today, he'd be ready to sleep on time, wouldn't he? So since we already had him upstairs, I decided to go up and suggest that someone—me, if necessary—read him a few stories until he was ready to drop off to sleep.

Half an hour later, I'd read Timmy a couple of the Dr. Seuss books Karen had left as part of his baggage and Michael had told him several charming bedtime stories involving llamas or big noisy trucks. I was just tucking him in with Kiki clutched in one hand and Blanky in the other and whispering "night-night" when Rob strolled in.

"Hey," he said, in ordinary tone of voice that sounded like a bellow compared to the soothing, hushed tones

I'd been using. "Grandad's on TV. Come on; it starts in five minutes."

"TV?" Timmy's head snapped up.

"Dammit, it's his bedtime," I said, waving the instruction manual. "I nearly had him settled down."

"Watch TV," Timmy said, popping up like a prairie dog peering out of its hole.

Dr. Blake strode in.

"This is educational," he said. "Come on, Timmy—you want to see the turtles, don't you?"

"Turrels! Turrels!" Timmy repeated. "Want see turrels!"

Rob picked Timmy up and hoisted him to the ground. Timmy sprinted for the door, collided with Dr. Blake's legs, and ricocheted out into the hall.

"Timmy, be careful," I called after him.

Blake tottered, and both Rob and I leaped to make sure he didn't fall over. Rob missed, but I caught Blake's arm and found myself supporting his whole weight for a few seconds.

"Damn," he muttered. He scowled at me, then righted himself. "Energetic little cuss, isn't he?"

He stomped toward the door.

"You're welcome," I said under my breath. I underestimated his hearing. He whirled around, still scowling, and put his hands on his hips.

"Yes, I'm an ungrateful old devil, aren't I?" he said. "I'm well aware of how lucky I was just now that it was you standing there instead of some wilting lily who couldn't keep me from falling on my keister. Now come watch my TV show."

With that, he stormed out.

Five

Since I've always found it difficult to sit still and watch television without something to keep my hands busy, I brought along a project to work on during Dr. Blake's documentary. I unearthed a suitably sized three-ring notebook, a hole punch, and some tab dividers, and was turning Karen's inch-thick sheaf of notes into a more organized manual.

"You'll miss half the good footage," Blake grumbled.

"We're recording it, aren't we?" I asked. "I'll rewatch it later, when I can give it my undivided attention."

That mollified him a little, though he did keep frowning whenever I rustled papers or snapped the binder rings open or closed.

"Your friend will probably be back to claim Timmy before you finish that," Rob said, during one of the commercials.

"If she is, great," I said. "But in the meantime, I'm tired of having to leaf through this whole wad of paper every time I need some bit of information."

"Quiet!" Dr. Blake said. "I'm on again."

At least Timmy seemed to be enjoying the show—an *Animal Planet* special on sea turtles, with a lot of emphasis on the problems they faced from poachers and smugglers. He spent the commercial breaks begging turtle rides from Michael and Rob. Fortunately, turtle rides were much less strenuous than horsie rides, since they consisted of sitting on the turtle's back while it crawled at a comfortable pace.

"I'm a turtle," Michael said, whenever Timmy urged him to go faster. "This is as fast as I go."

And I had to confess that it was interesting to watch the show with Blake in the room, and get some of the inside scoop. He beamed with pride during some segments, but he was clearly still outraged by the poachers and smugglers and frustrated by what I gathered were network limitations on how savagely he could condemn them.

"In some cultures," the on-screen Dr. Blake intoned, "sea turtle eggs are erroneously believed to have an aphrodisiac effect."

"Should have let me say which damned ignorant cultures," the live Dr. Blake muttered. "Bloody peasant superstition."

"This belief—which is completely without any scientific validity—has tragic consequences for the sea turtles," said the on-screen Blake.

"Tragic? Try criminal," the real Dr. Blake said. "If more people would think with their brains instead of their—"

"Dr. Blake!" Mother exclaimed, with a pointed look at Timmy.

Dr. Blake subsided into the occasional growl.

The final segment of the hour featured a raid on some suspected turtle-egg smugglers.

"This next part's quite dramatic," Dad assured us, while Dr. Blake beamed. The picture switched to Dr. Blake, crouching beside a ramshackle building, explaining in hushed tones how dangerous the upcoming raid could be.

"The smuggling of animals and animal products generates billions of dollars in profit every year," Blake was saying. "It's second only to the illegal drug trade—and very often, the same ruthless criminals are responsible for both. Which means that the turtle smugglers we're after today are probably also smuggling drugs using the same routes, the same carriers, and the same modus operandi. As a result, both the U.S. Fish and Wildlife Service and Drug Enforcement Administration agents have a keen interest in apprehending these dangerous lawbreakers—lawbreakers who have no scruples about turning their Uzis on the law enforcement officials who attempt to arrest them."

He glanced over his shoulder as if to make sure the Uzi-toting smugglers hadn't sneaked up on him while he was talking to us. I suddenly realized that the ramshackle building looked remarkably familiar.

"That's one of our sheds," I said. "What's our shed doing in your documentary?"

"It was while you were on your honeymoon," Dad said.

"You found armed turtle-egg smugglers in our shed while we were on our honeymoon?"

"No, but the raid took place at night," Dr. Blake explained, pointing to the screen, where blurred and out-of-focus shapes were dashing around haphazardly, accompanied by the occasional burst of gunfire. "We didn't get good footage."

"So you faked it using our shed!"

"We just needed a plausible-looking exterior for the intro. We don't actually say we're at the site of the raid."

"And our shed makes a plausible-looking smuggler's den? Didn't I hear something earlier about the squalid and filthy conditions the smuggled turtles were found in? Do you mean plausibly squalid and filthy?"

On screen, the picture cut to a DEA agent talking about a raid in which they had seized hundreds of kilos of cocaine along with other contraband, resulting in indictments of dozens of members of a major drug cartel.

"Oh, great," I said. "Now everyone in town's going to think we're part of a drug cartel."

"Don't be silly," Dr. Blake said. "Shh!"

"Other contraband," the on-screen Blake said, shaking his head. "Sea turtle eggs may be only an afterthought to the DEA. But to these magnificent giants of the ocean, their eggs represent the future, and the illegal trade in these eggs threatens the survival of one of the planet's most unique inhabitants."

The documentary cut to some footage of several turtles swimming across the screen with ponderous grace. The background music was more than a little reminiscent of the shark theme in *Jaws* and managed to give the impression that a pack of dastardly egg smugglers was lurking off camera, ready to pounce. Then, the music swelled to the sort of tragically doomed theme that usually means the movie's hero is walking off, chin high, to sacrifice himself for something or other. The turtles continued to swim stoically into the distance as the closing credits rolled in front of them.

"So what are you doing with our sheds this week," I asked. "Turning one of them into a replica of an alligator shoe factory? Or perhaps the lair of an ivory smuggler? Maybe reenacting one of the cockfights you raided?"

"We've already wrapped up those shows," Dr. Blake said. "And we'll only be using your shed to keep a few birds in. I doubt we'll need to do any filming there this time. Anyway—time I went home."

Since Dr. Blake had lost his driver's license about the time he turned ninety, these words were, as usual, a signal for someone to offer to drive him back to his hotel. Mother and Dad had offered to let him stay with them— for that matter, they'd also offered to let him stay with me and Michael. But he seemed to prefer the independence of staying at the Caerphilly Inn. Or perhaps he suspected, rightly, that staying with family wouldn't be nearly as comfortable as staying in a five-star hotel.

"Come on, Timmy," I said. "Bedtime."

Timmy, his eyes still glued to the television, moved about three inches toward the stairs.

"Timmy . . ."

"I'm coming," he said.

"Sometime tonight."

"I'm a turrel," he said, grinning up at me. "This is as fast as I go."

"What an enormous sea turtle!" Michael exclaimed. "I wonder if I can pick it up."

He swooped down and snatched up Timmy.

"I'll put him to bed this time," he said over his shoulder as he carried away the giggling toddler. "By way of apology for the fact that I'll be in more damned faculty meetings all day tomorrow."

Rob, as usual, ended up chauffeuring Dr. Blake. Mother, Dad, and Rose Noire kissed me good night and took off for the farmhouse.

I sat down and changed to the local news. The headline stories were the heat wave and a house fire in neighboring Clay County. No reports of fatal traffic accidents or unidentified female bodies turning up. I tried Karen's home and cell phone again before going upstairs.

From down the hall, I heard Michael doing an animated reading of *Yertle the Turtle*. I did my usual nighttime washing and toothbrushing routines. When I stuck my head out in the hall again, Michael had moved on to *Horton Hears a Who*. Timmy had already heard all dozen Dr. Seuss books on hand either during the day, at nap time, or during our first attempt to settle him down for the evening. I wondered how many he was good for this time.

I curled up in bed with Timmy's instruction manual. While I'd been punching holes in it and sorting it into tabs, I'd decided from its relative cleanliness—at least when I'd first received it—that Karen had probably prepared it especially for Timmy's visit with me. Was it possible that hidden in the midst of all the childcare instructions Karen might have let slip some clue to where she was and why she had disappeared?

Somewhere in the middle of a description of how to cook the fruit concoction I was supposed to administer to Timmy at the first signs of constipation, I must have dozed off.

Six

Michael woke up in a good mood. I woke up worrying about Karen.

"So what are my chances of talking you into embarking on a Timmy of our own," he said. I couldn't tell if those were the first words he uttered or simply the first that made it through my early morning fog.

"Arg," I said. "Let's talk about it later."

"Can I at least talk you into a practicing for the real thing?" he asked, in a tone that would normally have distracted me immediately. I could tell from his voice that he wasn't expecting my answer.

"We should talk about that later, too," I said.

"Did I say something wrong?"

"No, but the Timmy we already have is standing right here at my side of the bed," I said. "Good morning, Timmy."

"Kiki hungry," Timmy announced.

Michael sighed.

"And what would Kiki like for breakfast?" he asked, as he rolled out of bed.

"Pizza."

"Pizza? We'll have to see about that. Do you have pizza for breakfast every day?"

Timmy nodded.

"It's got protein," I said, sinking back into my pillow. "And if you give him the leftover supreme, it's even got vegetables."

"You're joking, I hope," Michael said. "Come on, Timmy. Do you like oatmeal?"

"Yuck," Timmy said.

I listened for a minute as their voices disappeared downstairs, and then I felt around the bedside table until I found my cell phone.

Karen didn't answer again. Of course.

I confess, I was preoccupied during breakfast. Not too preoccupied to notice that Michael was wonderful with Timmy. In spite of the page in Timmy's instruction manual warning that he was a fussy eater and refused to consume anything for breakfast but French toast with real maple syrup, Michael managed to get him to eat the same thing he usually fixed for the two of us—oatmeal seasoned with bits of raisin, walnut, and apple, and a side of yogurt. And while clearly he was doing his best to demonstrate what a helpful, fully involved father he could be for our own children, he also seemed to be enjoying himself.

I decided there must be something wrong with me. Everyone else found Timmy amusing and didn't mind helping out with him. Clearly I must have been lacking some important gene that would have made me adore small children uncritically.

Then again, everybody else was just helping out with him. I was the one responsible for him. "There just isn't anyone else I can trust," Karen had said. I found myself wishing she'd lingered long enough to tell me if there was anyone she particularly distrusted. If she had, at least I would have a little bit of information to give Chief Burke when—if—I had to report her disappearance.

And maybe the time for that report had come.

"Meg? Something wrong?" Michael asked.

"It just occurred to me that perhaps I should search for a certain missing friend," I said. "And maybe if I don't succeed in finding her, I should talk to Chief Burke."

Michael glanced at Timmy, who was pretending to feed the nuts and raisins to Kiki before eating them. Then he nodded.

Fortunately, before Michael raced off to his day's meetings, I managed to ingest enough food and caffeine to fuel my morning with Timmy. Transferring him from pajamas to day clothes, accompanied by a change of diaper, took over half an hour.

Rob showed up about the time I had Timmy theoretically presentable for meeting the outside world. This was early for Rob to be up and about, which probably meant that he'd slept upstairs in his sleeping bag. Well, at least he was handy.

"Here," I said, turning Timmy over to Rob. "Amuse him for a minute. I'm going to make one more try."

"Horsie-horsie!" Timmy said, holding up his arms in a not particularly subtle plea for Rob to pick him up and give him a ride.

"I think I can skip the gym this week," Rob said. He settled Timmy on his back, pawed the ground a few times with one foot, neighed, and trotted away. I picked up the kitchen phone receiver and dialed Karen's home number again.

Once again it rang unanswered. I let it go until the voice mail kicked in, then hung up. No sense leaving any more messages unless I had something to say. Something other than "Where the hell are you and when are you coming back to pick up Timmy?" I'd left enough variations of that already. Rob trotted through the kitchen again, prancing dramatically while Timmy squealed with laughter.

"No answer?" Rob asked. "What do you supposed has happened to her?"

With Timmy around, I couldn't exactly list the host of unsettling possibilities that came to mind. I didn't really think the running off to Bali thing was very likely, but what if she was deliberately trying to dodge me? What if something had happened to her? What if—

I hung up and dialed her cell phone. Again it rang until the call answer picked up. Rob and Timmy cruised into the kitchen again. Timmy's enthusiasm seemed unabated, but Rob was prancing a little less energetically.

"Dammit," I said, slamming down the receiver. "This is ridiculous."

"Dammit!" Timmy echoed. I winced.

"I'm going over there."

"And do what?" Rob asked, prancing in place by the counter.

"Find her, if she's there."

"And if she's not?"

"I don't know. Leave notes. Interrogate the neighbors. If I find her, I can apologize for Timmy's deteriorating vocabulary. If I don't, maybe I should drop by and talk to Chief Burke. Report her as missing."

"Don't you have to wait forty-eight hours for that?"

"I think they can waive the waiting period if there are suspicious circumstances," I said. "Like abandoning a toddler to the care of highly unsuitable persons. Timmy, want to go for a ride in the car?"

"Dammit!" Timmy shrieked, waving his arms with such enthusiasm that he almost knocked himself off Rob's back.

"You're going now?" Rob swung Timmy down to the floor and rotated his no-doubt aching shoulders.

"Immediately," I said.

Seven

Of course, immediately with a toddler isn't quite the same thing as immediately for an unencumbered adult. It took me half an hour to pack all the paraphernalia I thought I might need for a car trip with Timmy.

Diapers. A change of clothes for Timmy. A change of clothes for me, in case we had any more unfortunate food or diaper incidents. Baby wipes. A cooler containing a couple of sippy cups of milk, a couple of bottles of water, and some dried fruit, along with one of those blue ice things to keep it all from spoiling. A sandwich bag of Cheerios and another of trail mix. Toys. Books.

Kiki and Blanky, of course. I'd initially assumed that they were along to provide nighttime companionship, and perhaps to soothe an occasional moment of stress, but I'd now realized they were Timmy's constant companions. Though perhaps despite his cheery demeanor, Timmy's entire stay at our house had been one prolonged stressful experience. He'd stopped asking about Mommy, but that might be a bad sign rather than a good sign. I pushed that alarming thought out of my mind.

I also took along a first aid kit—not the little one I

usually kept in the car, but the big, industrial one I'd bought after the last time we had unwisely let Dad get his hands on a chain saw.

Michael and I had taken less baggage on our honeymoon.

It took another twenty minutes to get Timmy safely confined to the car seat, partly because the thing seemed to have at least half again as many straps as it needed and partly because although Timmy was quite happy to climb all over the front and back seats of my little Toyota, honking the horn whenever he could get near it, he wasn't all that keen on sitting in the car seat and began squirming incessantly as soon as I tried to strap him in, with the occasional ear-splitting shriek of protest. I finally had to get Rob to hold him down while I did up the buckles, and by the time we finished, my ears were ringing and I was more than half convinced that Child Protective Services would show up at any moment to arrest both Rob and me and confiscate Timmy.

"Want stay here," Timmy sobbed, once we had him in the car seat. I suddenly realized that maybe he wasn't just being obstreperous. The last time he'd been in the car seat, his mother had dumped him at my house. Did he think I was going to haul him off and leave him with yet another stranger?

"But I have to run some errands," I said. "And I thought you were going to come with me. Would you rather stay here with Rob?"

Rob looked panic-stricken. Timmy considered it.

"Come with you," he said, and settled back in his car seat. Rob breathed a sigh of relief.

"So, hold down the fort," I said to Rob. "And if Karen calls, find out where the hell she is. And if she shows up, call me and don't let her leave till I can get back."

"Roger," Rob said.

As I got into the car, Timmy was amusing himself by kicking the seat in front of him and singing "Dammit! Dammit! Dammit!" I squelched the kicking and, by way of distraction, shoved in a CD Karen had left as part of Timmy's baggage—a home-burned CD labeled "car music"—and turned on the stereo. A peppy rendition of "The Eensy Weensy Spider" echoed through the car as I drove off toward town. Normally I have nothing in particular against "The Eensy Weensy Spider," but this singer made it sound so cutesy that I couldn't wait for it to end.

Track two was a repeat of the same marzipan-sweet rendition of "The Eensy Weensy Spider." I skipped the track, only to find more of the same on track three.

Timmy had calmed down considerably, though, and was chanting "eensy weensy eensy weensy" in a comparatively quiet tone, so I gritted my teeth and drove on

A few blocks from Karen's house and twenty renditions of "The Eensy Weensy Spider" later, the program finally moved on to "Old McDonald Had a Farm." I had the sinking feeling that the CD would consist entirely of Timmy's five or ten favorite tunes, repeated fifteen or twenty times each.

I pulled up in front of Karen's small bungalow and got out. Timmy seemed oblivious to our arrival at his home, and continued happily singing "Moo moo here! Moo moo there!" and waving Kiki and Blanky in the air. I considered taking him out of the car seat—there were lights on, and I could hear the sound of a TV. But I decided I'd rather have Karen's help controlling him once I let him loose, so I figured out how to unhook the car seat from the car while still leaving him strapped inside—so that was why the thing had so many straps— and hauled him with me up to the door.

I set the car seat in a shady place beside the door, rang the door bell, and stood there for some moments, glancing back and forth between the door and Timmy. I heard a noise inside, and I noticed a slight shadow through the peephole, as if someone was checking me out. I smoothed my face into a smile and worked on looking harmless. The door finally opened and a short, twenty-something woman looked out at me with a slightly wary look.

"Yes?" she said.

"I'm sorry," I said. "This is 125 Hawthorne Street?"

I glanced back at the mailbox, and then at the house again. It was the house I remembered visiting, and this wasn't the kind of cookie cutter neighborhood where you could be one street over and not notice the difference. I even remembered the little planter beside the front door. The impatiens Karen had planted in it the last time I'd visited had given way to some plastic sweet peas.

"Yes," the woman said.

"I was looking for Karen Walker—" I began.

The woman's face changed dramatically the minute I said Karen's name, and she drew back a step.

"Just leave me alone!" she shouted. "She hasn't lived here for two years, and I already told you people where she went, so just leave me alone! I'll call the police on you if you don't go away."

She slammed the door.

"Not s'posed to slam doors," Timmy said, shaking his head as if to imply that he, of course, had never been guilty of such heinous behavior.

I stood, stunned for a moment. Yes, I was a little vexed with Karen for dumping Timmy on me so long, but I couldn't imagine why the woman would react to her name with such anger. Or was it fear?

After standing there in stunned silence for a few moments—well, silence except for the Timmy's soft chanting of "Moo moo here; moo moo there"—I rang the bell again.

"I said go away," the woman shouted through the door.

"I'm going!" I said. "Just tell me where to go!"

"I have the phone in my hand!"

"Fine, call the police if you like," I said. "But first, please tell me where Karen went."

"I told you already!"

"You told someone," I said. "Not me."

"Why do you need to know?" she said. Less loudly. It sounded as if she might be calming down a bit.

"Because she dumped her toddler on me last night and I want to give him back!"

The door opened a crack and she peered out.

"Her toddler?"

I pointed down at Timmy, who was talking to Kiki in a low tone, with a very earnest look on his face—in short, looking very cute.

"I hadn't seen her since shortly after Timmy was

born," I said. "Then yesterday morning she showed up, asked me to watch the kid for a little while, and that's the last I've seen of her. I'm worried. Do you know where she moved to?"

The woman studied me for a few moments. She glanced back at Timmy. I thought I saw her face soften slightly.

And there was a toy dump truck on the lawn. If this woman had kids of her own . . .

"He's distracted right now," I said, shaking my head and frowning sadly. "But being without his mother all day yesterday—and then overnight; going to bed without a goodnight kiss from Mommy—you can imagine! I have to at least try to find Karen. For Timmy's sake."

It sounded over the top to me—I'd put a small quiver in my voice, and you could practically hear violins playing in the background. But it worked.

"Wait here a minute," she said.

She closed the door and disappeared. Timmy tired of "Old McDonald's Farm" and began singing "The Eensy Weensy Spider" again.

The door opened again, and the woman handed me a sheet of paper. I glanced at it. An address. 1415 Stone Street, apartment 12.

"It's those apartments over behind the bus station," she said. "Those kind-of run-down ones."

"The College Arms?"

"Yeah, the Armpits," she said, snickering. "That's what most people in town call them, you know."

I knew the place. So did anyone who regularly read the police blotter column in the *Caerphilly Clarion*. If I were one of Caerphilly's finest and found myself run-

ning a little short of my monthly arrest quota, I'd just
mosey over to the College Arms and keep my eyes
open until a few of the part-time burglars or small-time
drug dealers in residence did something blatantly illegal so I could haul them in.

"What on earth is Karen doing living there?" I said.

"They're cheap," the woman said. "And maybe she
was hoping to shake all the people who're after her."

"What people? Bill collectors?"

"Yeah, I guess they could be bill collectors," she
said. "Me, I don't run up bills with people like that.
Look, I'm sorry about your friend, but I don't know
anything else about her. She doesn't live here anymore.
I told them where she went. I just want all those thugs
to leave me alone."

With that she shut the door.

I picked up Timmy's car seat and hauled it back to
the car. As I was buckling the seat in place again,
Timmy's mood shifted from cheerful into miserable.

"What's wrong?" I asked.

"Na mimo!" he said. Actually, he said a great deal,
but none of it was any more intelligible than "na mimo"
had been. I experimented with various solutions. No,
he didn't want a train or a ball. The relatively limited
investigation of his Pampers that I could make without
unstrapping him did not reveal any serious cause for
concern. I handed him the bag of Cheerios and a sippy
cup of milk from the cooler and that did the trick.

With Timmy contently swigging milk and munch-
ing Cheerios, I drove over to the College Arms.

Karen must have fallen on hard times to have moved
there. Was this before or after her husband left? And

what the hell did the woman mean about not running up bills with "people like that?" People like what—drug dealers? Loan sharks? The woman had said thugs. None of that sounded like Karen. Maybe the woman was mistaken about her forwarding address. Maybe someone else far less respectable had lived in the house briefly between Karen's departure and the woman's arrival.

At least I knew why Timmy hadn't shown any sign of recognition when we'd driven up. He wouldn't remember the bungalow on Hawthorne Street since he was probably less than a year old when they left.

He began getting excited as we pulled up in front of the College Arms, but I couldn't be sure it was the joy of homecoming.

"Fire engine!" he shouted, banging his sippy cup on the arm of the car seat and waving the Cheerios bag in the air with such enthusiasm that its contents scattered about like confetti. "Fire engine! Fire engine!"

"No, Timmy," I said. "Those aren't fire engines. Those are police cars."

Eight

The Caerphilly Police Department didn't have that many police cruisers, and I suspected all of them were on the scene, lights flashing. And there were a lot more civilian vehicles than usual in the lot and up and down both sides of the street. Vehicles that didn't really look as if they belonged at the Arms, whose residents drove either junkers or old trucks, if they were poor but honest, or brand-new high-end cars and SUVs if they were successful in their chosen felonies. So evidently something had happened here at the Arms to attract the attention of local law enforcement. Not an unusual occurrence. Possibly not even the first time the whole force had turned up here—but given Karen's apparent disappearance, finding them on site today seemed ominous.

I even saw a couple of campus police cars. Normally the Caerphilly police and the Camcops, as the students called them, were barely on speaking terms, but I saw a brace of Camcops talking amicably to Sammy Wendell, one of Chief Burke's deputies. I slowed down and waved at him. He waved back.

And while waving, I realized where all the police

activity was centered. The second stairwell. Apartment twelve. Wasn't that—?

I glanced down at the piece of paper I'd gotten on Hawthorne Street. Yes, it said apartment twelve.

"Oh, sh—oot!" I said, catching myself at the last moment before I taught Timmy another word Karen wouldn't thank me for when I turned him back over to her. If she was still around to—no, I wasn't even going to think that.

I pulled up to the next corner and stopped to mull things over—leaving the engine on, though, so I wouldn't stop the air conditioner or the wretched music. I needed to find out what was going on there—apparently in Karen's apartment.

"Go see 'leese car?" Timmy suggested.

"In a minute," I said.

Maybe I could get some information out of Sammy. Like our neighbor, Mr. Early, Sammy was infatuated with my cousin Rose Noire—who was a free spirit, and so far had barely noticed the existence of any of her suitors. As a result, Sammy was highly vulnerable to manipulation by any member of my large extended family who wanted a favor, or the answer to some question about police business that she really shouldn't even be asking. I tried to be the exception to the family rule, and only play the Rose Noire card in truly dire emergencies.

"'Leese car now?" Timmy repeated.

But with county and campus police swarming in and out of Karen's apartment after more than twenty-four hours during which she hadn't been seen, hadn't called, hadn't answered her cell phone or her home phone—this was a dire emergency, wasn't it?

Just then the car tunes CD segued from "Old McDonald's Farm" into Barney the dinosaur singing "I Love You, You Love Me." That settled it. Definitely an emergency. I cut the ignition, grabbed the diaper bag, and resigned myself to liberating Timmy from the safety of his car seat.

"Come on, Timmy," I said. "We're going to see the police cars."

Keeping a grip on Timmy's hand proved to be an impossible task, so I settled for getting a good grip on the waistband of his pants. The shirt collar would have worked better—I wouldn't have had to stoop so much—but I suspected that would work much as a choke chain did on Spike. Unlike most dogs, Spike never seemed to notice the first warning signs of strangulation, and I suspected Timmy would prove equally oblivious to pain. With Spike, we'd solved that problem with a harness that shifted the pressure from his throat to his chest. Did they make toddler harnesses? And if so, was it worth finding one for what I hoped would be the short remainder of Timmy's stay with me?

"Hi, Sammy," I called out, as we drew near. "What the heck's going on?"

"Hi, Meg," he said. "I'm sorry, but you can't come in here now."

I decided to play dumb.

"Drat," I said. "You guys would have to be making a big raid on this dump just when I need to take Timmy home."

I indicated Timmy, who was straining toward the nearest police car, repeating "'Leese car! 'Leese car!"

"Timmy?" Sammy said, looking down at the pre-occupied toddler. "He lives here?"

"His mother is my friend, Karen Walker," I said. "Apartment twelve. If I can't come in, could you get a message to Karen that I'm out here with Timmy?"

Sammy and the Camcops looked at each other.

"I'll go find Chief Burke," one of the Camcops said.

"So you've been babysitting the kid?" the other Camcop asked.

"She—no, Timmy!" I snapped, and grabbed him by the waist again. He'd been reaching toward Sammy's service revolver.

Just then Chief Burke came trotting up. Things must be serious—I couldn't recall when I'd seen the chief moving faster than his usual stately walk.

"This is Karen Walker's son?" he asked.

"Timmy," I said. "Timmy, say hello to Chief Burke. He's the boss of all the police here."

The remaining Camcop frowned. Timmy tilted his head and inspected the chief with interest.

"Hello," he said. "Want ride in the 'leese car."

"Do you indeed?" the chief said.

Timmy frowned and cocked his head, as if this was a test.

"Please?" he said finally.

"That's the magic word," the chief said, with a faint smile. "We need to talk," he added to me. "Sammy! Why don't you take Master Timothy for a ride in your cruiser?"

"I don't have a car seat," Sammy said, turning pale.

"I do," I said, holding out my keys. "My car's down the block."

"Make it a good long ride," the chief said. "Use the siren a lot. Stop for ice cream if you've a mind to."

"Yes, sir," Sammy said. He moved around so he could take Timmy's hand with his left, to keep him as far from the gun as possible.

"Fred, you want to go along, help Sammy?" the chief said, turning to the remaining Camcop. It was a question, not an order, but I could see Fred was frowning and digging in his heels. "Might be good to have another officer along, if the kid happens to let slip any information."

"Yes, sir!" Fred's face cleared, and he strode off looking very polished and military, especially compared with Sammy, whose gangly frame was contorted as he tried to stoop down so his hand was at toddler level.

"I gather all this has something to do with Karen," I said, gesturing to the herd of police vehicles.

"Ms. Walker's a close friend of yours?" The chief had taken out his notebook. And he was looking at me with suspicion. More suspicion than usual. Of course, usually all he suspected me of was snooping around and interfering with one of his investigations. This time . . .

"She's a friend, yes. I wouldn't say a close friend. I hadn't seen her in months."

"And yet she left her child with you."

"Close enough at one time that it didn't seem too odd leaving him with me for a little while—that's what she said, a little while, and it was clearly some kind of emergency. I assumed maybe an hour or two. But that was at eight a.m. yesterday. Around noon I started calling her, and not getting an answer, so I thought I'd come over today and see if I could find out anything."

He scribbled away in silence.

"Look, what's wrong?" I asked. "Has something happened to Karen?"

"I was hoping you could tell me," he said.

"Then she's not—" I stopped myself. I didn't want to say the word "dead." I didn't even want to think it.

"We haven't found a body, if that's what you mean," the chief said. "The place was broken into last night, and has been pretty thoroughly ransacked. Any chance you'd be willing to take a look around, see if anything's been taken?"

"I'm willing, but I'm afraid I wouldn't be very useful," I said. "I didn't even know she lived here. I went over to the bungalow she used to live in, on Hawthorne Street. That's 125 Hawthorne Street," I added, anticipating the chief's question.

"Bit of a comedown from Hawthorne Street," he said, glancing up over his shoulder at the College Arms.

I nodded. The town of Caerphilly didn't have much in the way of bad neighborhoods, but if there was anyplace within the town precincts that would make me surreptitiously click my door lock button before I drove through it, this two- or three-block stretch of Stone Street would be it.

"You might want to talk to the woman who moved into her old house," I said. "I don't usually think of myself as a very menacing presence, but she was afraid to open her door to me at first. I had to use Timmy to lull her suspicions, and I get the idea some pretty unsavory characters have turned up there looking for Karen."

The chief scribbled some more.

"Just how do you know Ms. Walker?" he asked.

"She was one of the first friends I made when I came to town," I said. "The first who wasn't really Michael's friend. And I got the feeling all of them were a little wary of me."

"Wary?" the chief repeated. I had to smile, because the word rather accurately described his usual attitude toward me.

"Well, they didn't know how long I'd be around— we were just dating then. And most of them were faculty or faculty spouses, and sometimes the college gets a little suffocating, you know?"

He nodded.

"I met her when I went by the college accounting department to drop off some form Michael kept forgetting to turn in," I went on. "Karen works there. At least she did work there. We started talking, and hit it off. She invited me for coffee. She helped me find my way around. Let me use guest passes to her gym until I found I was spending so much time down here that I might as well join myself. We did yoga classes there together at first, but after a while, we began drifting apart."

"Any particular reason?"

"No," I said. "We had common interests, but not a lot of them. And of course, that was about the time she met Jasper. Her husband. Ex-husband now, I gather. I guess if there was any one thing you could call a reason, it would be Jasper."

"You didn't like Jasper?"

"Not really," I said. "And it was mutual. That does have a cooling effect on a friendship, you know, when she says 'Isn't he wonderful!' and you have a hard time saying anything more than 'If you say so.' And I hadn't heard that they broke up. Maybe she was afraid I'd say 'I told you so.'"

"So you haven't seen Mr. Walker recently either?"

I shook my head.

"You have no idea what he did?"

"Do you mean did for a living, or are we talking about something in particular he did that brought him to your attention?"

He looked over his glasses at me.

"Sorry," I said. "I didn't mean to be nosy. He did some kind of tech work. I think Karen met him when he fixed her computer. Look, something's happened to Karen, hasn't it? I can understand now why she wasn't answering her phone, but she's not answering her cell phone either, and that's a bad sign."

The chief frowned for a moment.

"Try calling her again," he said.

I pulled out my cell phone and dialed Karen's number. I could hear her phone ringing in stereo—from my own cell phone, and from a nearby cruiser.

"Chief," one of the officers called. "The cell phone we found—"

"Just ignore it," the chief called back. "You can hang up now," he said to me.

I ended the call. The ringing in the cruiser stopped. We looked at each other for a long few seconds.

"Now let's go over what happened yesterday," he said. "In detail."

I winced. Chief Burke's appetite for details usually far exceeded my ability to remember them. This could take a while. I hoped Sammy was up to the job of entertaining Timmy for that long.

Nine

It was nearly eleven by the time Chief Burke finally let me leave, and even then I suspected he was only taking pity on Sammy and the other officers who'd been keeping Timmy busy. And he gave me no hint of what was really going on—surely that many police wouldn't turn out for a simple burglary. Even more frustrating, from the questions he'd asked he was clearly assuming that Karen was involved in something illegal. I found myself fuming. Yes, there were a lot of small-time drug dealers and petty criminals living at the College Arms, but there were also a few impoverished grad students and honest, hardworking, but badly paid people. Like single mothers whose husbands skipped out on them and weren't paying any child support, which I suspected was what had happened to Karen. And all the chief could do was ask about her known associates.

And was he looking for her? Looking for her effectively, that is? He seemed to be assuming she was a suspect, or at least what the media call a "person of interest." And while I didn't know much about police procedure, I suspected the way you looked for a person in jeopardy might be radically different from the way you hunted down a suspect.

Still fuming, I drove over to the campus, trying to stay patient while explaining to Timmy every few minutes that no, I couldn't turn on the siren because my car didn't have one. I found a semi-legal parking space a couple of blocks from the college administration building, liberated Timmy from the durance vile of his car seat, and slung the heavyweight diaper bag over my shoulder.

I thought of telling Timmy that we were going to Mommy's office, but decided maybe that was a bad idea. I'd had a home address for Karen that was two years out of date—what if my information on where Karen worked was equally obsolete? After all, she hadn't put her work number in Timmy's instruction manual. Did that mean she no longer worked at the college, or that she hadn't expected to be at the college during Timmy's stay with me, or perhaps that she didn't want me calling the college for some reason?

I was relieved to note, as we headed up the steps toward the administration building, that Timmy seemed to recognize the place, and pulled at my hand. That had to be a good sign. Surely Timmy didn't have enough short-term memory to recall the place unless Karen still worked there or at least had until very recently.

We strolled into the administration building. It was quieter than I'd ever seen it, but then I didn't recall ever having a reason to go there before the school year began. I ran into the occasional staff or faculty member strolling calmly through the halls. No one I actually knew, but we all nodded pleasantly, even the ones whose faces I didn't recall seeing around the town and campus for the last several years. After all, my presence here three weeks before the start of classes proved we were on the same team—staff, faculty, and their families. I wasn't one of the hordes of students and parents who would come swarming in after Labor Day, briefly and predictably overwhelming all the administration offices with their forms and questions.

I headed for the office where Karen had been working when I met her. Thanks to Timmy, I didn't have any trouble finding my way—all I had to do was keep a good grip on his hand. He knew the way. Better and better.

I knew from previous visits—like the one on which I'd first met her—that Karen sat at one of four vintage metal desks in a big room whose walls were lined with battered beige four-drawer file cabinets. And right inside the door, if they hadn't rearranged things, two cafeteria tables, placed end to end, served as a makeshift counter piled high with stacks and boxes of forms, all printed on the pale blue copier paper the Caerphilly College administration used to distinguish its official forms from lesser documents. I wasn't sure if I should just march in and ask for Karen or pretend to be looking for some form or other. I'd play it by ear.

I pushed open a door marked FINANCIAL ADMINISTRATION. Just as I'd remembered it, except that the file cabinets had multiplied so they not only lined the walls but served as low dividers between the desks. But the counter was there, and they'd even put out a couple of folding chairs so people could sit down to fill out forms. Now all I had to do was—

"Mommy!" Timmy shouted, and pulled himself out of my grip to duck under the tables and race toward the back of the room.

My heart gave a brief lurch of relief—she was all right! And then I realized that he hadn't seen Karen. He was heading for her desk.

"Oh, my God, it's Timmy!" someone exclaimed. I glanced over to see that the speaker was seated at one of the closer desks. Had been seated at the desk. Now she had jumped up and was frantically trying to clear everything off the top of her desk into her already crowded drawers.

It was Sandie, the tchotchke lady. Karen and I had laughed and shaken our heads over her during some of our lunches. Every square inch of Sandie's desk that wasn't covered with papers was filled with tiny breakable ornaments: bud vases, glass or china figurines of dogs and cats and fawns, tiny china frames with babies' pictures in them, snow globes, porcelain thimbles, miniature teapots and who knew what else. It was a veritable museum of things that should not be left within a mile of Timmy's busy little hands. I'd have thought the top of the desk was safe, but Sandie probably had more experience with Timmy than I did.

Luckily, Timmy ignored all the temptations on Sandie's desk and headed straight for Karen's. I was expecting a temper tantrum when he didn't find her there, but instead, he climbed up into her desk chair and sat there, clutching Kiki and his sippy cup, twirling the chair slightly, and looking expectant.

"Karen promised she wouldn't bring him in here again," Sandie fussed, as she continued clearing things off her desk. I knew how she felt; I'd spent most of the previous evening doing the same deck clearing at home. "She knows how he disrupts our operations."

"I'm sorry," I said. "Karen didn't tell me that—I guess she was in a hurry when she dropped him off. Is she here?"

"No," Sandie said. She paused in her tidying and looked up. "And let me tell you, Nadine is pretty burned up about that. If you know where she—"

"Sandra?" Sandie flinched slightly and returned to her tidying, so I deduced that the speaker meant her. I turned to see a tall, elegant woman in a gray suit standing in a doorway that led to an inner office. Nadine, I presumed.

"Hi," I said, in a deliberately light and cheerful tone. "I'm looking for Karen."

"Karen's not here," Nadine said. "And I'm sorry, but I'm afraid we cannot permit a toddler to stay in the office. Too disruptive."

She frowned slightly at Timmy, who was actually behaving quite well. He was turning Karen's desk chair around in slow circles, and yes, he was pushing against the desk and the file cabinets with his feet to do so, but they looked as if they had survived far worse abuse. For Timmy, he was being positively angelic.

Of course, perhaps Nadine had met him before in another mood.

"I'm sorry," I said. "I'll take him right out again. I must have gotten my signals crossed about where I was supposed to drop him off. She's not in today?"

"No." Nadine said. I waited, hoping she'd say something else, but she simply stood there, looking forbidding, with that faint frown on her face. Sandie was trying very hard to be invisible.

"Damn," I said. "Well, I'll get Timmy out of your hair. Could I give you a message in case you see her?"

"Perhaps you could write your message down," Nadine said, looking down her nose at me. "And leave it on her desk."

"Okay," I said, trying to look abashed. Actually, that was just what I was hoping she'd say. I'd spotted a sheaf of pink "While-you-were-out" slips spread out across Karen's desk.

I made my way through the forest of file cabinets to Karen's desk, ostentatiously pulling out my notebook as I did, and flipping to a clean page. Nadine walked over to one of the other empty desks and picked up a paper. It wasn't lost on me that from her new position she could keep an eye on me.

"Can I sit down, Timmy?" I asked. Timmy obligingly slid off the chair and crawled under the desk, where he began rummaging through various boxes and papers.

I took a moment to glance at the photos on Karen's desk. Several of Timmy at various ages, and one family group, with Karen and Jasper holding the infant Timmy. At least I assumed it was Jasper—Karen had covered the man's head by sticking a square cut from a yellow Post-it note to the glass.

I flipped up the sticky note—yes, that was the Jasper I remembered. Tall and angular, with long, straight brown hair pulled back into a ponytail. Decent looking, if you overlooked a slightly weak chin. And I'd always thought his smile looked a little forced.

I shook my head, dropped the tab back over his face, swung myself around with my back to Nadine, and began writing. I pretended to tap my left hand on the desk while I was writing, though what I was actually doing was flicking the "While-you-were-out" notes aside, one by one, so I could jot down all the names, numbers, and messages. Most of them were written in a round, loopy handwriting and initialed with an S, except for one that was written in a handwriting so tiny that you could have fit an entire short story on the small sheet of paper, and yet so precise I had no trouble reading it. Nadine, I suspected.

When I'd finished copying the names and numbers, I glanced under the desk.

"What are you doing, Timmy?" I said.

"Nothing," he said. He was almost telling the truth. He was just sitting under the desk, clutching Kiki and gently poking at my ankles with his foot. But as I bent down, pretending to check on him, I turned the notebook page I'd been writing in so I'd have a clean sheet.

"We're leaving in a second," I said. I quickly scribbled a note to Karen:

Karen—hi! Dropped by with Timmy. Please call me to let me know where I should bring him.

I added my home and cell phone numbers and underlined the word "please" several times. Then I ripped the sheet out of the spiral notebook and set it on top of the "While-you-were-out" notes.

"Okay, Timmy," I said. "Mommy's not here yet. We'll come back later when she's here."

Nadine frowned and opened her mouth, then closed it again, apparently realizing that any mention of a return visit was only intended to expedite Timmy's exit. She returned to the door of her office to watch us go.

"Sorry," I said, glancing down as we passed Sandie's now denuded desk.

Sandie's back was to Nadine. She didn't move her head, or smile, but she made some sort of frantic, incomprehensible gesture with her hands. I paused.

"Do you need any help putting stuff back on your desk?" I said.

"No thanks," she said, looking up and still gesturing. As a mime, she was a dismal failure. If she was trying to tell me something, it wasn't working. Maybe she wasn't signaling. Maybe she was just having some kind of stress-induced arm spasms.

I gave up trying to interpret her signals and reached down to take Timmy's hand. He shifted his sippy cup into his other hand to take mine and its top fell off, spilling the tiny amount of milk that he hadn't finished— maybe a tablespoon's worth.

"Oh, no!" Sandie whispered. A little melodramatically, if you asked me. It was milk, not blood.

"I'm sorry," I said. I stooped down and began mopping at the spill with a tissues from my purse. "Do you have any paper towels? Because I could run to the ladies room if—"

"This is one of the reasons we cannot allow children here," Nadine said. She squatted down and began to spray Windex on the remnants of the spill and mop around with giant wads of paper towel. "Apart from the potential damage to the facility, it constitutes a serious safety hazard."

Damage to the facility? The floor was linoleum. And yes, spills could be a safety hazard, but so was knocking people down in your haste to clean up spills. My ribs still smarted where she'd elbowed me out of the way.

"I'm so sorry," I said aloud. "I'll take him away right now."

Nadine didn't answer. By this time, she'd sprayed Windex on an area at least five times larger than the original spill, and showed no signs of slowing down. I grabbed Timmy's hand, made sure his sippy cup was upright, and tiptoed out.

Outside in the hall, I stopped to adjust the Velcro on one of Timmy's shoes. It didn't really need adjusting, but it put me out of Nadine's sight and still visible to Sandie. I was hoping Sandie would notice me, and wondering if I should try to contact her to find out why she was signaling me so urgently. Should I call her up? Lie in wait until Nadine left and then return?

At first, Sandie didn't see me—presumably because she was focusing on Nadine's cleanup efforts. I could tell when Nadine had finished because Sandie relaxed slightly, took a deep breath, and glanced out the doorway as if contemplating escape. She saw me crouching outside and luckily she got the hint.

"Nadine, I'm going over to the cafeteria as soon as I finish this batch of receipts," she said. "Can I bring you back something?"

Apart from the initial no, I didn't quite catch Nadine's answer, but the tone of polite contempt came through loud and clear. No campus cafeteria food for her. I stood up and turned to leave. Probably time to fuel up Timmy again. We'd head for the cafeteria, too.

As we passed the open doorway, I glanced in to see that Nadine had decorated the site of Timmy's spill with one of those yellow CAUTION! WET FLOORS! signs that cleaning staffs use. Sandie looked up, saw me looking at the sign, and rolled her eyes.

Ten

I did my best to talk Timmy into grilled chicken and broccoli for lunch, but he held out for hamburger and French fries. I gave up. Let Karen guide him back onto the path of responsible nutrition when she showed up again.

"Make that two burger platters," I told the student behind the counter. "With a lot of lettuce and tomato on the side."

I even figured out a way to get Timmy to eat the lettuce, by stuffing one leaf sideways into my mouth and waggling it up and down while I chewed on the other end and gradually sucked the whole thing into my mouth. It was messy and a little gross, but Timmy was charmed, and while imitating me, he finished off all his lettuce and the balance of mine. That counted as one serving of fruits and vegetables, right? Perhaps I could figure out something equally entertaining to do with the tomato slices. Then again, Timmy seemed to consider French fries mainly as a vehicle for conveying vast quantities of ketchup from his plate to his mouth. He often loaded one French fry three or four times before it disintegrated to the point that he couldn't reload it with ketchup and reluctantly ate it. Surely a quarter bottle of ketchup would count as another serving, wouldn't it?

I was about to try a game of wheeling a tomato slice around my plate and into my mouth when Sandie appeared at the other side of the table carrying a tray.

"Boy, did you upset Nadine," she said, as she sat down.

"I'm sorry."

"Don't be," she said, with a shrug. "Nobody likes Nadine."

"Then would you like me to go back and annoy her some more? Maybe sneak in and spill some molasses on the floor?"

She giggled and shook her head. She cast an ostentatiously jealous look at our hamburger and fries, then sighed.

"Want fry?" Timmy said, offering her one of his largest.

"No thanks," she said. "Not that I wouldn't love one," she added to me. "I've been on this diet forever. Doomed to nibble lettuce like a rabbit for the rest of my life."

I nodded sympathetically. Since she was busily emptying four packets of blue cheese dressing on an enormous Cobb salad, I found myself wondering whether my lunch was all that much more fattening than hers, but I'd learned long ago to keep my mouth shut about other people's diets and pray that they did the same about mine.

"When Nadine gets over being ticked at you and Karen, maybe I'll ask you to come back and rile her up again," she said. "Right now she's just ignoring me, and that's the way I like it. So Karen left Timmy with you?"

When he heard his name, Timmy grinned broadly, revealing all the bits of ketchup-daubed French fry he was chewing. Sandie and I both averted our eyes.

"Don't chew with your mouth open," I reminded him. "Yes, Karen asked me to take care of him for a little while. That was yesterday morning. I'm getting a little frantic."

"I can imagine." She glanced over at Timmy, who was jamming a fry against Kiki's stitched mouth.

"You have to eat *something*, Kiki," he said. More of a sentence than he usually constructed, so I suspected he was echoing something he'd heard repeatedly from Karen.

"It's probably because of her husband," Sandie said. "She found out Friday he was back in town."

"Her husband? Jasper? They're still married?"

"She filed for divorce when he ran out on her, but it takes a while, especially if you can't find the jerk to get him to sign any papers. So when she heard he was back, living at his uncle Hiram's old house, she said she was going to go out and get him to sign something."

"Don't people usually get a lawyer or a process server to do stuff like that?"

"Yeah, but she didn't have a lot of money," Sandie said. "I guess it's cheaper if you do it yourself. Anyway, she was going to go out and see him."

"Did she say when?" I could feel the hairs standing up on the back of my neck. If Karen had left Timmy with me because she was going to see her estranged husband—and hadn't returned . . .

"She was talking about it Friday afternoon," Sandie said. "I assumed she meant to do it over the weekend. And then when she didn't come on time yesterday morning, I thought maybe she'd taken the morning off to do it. Then Nadine went on the warpath—she's a real stickler about unexcused absences."

I imagined Nadine was a real stickler about a lot of things. Escaping the Nadines of the world was one of the main reasons I'd chosen blacksmithing over more secure but confining jobs.

"Maybe that's what she's doing," I said. "She dropped by my house about eight in the morning yesterday."

"You've seen her a lot more recently than I have, then," Sandie said. "She left Friday afternoon, just like usual, and that's the last I saw of her."

Her face was solemn, and the words sounded a little rehearsed, as if she had already practiced saying them for CNN, should the occasion arise.

"Do you know her husband?"

"Jasper? Not that well. Of course, his parents were from around here."

Clearly she didn't like him, or she'd have said Jasper himself was "from around here." Still, he was a native, even though an unlikable one. And so was Sandie, from her words—though come to think of it, I could have guessed that from her voice, with its subtle hint of an accent.

"He didn't stick around much after his parents died," Sandie went on. "They sold the farm and all. So I think everyone was surprised when he moved back here again. Got a decent job at the college, in the data support center. Though he didn't hang onto it for long. That's how he met Karen, you know. They were putting in this big, automated bookkeeping system and Karen was the one from our department who worked on the conversion."

"Do you have any idea why he was fired?" I asked.

Sandie shook her head.

"Whatever it was, Karen was real upset about it," she said. "But she never did say much. It was about that time they broke up, though—and good riddance to bad rubbish. I'll say one thing for Jasper—he makes my ex look good, and that takes some doing."

The newly returned Jasper Walker was starting to sound more and more suspicious.

"Kiki got a boo-boo," Timmy announced. I dug into my purse and handed him a Band-Aid. Not for the first time—in my opinion, Kiki was a hypochondriac.

"You said Jasper was living at his uncle Hiram's house," I said aloud. "Do you know where it is?"

"Out in the woods somewhere near the Clay County line. Hiram Bass—Jasper's mother's sister married one of the Clayville Basses."

To someone "from around here," that snippet of genealogy probably told volumes about Jasper and his family, but all it told me was that my quest to find Karen was probably going to lead Timmy and me to the county property records office, to locate Hiram Bass, and then out into the more rural end of the county.

I noticed that Sandie was looking at Kiki and frowning. Well, yes, Kiki wasn't exactly in pristine condition. If Karen didn't show up by bedtime tonight, I was going to try stealing Kiki after Timmy had dropped off to sleep and putting her through the washer and dryer. Or maybe Sandie was expressing disapproval of the number of Band-Aids festooning Timmy's hands and Kiki's paws. Well, yes, I suppose I had made a mistake, letting Timmy find out that I routinely carried Band-Aids in my purse.

"Thanks," I said. "You've been a big help."

"I should be getting back," she said, with another disapproving glance at Kiki. "But please keep me posted on how you're doing."

"Will do."

Though when I got back to the car, I wondered if taking Timmy along on my visit to Jasper was such a great idea. For that matter, if Karen had disappeared after going out to see Jasper, maybe going out there myself wasn't such a great idea.

Maybe I needed to find out a little more about Jasper first.

I had a lot of trouble getting Timmy back to the car—I practically had to carry him down the sidewalk. Not that he was being deliberately uncooperative, but he had clearly hit the wall and was falling asleep on his feet. When I got him strapped in, I consulted his instruction manual and remembered that after lunch was supposed to be story and nap time.

I shoved in the car songs CD to substitute for the story, but with the volume turned down so it wouldn't interfere if he decided to start his nap immediately. Then I turned the car homeward. While Timmy was napping, I'd see what I could find out about Jasper.

Eleven

About a mile from our house, the road from town ran up onto a ridge, giving motorists a sweeping view of the landscape for several miles around—including our house and the sloping part of Seth Early's pasture that lay across the road from us. Michael always said that he loved that first sight of our house waiting for him at the end of his drive home from the college. I was usually more interested in getting a preview of who and what might be waiting for me when I arrived at the house. A couple of times, the ridge had let me spot some unloved relative's car parked in front of the house, giving me a chance to remember that I hadn't quite finished all my errands yet.

Today, I could see that Seth Early was skulking across the road from our house, behind the hedge and fence that separated his pasture from the road. I found that reassuring. Mr. Early reacted with great alarm to even the most harmless of breaks from routine, suspecting innocent-seeming delivery men and lost motorists of having sinister designs on his prize Lincoln sheep. Surely anyone who actually meant us harm would raise Mr. Early's hackles and inspire him to call the Caerphilly police long before the intruder could do anything.

I thought of waving to him when I pulled up at the house, but I decided against it. He probably thought he was cleverly concealed and I didn't want to spoil his fun.

Timmy was fast asleep in his car seat, presenting me with a dilemma. I suspected that, like sleeping dogs, sleeping toddlers should be left undisturbed. I needed Timmy's nap at least as much as he did. But the thermometer was a blistering ninety degrees outside.

I parked the car in the shade and left the air conditioning running while I pondered the problem. I decided that I could probably get the car seat out of the car without waking him, but hauling him upstairs and transferring him to the crib probably wouldn't work. So I opened all the doors and prepared to wait until he awakened by himself. Just to be safe, I dragged a portable fan and an extension cord out of the kitchen and set them up so the breeze would blow gently across Timmy's car seat. The resulting breeze was actually a considerable improvement over what the window air-conditioning units had achieved in the house, so I fixed myself a glass of lemonade and settled down beside Timmy to enjoy it.

I had almost fallen asleep when I heard a noise at my elbow.

"Psst!"

I opened my eyes to find Seth Early standing beside the car. I put my finger to my lips and led him about fifteen feet away so we wouldn't wake Timmy.

"How do I get in touch with Homeland Security?" he said.

"Why would you want to?" I asked. "I mean, what's up?"

"Remember that guy you told me about? The one who's been hanging around here?"

"Hanging around here? I only saw him that one time."

"He's been hanging around here. Swarthy-looking guy. Definitely not from around here."

Swarthy-looking? Considering how brown Seth Early was from all his outdoor work, I wondered how deeply tanned someone had to be to qualify as swarthy in his eyes.

Could it be Jasper, Karen's ex? I called up his image from the photo on her desk.

"Was he tall and skinny? Long brown hair in a ponytail? Weak chin?"

"No, that's not him. This guy was shortish, with short hair."

Not Jasper, then. But perhaps one of the thugs who had been hanging around, looking for Karen? And did Seth Early actually know what swarthy meant? Maybe he thought it merely meant thuggish or suspicious.

"Did you call the police?" I asked aloud.

"They said they'd drop by later. They haven't, though. Wouldn't do much good; the guy's gone now. But he'll be back, I suspect."

"If he comes back, call them right away," I said. "And remind them that you live across the street from me, and that I'm baby-sitting Karen Walker's son."

"You think that'd make a difference?"

"After today it will," I said. "Her apartment was broken into. Lots of cops there. At the moment, anything related to Karen is probably high priority with Chief Burke."

He shook his head doubtfully and ambled off to return to his vigil.

Even though Chief Burke had made Seth Early give up carrying his shotgun around, I felt a little better knowing he was keeping watch across the street.

But he'd ruined my chances of napping. I walked over to make sure Timmy was still cool and comfortable, then sat down under a nearby tree and pulled out my cell phone. I was stuck here until Timmy woke up, but maybe I could make good use of the time.

I called Jack Ransom. Jack was technically the second-in-command at Mutant Wizards, the computer gaming company Rob had founded. In reality, Jack ran the company, since Rob had no managerial, business, or computing skills whatsoever. From the company's point of view, Rob more than justified his existence by providing a steady stream of oddball ideas that, more often than not, could be turned into successful computer and video games by Jack's legions of programmers and graphic designers.

But unless the staff needed him to come in to brainstorm for them or impress some important client, Mutant Wizards ran just fine without Rob. In fact, having Rob on site usually proved so disruptive that the staff went to great lengths to keep him away. Most of the time, he was content to live the life of a dilettante, but every so often he'd have a brief attack of guilt and vow to be more industrious. One of my unofficial jobs, as a member of the Mutant Wizards board of directors, was to detect Rob's guilt trips in their early stages and side-track him into something else.

These days I saw a lot more of Jack than Rob did—we'd arranged to give me a bunch of corporate titles that meant I could sign off on documents when Rob was nowhere to be found. Luckily, seeing Jack was a lot less stressful now that he'd gotten used to the idea that Michael and I were not breaking up anytime soon and he would not be getting a dramatic promotion from understudy to leading man in my life—his metaphor, not mine.

And Jack was very plugged into Caerphilly's relatively small tech community. Jasper was a techie. If Jack didn't have the lowdown on him he would know someone who did.

"Jasper Walker," Jack repeated. "Yeah, rings a bell. We interviewed him a couple of times. He had a great resume—too bad he must have stolen it from someone who actually has a functioning brain."

"So you weren't impressed?"

"Only by his gall in repeatedly applying for positions for which he was totally unqualified. How did you meet Jasper, anyway?"

"I didn't; a friend did."

"Steer her away from him, then; the guy's bad news."

"Too late—she married him."

"Bummer."

"And I think he's dragged her into some trouble. I desperately need to find out what. Could you maybe ask around, figure out what he's up to these days—Is he still working over at the college's data support center? If not, what happened? Is he in some kind of trouble?—stuff like that."

"Can do. In fact, why don't you drop by here this afternoon—anytime after two. We have a programmer who used to work with Jasper. I remember it really shook the kid up when he saw Jasper in the waiting room, and he was visibly relieved we weren't hiring him. He just said they didn't get on, and it wasn't important, since I wasn't hiring Jasper anyway. But I bet he knows more, and you could probably get it out of him."

"It's a plan."

I settled back to wait until Timmy woke up. I took out my notebook that tells me when to breathe, as I called my giant to-do list. I tried, without much success, to find a few items in the to-do section that could be done while waiting for a napping child to wake. Clearly, before embarking on motherhood, I needed to get better at making good use of small windows of time when I couldn't go anywhere. And also at rearranging my life at a moment's notice.

Timmy finally awoke around two-thirty, but thanks to diaper changing and snacks and such, it was closer to three-thirty by the time we hit the road, and I was overdue for some adult conversation.

Twelve

I found a shady spot in the Mutant Wizards parking lot and led Timmy inside to find that the reception room had altered dramatically since last week. The furniture was unchanged, but it had been rearranged in a much more efficient layout, and most of the clutter and tchotchkes had gone. The waiting room now looked chic, modern, and uncluttered—exactly the sort of decor I'd always thought we needed for the reception room in the first place. And a lot easier to keep Timmy safe in, for that matter.

"Morning, Apple," I said to the receptionist. "I see you've been doing some redecorating."

"More like undecorating," Apple said, with a sniff. "I told Jack I was sick and tired of seeing all those bamboo flutes and Chinese dragons all over everywhere, and I was going to put them in a closet for a while and see if anything horrible happened. And so far nothing has."

"Not a believer in feng shui, then?"

"Feng shui's okay within reason, but the place was starting to look like a souvenir stand in Chinatown."

"No kidding," I said. And then I felt a stab of guilt. I

reminded myself that family honor didn't require me to defend Rose Noire's feng shui expertise—she'd installed the flutes and dragons and hundreds of other feng shui cures after we'd had a murder on site. And it was true that Mutant Wizards had not experienced any further homicides, but then neither had any of the buildings in town that Rose Noire hadn't feng shui'd. "I'm glad you kept the fish tank, though," I added.

"The guys like the fish tank," she said.

So did Timmy. He hadn't made a sound since he'd walked in and spotted the tank. He was now six inches away from the glass and staring avidly—about the longest I'd seen him stay in one place when not asleep or securely strapped in. I scrutinized the tank, but it looked fairly sturdy and well balanced. Though I noticed that even the fish tank had changed.

"Different fish, I see."

"Piranha," Apple said. "A lot more interesting. Especially at feeding time. The guys love that. You want to see Jack, right?"

I nodded and went over to keep a closer eye on Timmy. At the moment, he had his nose plastered against the tank and was staring cross-eyed at the deceptively ordinary-looking fish inside. But I wouldn't put it past him to find a way to put his head into the tank if I turned my back on him, or perhaps pull it down on top of himself. And I reminded myself that telling Timmy to stay away from the tank would almost certainly make him more interested in it.

"Good grief," Jack said, as he strode out into the reception area. "Has Rob forgotten to tell me something very interesting? Have you and Michael—?"

"He's not ours," I said. "He's only temporary."

"Taking a test drive to see if you like the model? Smart move."

"Actually, I'm looking for his mother. And his father, for that matter. That's why I called you."

"Oh, God," he said. "You're not going to ask me where I was on the night of November 13th and pull out a Q-tip to sample my DNA, are you?" I could tell he was clowning. Possibly for the benefit of Apple, who was drinking in our conversation.

"Nothing so dramatic," I said. "I know his father's identity; it's his whereabouts that are in question."

"Yeah, I figured. I may have something for you. Come on."

He turned to go into the main office area.

"Wait—you're not leaving him here, are you?" Apple protested.

"Of course not," Jack said, though clearly he had been about to. He strode over to Timmy, picked him up and lifted him up over his head. Timmy squealed with delight, as he usually did at becoming airborne.

"Whoa," Jack said, pretending to tap Timmy's head against the ceiling tiles. "Would you look at this kid! He's too big for our office—even taller than I am. Come on, Timmy; we'll find some way to make you useful."

He set off down the hallway, alternately lifting Timmy up near the ceiling and waving him down along the floor. Fortunately, Mutant Wizards wasn't the sort of place where a squealing toddler would prove much of a disruption to the working day. Only two or three employees stuck their heads out as we passed, and they didn't seem annoyed, just curious.

Jack stopped at a cubicle and set Timmy down.

"Here, Hal. I've got a test subject for you."

Hal, a sleepy-looking thirty-something Asian man, regarded Timmy with greater enthusiasm than most people would have shown at having a two-year-old suddenly dropped off in their office.

"Test subject for what?" I asked, feeling suddenly protective.

"Kiddy games," Hal said.

"New game line we're experimenting with," Jack said. "Educational games for preschoolers. Hal, why don't you and Muriel see if Timmy likes any of the prototypes."

Muriel, apparently, was the young woman with the purple hair sitting in Hal's cube. She examined Timmy with calm interest.

Now that Timmy was on the ground, he was starting to look a little anxious at being in a strange place, surrounded by strangers. He grabbed my leg and I found myself feeling curiously protective.

"It's okay, Timmy," I said, leaning over and putting my arm around him. "Hal and Muriel are going to show you some computer games. Would you like that?"

Timmy nodded, a little tentatively.

"Do you like tractors?" Hal asked. "And trains?"

Timmy nodded with a little more enthusiasm.

Muriel hitched herself closer to one of the four computers crowded into the cubicle and tapped a few keys. A brightly colored, highly detailed cartoon of a tractor appeared on the screen.

"Tractor!" Timmy said, sounding happier.

Muriel tapped a few more keys and the deep growl of a tractor motor filled the cubicle.

"Oh, much better sound effects," Jack said.

Timmy let go of my leg and took a couple of tentative steps toward the computer.

Muriel tapped a few more keys, and the view on the monitor pulled back to show that the tractor was in the middle of a kind of obstacle course littered with other mechanical objects.

His eyes glued to the monitor, Timmy walked over and leaned against Muriel, in what for him was a relatively subtle hint that he wanted her chair. A minute or so later, Timmy was installed in the desk chair with a mouse in his tiny hands and Muriel leaning over his shoulder pointing out things on the screen while Hal scribbled notes on a clipboard.

"That should keep him busy for a while," Jack said. "And Hal's been asking for some more kids to test the games on."

"Great," I said. "The baby-sitting service alone is worth whatever bribe I promised you. And if you have any information about Jasper Walker . . ."

"I not only have information," he said. "As promised, I have someone who used to work with Jasper. Someone who can't stand him, which means we'll hear all the dirt."

"Great," I said. "Though I might be more impressed if you'd found one of the very small number of people who actually like Jasper."

We'd reached Jack's office by that time. A slight young man with olive skin and a shaved head, who had been sitting in the guest chair, popped up like a jack-in-the-box the minute we entered.

"Meg, this is Ashok, from our User Experience Division," Jack said. I was relieved; apparently Jack had finally broken the habit of calling it the Idiotproofing Division. "Ashok, Rob's sister, Meg."

"Great to meet you," Ashok said. He was wide-eyed, and the hand I shook felt a bit damp. No doubt he was nervous, being called into Jack's office to meet the CEO's sister. He was probably a relatively new employee, which meant he'd barely met Rob. We'd figured out that the less contact the rank and file employees had with Rob, the easier it was to keep intact their belief in the corporate myth that Rob was a business mastermind and a computer genius.

"You know Jasper Walker?" I asked.

He nodded.

"I actually worked under him for a little while," he said. "Not that many places in Caerphilly for programmers to work. It's a small world."

"A small, small world," I said. And then I winced. Thanks to Timmy's car tunes CD, I could barely keep myself from singing those words to the increasingly familiar tune.

"When I graduated, I got a job in the college's systems support department," Ashok went on. "Walker was my project leader. We were taking this COTS accounting software and trying to integrate it with all the legacy systems."

"COTS means a commercial, off-the-shelf program," Jack translated.

"Sorry," Ashok said, looking anxious.

"Okay," I said. "And legacy systems, if I remember correctly, are all the programs that have been around since the dinosaurs roamed the earth that the college is too cheap to replace."

"Yeah," Ashok said, smiling slightly, and looking a little more relaxed. "Anyway, it was the project from hell, right from day one. And Walker was a total idiot. The only reason our boss kept him around was that Walker had an in with some woman in accounting and could get her to sign off on stuff. Stuff that didn't actually work, or at least not the way it was supposed to. I mean, if you ask me, it was a total scam."

I winced slightly. Did this mean that Jasper had taken advantage of Karen? Or that Karen had been unwise enough to help her husband cover up his department's failure?

"I gather he's not working there anymore, either," I said. "Did he leave voluntarily or . . ."

"Fired," Ashok said. "I guess they finally figured out what an idiot he was. I was gone by that time—bailed as soon as I could land the job here—but I heard about it from some of my friends who were still there. It was just a few months later. Jasper was out, and a lot of other people with him, so there must have been some kind of stink, but nobody really knew exactly what happened. But I bet it had something to do with what happened today."

Ashok paused dramatically. Jack and I looked at each other and then back at Ashok. Jack broke down first.

"And what happened today?" he asked.

"The police," Ashok said.

Thirteen

"Police?" I echoed.

"They showed up at the college data center an hour ago," Ashok said. "And they've been seizing files and hardware and interrogating people ever since. And they're asking a lot of questions about Walker."

"Damn," I said.

Ashok's face fell and he looked at Jack as if for reassurance.

"Sorry," I said. "That was directed at Walker, not you. How did you hear about this so fast, anyway?"

Ashok visibly relaxed.

"Some friends texted me the news about an hour ago. They couldn't even IM me because the police had seized their computers."

Text, IM—I found myself wondering if it would ever occur to any of them to pick up the phone and call each other to gossip, which would be my first instinct. And was the fact that I thought this a sign of culture clash or generation gap?

"What could he possibly have done?" I wondered aloud. "I mean, it must be something big, or the police wouldn't be that hot about it, but if it's big, it's hard to believe it took them two years to discover it."

Unless, of course, someone who still worked at the college had been covering it up for two years. Someone like Karen. Had she disappeared because she'd been covering up for Jasper and knew the police were about to pounce? Or had the crime come to light because her disappearance interrupted her cover-up? Of course, it was always possible that she'd disappeared for some other reason, and the police raid on the data center happening just after her disappearance was only a coincidence. Possible, but not, alas, very likely.

"What kind of system was Walker working on?" Jack asked. "I don't mean the technical specs—what was it designed to do?"

"Financial stuff," Ashok said. "Keeping track of vendors and contracts and generating checks and electronic payments and a lot of stuff with bank accounts and investments. Sort of a complete system for all the money stuff. Sorry," he said, seeing both Jack and me frown. "I know that's kind of vague, but Walker just treated me like a code monkey, and I tried to keep my head down. He didn't like it if you asked too many questions."

"No, if I were an embezzler, I'd try to keep my staff from learning too much," Jack said. "Especially if I'd been lucky enough to get my larcenous little paws on the code that runs the college's central financial systems. Talk about a gold mine."

"But if Jasper's been gone for two years, then he has to have a confederate who's still on the inside, right?" I asked.

From the look on Jack's face, I suspected he understood why I was asking.

"Not necessarily," he said. "He could have left himself a back door. A way of getting back into the system without anyone knowing about it," he added, before I had to ask.

Ashok looked solemn.

"That was one of the rumors that went around when they fired him," he said. "That they'd uncovered a back door he'd coded into the system."

"They'd have fixed that, surely, after he was fired," Jack said.

"Yeah but what if Jasper was sneakier than any of us realized," Ashok said. "What if he programmed an obvious back door—maybe a couple. And when someone found them and fired him, all he had to do was sit and wait till the system went on-line and he could milk it."

"Not sure that's plausible," Jack said, shaking his head.

"It's a classic game technique," Ashok said. "Put the players off guard by giving them a trap that's easy to avoid. They're so busy patting themselves on the back, they don't notice until the last minute when you spring the real challenge."

"Yeah, but the first thing any sane IT department would do if they found one back door is search for others. Of course it's also possible that they focused too much on looking for back doors and overlooked other sneaky things he could have done."

"Like having a confederate to let him in the front door."

"It's possible," Jack said. "Of course, it's not the only

possibility," he added. No doubt he'd seen the look on my face at Ashok's suggestion and remembered who Jasper's confederate might be.

"And it's not as if they have anyone left over there with the brains to spot a back door," Ashok said. "Of course, I think there's still a limit to how long you could get away with working a back door, unless you had someone on the inside to help you cover up."

"That's true," Jack said. "Sorry," he added to me. "But if I were the police . . ."

"You'd be looking closely at Karen," I said. "So would I."

"Wow," Ashok said. "Maybe Walker was smarter than he looked after all."

"Smarter, no," Jack said. "Just sneakier. Look, if you hear anything else juicy . . ."

"I'll tell you, right away."

"Tell Jack and me," I said. I pulled a sheet from my notebook, scribbled my cell phone number, and handed it to him.

"You bet," he said, beaming again. "I'll text some of my friends right away."

"Thanks, Ashok," Jack said.

Ashok shook hands with me and left with a positive bounce in his step, his fingers already flying over the keys of his cell phone.

"Not good news," Jack said.

"No," I agreed. "But useful news. Hang on, I need to make a call."

"I'll check on Timmy."

"You don't have to leave," I said.

"No, but I want to make sure your temporary toddler

hasn't traumatized my programmers too badly," he said.

He slipped out of the office as I dialed Sandie's number.

"Financial Administration," she said.

"Hi, Sandie," I said. "It's Meg Langslow."

"I'm sorry, you have the wrong number," Sandie said.

"No, Sandie, remember me—I was in there this afternoon."

"It's okay, Nadine, it's only a wrong number," Sandie said, her tone slightly muffled.

"Okay," I said. "I get it. You can't talk right now. Can I call you back at another number?"

"Just a minute, let me get my college directory," Sandie said. "Do you have a pen?"

After I assured her that yes, I had a pen, she recited a number. I jotted it down, Sandie reassured me that it was no trouble at all, urged me to have a nice day, and hung up.

"Now that was weird," I said aloud. "Something's up."

"Up where?"

I looked up to see that Jack was back.

"At Karen's office, by the sound of it."

"The police show up there, too?"

"I don't know—my source there wouldn't talk to me. She did give me a phone number, though. I'm wondering how long I should wait before—"

My cell phone rang. The display showed the number Sandie had just given me.

"Hello?"

"What did you do?" Sandie exclaimed. "Half an hour after you left, the police came in and they've been going through Karen's files ever since and Nadine is just about ready to spit tacks!"

To my relief, she didn't sound mad. In fact, she sounded as if she was having a lot more fun than she had been before my visit.

"I didn't do anything," I said. "I went home so Timmy could take his nap. I was just calling to see if Karen was back."

"Well, you must have done something. Did you talk to anyone before you came over here?"

"I didn't tell anyone I was coming over to see you," I said. "That was an impulse. Poor Nadine! After she was so welcoming and helpful, too."

Sandie giggled.

"Look, I should get back," she said. "I'm only out here having a smoke, which I shouldn't be doing because I'm supposed to be trying to quit, but that was the only way I could leave the office without it looking odd, and I guess backsliding's a pretty normal thing to do, with all this going on. But Nadine will get antsy if I take too long."

"I appreciate you calling me back," I said. "Let me know if anything else happens."

"Will do," she said. "Yipes, I think some more cops are arriving. Bye."

"Damn," I muttered. I looked up to see Jack raising one eyebrow quizzically. "The cops are also swarming all over Karen's office. This is not looking good—Karen dumps Timmy on me, then disappears, her apartment is burgled or vandalized, and now they're searching her

office and her husband's former place of employment
and—damn!"

"You're thinking she's involved in whatever Walker
did, then?" he asked. "And dumped Timmy on you
while she makes a getaway?"

"It doesn't sound like Karen, but who knows?" I said.
"There's always the possibility that it's her husband who
has done something wrong, and she's getting dragged in
because of him. By the way, how's Timmy?"

"Timmy's fine. In fact, Timmy's over the moon. Hal
has invented a simple game that allows the player to drive
a truck or a tractor around and crash it into things."

"Sounds like something Rob would love."

"Oh, he does," Jack said, with a grin.

"Timmy's going to hate it when I try to drag him
away," I said, with a sigh.

"So why rush?" he said. "Surely you can do some of
your sleuthing from here?"

"If I were cyber-savvy, I could."

"Or if you had a cyber-savvy assistant." Jack pulled
his chair up to his desktop computer and twiddled his
fingers over the keyboard as if impatient to begin.

Fourteen

"Okay," I said. "Can you find out where Jasper lives? Or if he's not findable, his uncle, Hiram Bass?"

He could, quite easily. Jasper wasn't in the phone book, but Hiram Bass was listed, at 14953 Whitetail Lane. Jack even printed a map to get me there.

"How are you at phone numbers?" I asked.

"Have you ever heard of a reverse phone directory?"

"Do you have one?" I glanced at his bookshelves.

"There must be a dozen of them on the Web," he said.

"Okay," I said. "I've got four numbers. One appears to be her dentist, calling to confirm an appointment on Tuesday. I suspect she didn't make that one. But let's make sure it really is her dentist."

I handed the slip to Jack, who typed the numbers into something and then nodded.

"Yes, that's Dr. Payne. I go to him, too. Next."

"Next is Pete, with a college exchange," I said, handing him the next two. "Actually, he called three times, the last time asking her to call back ASAP."

"Peter Willoughby in the computer support division," Jack said. "Want his office number?"

"Please. Although from what Ashok told us, today probably isn't the best day to visit Mr. Willoughby. Next, someone named Trey."

Jack typed, then shook his head.

"Cell phone," he said. "I'm sure there's a way to find the owner, but I'm afraid I don't know it."

"Well, there's an easy way to find out," I said. I pulled out my cell phone, dialed the number, and listened while it rang.

"No answer," I said, after about seven rings. "And looks as if Trey hasn't set up his or her mailbox."

"Feckless," Jack said. "When will people learn to use technology effectively?"

I decided not to mention that it had taken me six months before I'd gotten around to setting up the mailbox for my own cell phone.

"And the last one is from Jasper, according to the message. Let's see if he answers."

I dialed and we both waited. Eventually his voice mail kicked in and I hung up.

"No answer," I said. "And under the circumstances, I'm not sure I want to leave a friendly message for the guy. Wish I had a nickel for every minute I've spent listening to phones ring over the last two days. Anyway, that's the lot. Not much use."

"Sorry about that. Anything else you want me to investigate?"

I thought about it for a moment.

"Yeah," I said. "Nadine."

"Nadine have a last name?"

"Probably; most people do. Unfortunately, I don't

know it. But she works in the college's Financial Administration office. She's Karen's boss."

"Let's check the college Web site, then."

After a few minutes of typing, interspersed with frowns and the occasional muttered insult at the amateurism of the college's Web site designers, Jack broke into a smile.

"Here we are. Nadine Hanrahan. Office in the third floor of Grover Pruitt Hall."

"That's her," I said.

"What do you want to know about her?"

I frowned. Jack waited, patiently.

"I don't know," I said, after a few moments. "I'm not even sure why her name popped into my head when you asked who else I wanted you to investigate."

"Maybe your subconscious finds her suspicious."

"Yeah," I said, slowly. "Or it could just be that my subconscious doesn't like her. I know my conscious doesn't. She's exactly the kind of college bureaucrat who makes Michael's life miserable. Now that I've met her, I understand why everything that comes through the Financial Administration office takes so much paperwork and hassle. What else *can* you find out about her?"

"I could probably figure out where she lives. You could flamingo her yard."

"It's a thought," I said, with a laugh. "Actually, I'd really like to flamingo Michael's department head's yard, but only if he never finds out I had anything to do with it. But yes, let's see where she lives."

"Nadine seems to have an unlisted number," Jack

reported after a little bit of typing. "Let me check the county property records. Ah, here she is. In Westlake."

"Westlake? Are you sure?"

"See for yourself." He turned the monitor so I could see the record on Nadine's home. My eye landed on the purchase price and my jaw dropped.

"Two million dollars!" I exclaimed. "Holy cow! Working in financial administration must pay a whole lot more than working in the drama department."

"I doubt it," he said. "And it's just her on the property record, so it's not like she's got a husband who's a real estate tycoon or anything."

"Maybe she divorced some rich guy and got the house in the settlement?"

"No, she bought it outright eighteen months ago," Jack said. He pointed out the place on the screen where I could see for myself. "Of course, it could still be loot from divorcing the rich guy if she got a cash settlement and decided to sock it away in real estate."

"Yes, but eighteen months ago," I mused. "That's very soon after the college fired Jasper Walker, possibly without taking a careful look at the code he left behind. Look, tell me if this sounds like wishful thinking because Karen's my friend—but if Karen's involved in the embezzling scheme, where's her share of the loot? She's living in the College Arms and driving a fifteen-year-old beater—does that sound like an embezzler's lifestyle? And here's Nadine in a two-million-dollar mansion. Which one of them looks more like an embezzler?"

"Nadine, no question," he said. "Ashok's rumor just said that Walker had an in with some woman in Financial Administration—it didn't specify who the woman was. Could have been Nadine as easily as Karen."

"Yes, and since Nadine runs the whole office, it would be a lot easier for her to cover something up for two years," I said. "Of course, there's still the whole question of why Karen ran away, and who she's running from. From Jasper, or Nadine, or the police or what. I need to find her. Preferably before the police do. Even if she didn't before, by now she really needs a lawyer."

"Anything else I can look up for you?"

"Not that I can think of," I said. "But I'll let you know. Thanks a lot for the info. I'll take Timmy off your hands now; I'm going to go out and see if I can find Jasper's uncle's house."

Fifteen

Timmy wasn't too happy to leave the tractors and the fish behind—in fact, he pitched a fit that probably registered about 7.5 on the Richter scale over at the college's geology department and earned him a time-out. At least I assume making him stand in a corner and be quiet was something like what parents did when they talked about giving their kids time-outs. Between that and a promise that we'd come back soon if he behaved, I finally managed to maneuver him out to the car—where he promptly fell asleep as soon as I started the engine. His instruction manual didn't mention the possibility of a second afternoon nap—was this a sign that he was getting ill? Or only that we'd have a hard time getting him to settle down at bedtime? Time would tell.

Of course, his instruction manual also hadn't mentioned the concept of time-outs, or any other hints on what kind of discipline he was used to. Did Karen simply let him run wild? Or did she assume that was one of the things everyone already knew? I made a mental note to skim one of Rose Noire's childcare manuals when I got home, to make sure time-outs hadn't been redefined as cruel and unusual punishments since my nieces and nephews had outgrown them.

In the meantime, I followed the map Jack had printed to Jasper's uncle's house—which was at the far end of the county, where most of the land was too swampy to farm and had been given over to raising pines for the pulp mills or just left alone. The directions were admirably precise, but every time I turned I found myself on a smaller road with the houses farther apart—if they were visible at all.

I finally found 14953 Whitetail Lane. Its mailbox stood beside another mailbox at the head of a dirt lane that led off into the deep woods. No name on the mailbox, only the number, but the lane's other resident made up for 14953's terseness by providing not just a number and a name on the mailbox—14955, Aubrey Hamilton—but two other signs. One, nicely painted, advertised the Prancing Poodle Kennels (A. Hamilton, proprietor), with what looked like a conga line of purple poodles against a pink background. The other, less professionally painted and unillustrated, proclaimed that the Belle Glade Bird Farm had canaries, parakeets, and cockatiels for sale. The bird farm sign looked brand new while the kennel sign was so weathered and faded that it looked as if the poodles had been prancing for decades. I deduced that Aubrey Hamilton had either recently added bird breeding to the longstanding kennel's operation or perhaps had given up dogs for birds.

The dirt lane looked badly rutted and little used. I glanced back in my rearview mirror. Timmy was still asleep. Odds were he'd wake up once I left the road. Ah, well; at least I'd had half an hour's respite. And it was getting hot out here in the sunshine—odds were it would be cooler in the woods.

I eased the car into the lane and lurched along at five miles an hour. It was like entering a green tunnel, as the dense woods closed around us. At first I could see the entrance, an arch of sunlight slowly shrinking in my rearview mirror. And then I went around a curve in the lane and the entrance disappeared.

"Truck!" Timmy exclaimed. I glanced in the rearview mirror. No truck visible behind me, but then I realized that Timmy was pointing to the right of the car. He had good eyes—there was, indeed, a truck by the side of the road, or at least the skeleton of a truck. It was so completely overgrown with vines that I hadn't immediately spotted it, but now I could make out the shape. Probably a surplus army troop truck, to judge by the patchwork of olive drab paint and reddish brown rust on its frame and hood. Maybe even World War II surplus, by the shape of it.

"Truck," I echoed.

To the left of the road I spotted another truck—this one a pickup, slightly newer and less decrepit than the first, and with a correspondingly less dense mat of vines concealing it.

"Truck!" Timmy said. He was bouncing up and down as well as he could in his car seat and pointing happily. "Tractor!"

"Yes," I said. "A truck and a tractor."

Just beyond the pickup was a partially disassembled front-end loader. Up ahead on the right was an abandoned Airstream trailer. Beyond that were a pinball machine, a rusty horse trailer, and a convertible that would have qualified as vintage if it hadn't been visibly falling apart.

"It's like a mechanical elephant's graveyard," I said aloud.

We proceeded along the lane for another half a mile, accompanied by Timmy's regular cries of "Truck!" "Tractor!" and "Car!" Occasionally I'd see what looked like the beginning of a smaller lane, or perhaps a driveway, to one side or the other, but they always petered out in the vines or ended abruptly with a truck carcass. The farther we drove back into the woods, the more densely the vines covered the hulks of rusting machinery, making them harder and harder to identify. Farther from the road, I could see small hillocks completely covered with vines like modern burial mounds.

Then the road split. Another haphazardly lettered sign for the Belle Glade Bird Farm pointed to the right. I eased the car to the left.

The car and truck skeletons began appearing more densely. Ancient vine-covered hulks alternated with vehicles that looked as if they were actually in running condition, or had been within living memory. I also saw stocks of lumber, cinder blocks, bricks, and other building supplies. Flocks of oil drums were scattered here and there, along with enough car batteries to power a small city if they were still alive, which seemed unlikely.

Finally, a few hundred yards along, I spotted the house—more like a low, rambling shack with a small clearing to serve as the front yard. Here, the construction and automotive junk gave way to a more general collection of household debris: old appliances, aban-

doned pots and pans, remnants of furniture, and rags
that might once have been garments or linens. The junk
flowed up onto the front porch and around the sides of
the house, though it was mostly clear of the driveway,
which meandered up to the porch and then curved away
again. I followed the driveway and stopped the car at
the foot of the porch steps.

Hanging crookedly by one nail over the front door
was a carved wooden sign that said BASS'S TAVERN:
FREE BEER TOMORROW. A high school shop project, by
the look of it. At least I was probably in the right place.

Timmy was still excited by the cars and trucks, but
he didn't seem to show any interest in the house. No
cries of "Daddy!" Of course, if Sandie was right, odds
were he didn't remember being here, if he ever had
been. In fact, odds were he hardly remembered Jasper.

I parked at the very foot of the front steps and, after
considering my options, reluctantly released Timmy
from his car seat and picked him up. Clearly if I were
going to spend much more time trying to trace Karen's
whereabouts, I needed someone to ride shotgun and
take care of Timmy while I snooped. I climbed carefully onto the front porch, which turned out to be a lot
more sturdy than it looked, and knocked on the door.

A lean brownish gray dog ambled out of the woods
onto the porch, where it stood looking up at me. Great.
Just what I needed—a watchdog between me and the
car.

"Doggie!" Timmy exclaimed, squirming to be put
down. "Want doggie."

"But doggies chase kitties," I said. "You don't want
the doggie to chase Kiki, do you?"

He frowned and pondered that. The dog sat down as if waiting for me to let him in.

I knocked again and then stood on the porch for a few moments, listening for footsteps or any other sound from the house and hearing nothing but bird songs, insect buzzes, and the whining drone of a window air-conditioning unit laboring to keep the small house cool in the humid Virginia heat.

The dog wagged his tail slowly whenever I glanced at him.

I squatted down and held out my hand. He came over to me, unafraid.

"Nice doggie," Timmy said. The dog seemed friendly enough, so I didn't interfere when Timmy reached out to pat him. And I didn't mind at all when the dog began licking Timmy instead of me.

While Timmy and the dog made friends, I looked at the tag attached to the dog's collar. His name was Scout, and anyone who found him was urged to call J. Walker. I pulled my notebook out of my pocket and checked the phone numbers I'd written down from Karen's "While-you-were-out" stack. Yes, the J. Walker number matched the one Jasper had left when he called her office.

"Good boy, Scout," I said. I reached in my other pocket and found a couple of cheese crackers I'd picked up from the floor of the car. I offered Scout one. He took it eagerly, but it seemed like normal canine eagerness, not the desperation of an abandoned and starving animal.

I knocked several more times. I called out, "Mr. Walker? Jasper? Mr. Bass?" a couple of times.

No answer.

I peered into the front window. The house was—well, empty wasn't the word. Less junked up than the yard, but not by much. But empty of people, as far as I could see. Not unoccupied, though. On a coffee table in the living room I could see a pizza box and a couple of beer and Pepsi cans, none of them dust-covered. Someone had been here recently.

Scout followed as I left the porch. He seemed happy to have me around. I wanted to circle the house, maybe find someplace to climb in, but I couldn't very easily do that carrying Timmy. Too much junk to trip over, not to mention the undergrowth to wade through. No wonder Sherlock Holmes had stayed a bachelor.

Just then, Timmy threw his head back and began uttering wordless howls of misery.

I set him down and squatted down beside him so I could get a better look at him. And also to get his mouth a little farther from my ear.

"It's okay," I said, while scanning for injuries.

He sniffled for a few seconds and then hurled himself back into my arms. He didn't feel overheated—if anything, a little chilled, so perhaps I'd been overdoing the car air conditioning on his account. And judging from the Hansel and Gretel-style trail of Cheerios leading from the car to my feet, he couldn't have eaten enough to give himself a stomach ache. Okay, he was genuinely upset—though I couldn't tell why. I sat on the ground for perhaps twenty minutes, rocking him and murmuring whatever soothing words came to mind. Scout sat beside me, whining, wagging his tail, and intermittently licking whatever parts of Timmy he could reach.

About ten seconds after the crying finally subsided, Timmy popped his head up.

"Juice?" he asked. "Please?"

I took him back to the car and fished in the cooler for another sippy cup. He grabbed it with both hands and began gulping the contents with the sort of intensity you'd expect from a traveler who'd just crossed the Sahara. With him safely occupied, I set him down at my feet and glanced back at the house, wondering if it might be a good idea to see if I could pick one of the locks and snoop inside. No, probably not—I'd have to take Timmy with me, and even if I managed to snoop without leaving traces, I suspected I couldn't keep him from doing so. Besides—

Never turn your back on a two-year-old. I heard Timmy smack his lips and sigh with satisfaction, and by the time I glanced down, he was vanishing into the shrubbery.

I spent what seemed like an half an hour playing tag with Timmy. Timmy and the dog, who seemed to think we'd invented a really superior game. The two of them were better suited to darting through small openings in the vines and shrubbery, and more uninhibited about crawling onto and into dangerous bits of rusting machinery.

I finally sat down in a clearing, out of breath and rapidly losing my temper. Maybe I was going about this the wrong way. Maybe I should go back to the car and find some bait. Some Cheerios, or maybe a candy bar. I had a few Snickers bars in the cooler, in case I needed a sudden jolt of energy. They weren't on Timmy's approved diet—in fact, candy bars of any kind were on the list of things he wasn't supposed to have under any circumstances. But if Karen was going to be that persnickety about his diet, she should stick around to supervise it herself.

Just then Scout stuck his head through some shrubbery and pulled it back. I pretended not to notice.

"I'll just have to go back without him," I said.

Scout stuck his head out again, as if he thought I might be talking to him.

"No idea where he's gone."

The shrubbery behind the dog rustled as if he were wagging his tail. From somewhere to my left, I heard a slight giggle.

"I should probably just go home for dinner," I said.

"Want dinner," came a voice from the shrubbery.

I peered in the direction the voice had come from.

"Timmy?" I asked. "Is that you?"

He giggled, and stuck his head out from behind some leaves. Then he ducked in again and giggled.

The leaves, I noticed with a sinking feeling, were poison ivy.

Sixteen

I managed to extricate Timmy from the poison ivy grove with promises of chocolate, though I had to wade through some of it to get back to the car. I postponed any notion of picking the lock and snooping inside Jasper Walker's house. I knew that if I could get home and wash the poison ivy oil off myself and Timmy immediately, we might have a chance of escaping an outbreak of the dreaded rash. Then again, either I was having psychosomatic itching or it was already too late. For me, anyway. Dad always said that children didn't develop sensitivity to poison ivy until after they'd been exposed several times, so Timmy would probably be all right. Then again, active as Timmy was, he could have already used up his immunity. I strapped him into his car seat and took off.

But as I reached the fork in the driveway, I saw the tail end of a red pickup truck disappearing in the direction of the canary farm. I hesitated. Washing off the poison ivy oil was important. So was finding Karen.

What the hell, I decided. I might not find the denizens of the canary farm home another time. The car and truck skeletons strewn on either side of the road made it difficult to turn, but I finally managed it. As we rattled down the lane, I told myself that if Aubrey Hamilton was a friendly soul, maybe I'd even beg the use of a bathroom to wash off the poison ivy oil. Come to think of it, the first aid kit probably contained some Fels-Naptha soap, which Dad recommended for that purpose.

I pulled up behind the pickup in front of a large, comfortable-looking farmhouse. The grass was a little unkempt, but the house itself looked in good repair, and the white board siding had been painted not that long ago. To the left and a little behind the house was a large barn, also in good repair, as was the fence around the barnyard.

A man came out of the house and stood at the top of the steps looking down at me as I got out of the car. He was youngish—probably around twenty-five—but had a faintly worn air about him, as if life hadn't treated him that well. And if we were friends, I'd have tried to convince him that nature had not designed him to wear a goatee—it made his already pointy chin look even pointier.

"Can I help you?" he said. He leaned on the top rail of the porch. He looked ill-at-ease but not unwelcoming, as if his country dweller's ingrained suspicion of unexpected visitors was at war with his hope that we might be here to buy canaries.

"You must be Aubrey Hamilton," I said. I strode over and shook his hand. "You run the canary farm, right?"

"Are you looking to buy a bird?" he asked. A little too eagerly—I wondered if perhaps the bird business wasn't going too well.

"Sorry, no," I said. "I'm looking for the guy who lives next door. Mr. Bass. Have you seen him recently?"

Hamilton shook his head.

"What do you want with the old guy, anyway?" he said. Was he frowning in suspicion of me, or in disbelief that anyone would voluntarily seek out his neighbor's company?

"I'm actually trying to find his nephew, Jasper Walker."

The frown deepened. Definitely suspicion.

"Jasper is or was married to my friend Karen," I went on. "And she left her son Timmy with me yesterday."

I indicated the car, where Timmy was chugging his juice. Hamilton barely glanced at him.

"Karen said she would just be gone for a little while," I said. "And that was yesterday morning. She's not answering my calls. I'm checking anyplace she might have gone and anyone who might have seen her."

"I haven't seen anyone next door for days," he said. "Sorry."

"Ah, well," I said. "Look, this may sound odd, but— Timmy got loose and wandered into a patch of poison ivy. I'd really like to wash him off. The sooner I do that, the less chance that he'll develop a rash."

Hamilton hesitated, clearly torn between a reluctance to appear inhospitable and an even stronger reluctance to let a wayward toddler into his house.

"We could just use that," I said, pointing to a green garden hose neatly coiled and hanging from a hook by the side of the house.

"Okay," he said. "Let me bring you a towel."

"He might have invited us in," I grumbled to Timmy as I stripped his clothes and diaper off.

Though once I began soaping him up and rinsing him off, I realized that it was an extraordinarily messy project, and I'd have been mortified at doing it inside a stranger's house.

"Sorry to put you to this trouble," I told Hamilton when he returned with the towel. "But you probably know how bad poison ivy can be for a little kid."

"No trouble at all," he said, though clearly he was getting tired of having us underfoot. He kept glancing over at the barn.

"Is that where you keep the birds?" I asked, pointing to the barn.

"What?" he said, looking startled.

"Your canaries. Is that where you keep them?"

"Yeah," he said. "Canaries, cockatiels, and parakeets. Are you interested in buying—sorry, you already said you weren't."

"How's business?" I asked.

"Slow," he said. "The market's depressed. Too many breeders. Damned things are eating me out of house and home. I could give you a good deal on a pair of cockatiels, if you like."

"Sorry," I said. "I'm not much of a bird-fancier. But I'll ask my family if anyone's in the market for a pet bird."

He nodded gloomily.

"Maybe you should have stuck to poodles," I said.

"Poodles?"

"The Prancing Poodle Kennels," I said. "I gather you're not breeding poodles anymore?"

"No money in poodles either."

"So when was the last time you saw Jasper Walker?" I asked.

"I don't know," he said. "Why?"

"I'm still trying to find him. Have you seen him within the last few days?"

"No," he said. "Not for months. I didn't even know he was back in town. Last I heard, he'd gotten fired from his job at the college and gone up to D.C. to look for work."

"Have you seen anyone over there lately?"

"No," he said. "I wouldn't expect to. Old Mr. Bass is in the nursing home, you know. Place has been empty for years."

I nodded. Apparently Jasper—or whoever had left the beer cans and pizza box—had been coming and going unseen. But maybe I should keep that to myself for now.

"Thanks a lot," I said, handing him the towel. "And if you see anything of Jasper or Karen, could you give me a call?"

I wrote my cell phone number on a sheet torn from my notebook and handed it to him.

"Okay," he said. "But I don't expect I'll see anything. It's—hey! Get away from there!"

I turned to see Timmy crawling through the barnyard fence. I gave chase, and managed to catch up with him before he reached the barn.

"Want see horsie," Timmy complained as I picked him up.

"There aren't any horsies there," I said. "Just birdies. Sorry," I added to Hamilton, who had only just caught up with us, and was seriously out of breath. "You turn your back on him for a second and he's gone."

"I understand," he said.

"Want see birdies," Timmy said.

Hamilton looked uneasy. He kept glancing at the barn and then back at Timmy.

"Look, I know he'd like to see the birds, but the last time a kid got in there he opened all the cages. Took us hours to catch the damned birds again."

"I understand," I said. "I doubt if Timmy's old enough to open cages, but it's time I got him home anyway. Thanks a lot."

Hamilton stood in the barnyard watching as I carried Timmy back to the car, wrestled him into clean clothes, strapped him into the car seat, and drove off.

"Is he hiding something, do you think?" I asked Timmy. "Or is he just not a sociable kind of guy?"

"Doggie," Timmy said.

Was that an incisive insult to Aubrey? No, Timmy had spotted Scout lying in the middle of the driveway to Hiram Bass's house. He lifted his head when he saw us, and his tail thumped a couple of times, and then, when we drove by, he put it back on his paws again.

"If you're still here when I come back, I'll call the animal shelter," I said as I watched the dog in my rearview mirror.

Back at home, I managed to get in a quick shower while Timmy took the shoelaces out of several pairs of Michael's shoes. I was down in the laundry room, putting our potentially poison-ivy contaminated clothes into the washer while Timmy ran around wearing nothing but a diaper, with a torn pillowcase over his head, pretending to be a ghost, when my cell phone rang. It was Michael.

"So do you think you can find a baby-sitter for Timmy tonight?" he said.

"Possibly, if I recruit someone from a few counties away, where he's not already notorious," I said. "Please don't tell me you scored tickets for something so hot that I'll hate Timmy forever if he makes me miss it."

"Actually, I was trying to arrange a dinner with Dr. Driscoll and his wife. At the Caerphilly Inn. I'm the department rep to one of his committees this year, and I'm supposed to ingratiate myself."

Granted, the prospect of dinner at the Inn was mouth-watering, but was Michael really expecting me to play charming faculty wife tonight? With Timmy on my hands and Karen's disappearance on my mind?

"You'll love the Driscolls," he said. "He's an avid bird-watcher—over eight hundred species on his life list. He'll tell you all about it if you ask. And his wife needlepoints and arranges flowers. They're elderly, and go to bed early, so I agreed we'd meet them there at five-thirty. That way they can still drive home before dark."

"You're telling me this so I won't mind missing dinner at the Inn to stay home and take care of Timmy. Who is this ghastly Dr. Driscoll, anyway?"

"Head of the financial administration department."

"Karen's department? Okay, you're on. I'm sure somebody around here owes me a favor."

"Let's hope it's a big favor," he said.

Seventeen

Usually most of my family could be convinced that they owed me multiple favors, but apparently I'd burned through a lot of those in the past couple of days. Dad and Dr. Blake had plans—presumably plans connected with whatever crime against wildlife my grandfather would be exposing in his next documentary. But when I asked what their plans were, they both changed the subject. Rose Noire was driving Mother up to Washington for a flurry of visits to antique stores and fabric stores and at the last minute they'd decided to go up the night before, to get an early start. As they scurried out the door, they assured me that their change of plans had nothing to do with Timmy.

I finally cornered Rob.

"Gee, I'm really sorry," he said. "But—"

"After all, you should at least try to help out with things if you're going to be practically living here," I said.

"I'm not practically living here," he protested.

"Oh, so I can throw away that pile of stuff in the closet of the bedroom on the third floor?"

It still took me fifteen minutes of my best guilt-inducing

persuasion plus the reassurance that I'd probably be home by 9 P.M. if not much earlier, but I broke him down.

By the time I'd gone over the most important sections of Timmy's instruction manual with Rob and reassured Timmy that even though I was going away for a few hours, Uncle Rob would be happy to play horsie-horsie with him all evening, I barely had enough time to throw on presentable slacks and a nice blouse before taking off for town.

I was walking out the door, car keys in my hand, when a complication hit me.

"I'll need to take your car," I said.

"Why?" Rob was still a little protective of his latest automotive toy, a Porsche convertible that had yet to acquire its first real scratch.

"What if something happens and you need to take Timmy someplace?" I said. "Like to the emergency room?"

"He can ride in the Porsche."

"It doesn't have a back seat to put the car seat in," I said. "And trust me, even if it did, you wouldn't want Timmy riding in your Porsche."

Rob digested that for a moment.

"Yeah, but what are the chances I'll actually have to take him to the ER?"

"Slim," I said. "So what does it matter if you're staying home with an aging tin can or a brand new race car in the driveway?"

He eventually gave way to common sense, but he was still sulking when I drove off. Or maybe just worrying about whether I could drive his car.

I had to admit, the Porsche was quite a change from

my reliable but aging Toyota. And after two days of
driving around with a car seat in the back, feeling as if
I spent more time looking in the rearview mirror at
Timmy than at the road ahead, being in the car alone
would have been exhilarating all by itself. Throw in the
sense of power and freedom of driving a hot car with
no roof—well, I found myself playing fast and loose
with the speed limit on one long open stretch. Fortunately I had slowed to a relatively sedate five miles
above the speed limit by the time I passed Chief Burke,
stopped by the side of the road, apparently talking on
his cell phone.

Looking in the rearview mirror, I thought I saw him
frowning at me, though his face disappeared in the
distance too soon to really tell.

Well, a frown was normal for Chief Burke when
he was in the middle of an investigation. No particular
reason for him to be frowning at me, was there?

I pushed the thought from my mind to enjoy the rest
of my drive. And I had to admit, the most beautiful
part of it was the last mile, from the gate of the Caerphilly Inn to the hotel's wisteria-draped front door. The
rest of the county was looking a little bare and baked
by a long, hot, dry summer, but the Inn's driveway was
cool and leafy under the overarching shade of the trees
on either side, and patches of bright summer flowers
appeared at charmingly unpredictable intervals. Now
that I'd started to try my hand at gardening, I had
gained a new appreciation for how expensive and labor-
intensive the Inn's low-key landscaping really was.

But I felt a lot less intimidated by the Inn now that
my recently discovered grandfather had taken up

semipermanent residence there. He terrorized the staff
on a regular basis, but they clearly adored him, which
either meant that they thought his bark was worse than
his bite or that he tipped hugely. Possibly both. At any
rate, with Dr. Blake in the picture, I felt a lot less worried these days that they'd do something dire like tow
my battered car for dripping oil on the spotless white
gravel of their parking lot. The locals debated hotly
whether the Inn had its gravel power-washed annually
or just replaced it. And of course Rob's practically new
Porsche shouldn't offend the Inn's sensibilities at all.

I glanced down at my clothes. The black slacks that
had looked okay at home suddenly seemed dowdy, and
flecked with bits of Spike's fur. And was that a spot of
yogurt on the left knee? Maybe I should have worn a
skirt. And heels. And—

Okay, so the Inn still had the power to intimidate.

I nodded to the desk clerk as I strolled through the
lobby toward the restaurant.

"Shall I tell your grandfather you're here?" he called.

I waved, smiled, shook my head, and pointed to the
dining room. He waved, smiled, and nodded in return.

Michael was already seated at a table with a view of
the lush expanse of the Caerphilly Golf Course, sipping a glass of red wine. He leaped to his feet when he
saw me.

"You look marvelous," he exclaimed, and leaned
over to kiss me with far greater decorum than usual.
Probably the civilizing influence of the hotel. I could
see the maitre d' beaming with subtle approval. Such a
well-dressed, well-behaved young couple.

Yes, it was definitely yogurt on the knee of my pants,

with tufts of dog-hair stuck in it. But the blouse was fine. I'd feel a lot more at ease once I got my unprepossessing legs under the tablecloth.

"I look okay," I said. "Imagine how marvelous I could look if—Yow!"

I'd started to sit down while talking, and didn't realize that the waiter had pulled out my chair for me— pulled it so far out and with such a flourish that when I tried to sit down where I'd last seen the chair, I landed on the floor in a heap.

I spent the next several minutes assuring the waiter and the maitre d' that yes, I was fine, and no, I didn't want the hotel doctor to check me out, and for heaven's sake, we didn't expect them to pick up our check.

"They're like sharks," I said to Michael in an undertone. "One drop of blood in the water—"

"Is madame injured?" Now it was the hotel manager at my elbow.

We finally agreed to accept a bottle of wine as suitable recompense for my injury. The hotel staff were still hovering solicitously over us when the Driscolls arrived.

Dining with the Driscolls was like dining with someone's grandparents. We managed to fill the first few minutes of the dinner with discussions of what each of us planned to order. But all too soon, the waiter took our orders and whisked away the menus, stranding us without any obvious means of conversation.

Michael and Dr. Driscoll fell back on college politics, and I hit on the notion of telling Mrs. Driscoll about our recent elopement and honeymoon. Either I'd found a subject dear to her heart, or she was as relieved as I was to have found something we could talk about. At any rate, she listened with a grandmotherly smile, making the occasional chirping comment, and happily sipping first a glass of the excellent wine Michael had initially ordered and then a few glasses of the even more excellent wine the maitre d' brought by way of apology. By the end of the salad course, I suspected Mrs. Driscoll would happily have listened to me read her the Caerphilly phone directory as long as I kept her glass filled.

By the time we reached the main course, though, I was eager to change the topic. I searched around for a ploy.

Eighteen

"Do you mind if I call home?" I asked, pulling out my cell phone and glancing apologetically around the table. I moved a few feet away and dialed Karen's number. Not that I really expected her to answer it, but I'd dialed it so often in the last couple of days that it was the first number that came to mind. I let it ring for a while, turning my back to the table so the Driscolls couldn't see that I wasn't talking to anyone, and then returned to my seat.

"Sorry," I said. "My brother Rob is baby-sitting, and I'm a little worried. He's not very experienced."

"Oh, you have children?" Mrs. Driscoll asked. And then a puzzled and slightly alarmed look crossed her face—no doubt as she recalled the scant two months since our wedding.

"Not yet," Michael said. "We're taking care of a friend's child. In fact, you probably know her—Karen Walker. Meg, isn't Karen in Ambrose's department?"

"Young Timothy?" Mrs. Driscoll exclaimed, a relieved smile spreading over her face. "My goodness—he's quite a handful, isn't he?"

"You have no idea," I said.

Dr. Driscoll looked troubled.

"Do you know where she's gone?" he asked.

"No idea," I said. "She dropped Timmy off with me Monday morning and I haven't heard from her since. Not that I can convince Chief Burke of that."

"Isn't it shocking?" Mrs. Driscoll said, shaking her head. "Ambrose has had the police in his office all day."

"You'd think they suspected me of something," Dr. Driscoll said.

"Well, Chief Burke's not with the college," Michael said.

"Precisely!" Mrs. Driscoll said, beaming as if Michael had said something particularly significant. Dr. Driscoll nodded solemnly and folded his hands on the table.

"I really don't think Chief Burke quite grasps the situation," he said, in a voice that had probably lulled generations of his fellow college staffers into gentle naps during financial meetings. "Karen is not the sort of young person to get involved in some kind of sordid embezzlement scheme. In fact—are you familiar with the unfortunate events we experienced two years ago?"

"Not really," I said.

"Not to go beyond this table," he said, holding up one forefinger in warning. "But as I tried to explain to the police—"

"And were absolutely ignored," Mrs. Driscoll put in.

"Two years ago, Karen came to me with very disturbing news," Dr. Driscoll said. "She and her husband had separated—a very sad business."

"Speak for yourself," Mrs. Driscoll said. "Nothing

sad about it. If you ask me, getting rid of that rascal was the smartest thing she ever did."

"Yes, of course. I meant the marriage. I think she knew it was a mistake almost from the first. At any rate, she told me that she was packing up some things he'd left behind after she asked him to leave—"

"Kicked him out on his ear, you mean," Mrs. Driscoll said. "If she'd asked him to leave, he could have packed up his own things."

"And she found some information that troubled her—information that seemed to indicate that her husband had been misusing his computer skills and the knowledge of our financial systems that she had helped him to acquire."

"He was embezzling," his wife said. "He hadn't taken much yet, but if she hadn't turned him in, he'd probably have taken the college for millions."

"I think we would have caught him before he stole quite that much," Dr. Driscoll said, frowning at her.

Mrs. Driscoll looked at me, rolled her eyes, and took another deep sip of her wine.

"At any rate," Dr. Driscoll continued, "Karen was instrumental in saving the college from substantial losses. Unfortunately, we weren't able to bring the matter to trial—"

"Hired himself a hotshot attorney who tried to make it look as if Karen was involved, too, the son-of-a—"

"Mabel!" Dr. Driscoll looked over his glasses at his wife, who shrugged and took another gulp of wine.

"You all backed down," she said. "You should have taken the jerk to court. He did it. You all knew that. Bastard should be in jail."

"Perhaps we did make a mistake," Dr. Driscoll said, with a sigh. "Karen's absence has me worried. Obviously her estranged husband has reason to resent her. What if Walker is responsible for her . . . disappearance?"

"I wouldn't put it past him," Mrs. Driscoll muttered.

"But if this all happened two years ago, what were the police investigating today?" I asked.

Dr. Driscoll looked embarrassed.

"It begins to look as if we may not have done as good a job of investigating Mr. Walker's crime as we thought," he said. "We handled it internally, of course—more discreet that way."

Michael nodded sagely, and I wondered if, like me, he was having to bite his tongue at the notion of handling an embezzler discreetly—instead of bringing his crimes into the open, trying to have him prosecuted, and generally doing everything possible to reduce the chances that anyone would give him a chance to embezzle again.

"It appears that far from terminating with his employment, his crime has been, well, ongoing," Dr. Driscoll said. "The police even seemed to think Karen was involved."

"Idiots," Mrs. Driscoll muttered.

"They have to investigate every possibility, you know," he said. "And it really doesn't look good, her running away like that, just when the whole thing came to light. If you see her—"

"I know," I said. "She needs to come back, talk to the police, and clear her name."

"If she *can* come back," Mrs. Driscoll said. "What if something has happened to her?"

No one quite knew what to say to that, and luckily, before the awkward silence dragged on too long, the waiter came around to ask us if we wanted dessert. And along with dessert, another distraction arrived.

"Meg! Michael!" It was Dr. Blake, striding up to our table. "What brings you here?"

"The food," I said.

"How are you, Dr. Blake?" Michael asked, standing up to shake my grandfather's hand. "Have you met Dr. and Mrs. Driscoll?"

"Dr. Blake!" Ambrose Driscoll had bounded to his feet and was staring with awe at the new arrival. "What an honor to meet you! I can't tell you how much I admired your article in *Audubon* magazine on the plight of the Blue-throated Macaw!"

"Thank you, thank you," Dr. Blake said, shaking hands vigorously with Dr. Driscoll. "Are you a birding man yourself?"

"Only an amateur, compared with you," Dr. Driscoll said.

"Dr. Driscoll is too modest," I said. "He has a life list of over eight hundred birds."

Dr. Driscoll beamed with delight.

"Yes—814, to be precise," he said. "How kind of you to remember."

"Marvelous!" Dr. Blake exclaimed. "We need more concerned birders—if only I could interest these young people in the cause!"

I sat back to let my grandfather charm the Driscolls and enlist them in his legion of supporters who would write letters to Congress and checks to the Montgomery Blake Foundation whenever their leader rallied them. I'd spotted something interesting.

Blake was dressed in his customary garb—cargo pants, cotton shirt, and fishing vest, all in muted earth tones, and hiking boots. He wasn't wearing his pith helmet, but the pockets of his vest bulged, as usual, with random bits of junk and gear. All of this was perfectly normal—he wore the same outfit whether he was slogging through the jungle, appearing on CNN to denounce some corporation's environmental record, or sipping wine at the bar of the Caerphilly Inn.

But behind him I could see the door to the hotel lobby. As Blake was holding forth in his most charming manner, I saw Dad stick his head in, look left and right, and then duck back out. And then I saw him creep past the doorway in the most dramatically furtive manner imaginable. And he was wearing an over-the-top outfit similar to Dr. Blake's.

A few moments after Dad disappeared, Dr. Blake wished us all a good evening and shook hands all around. I followed him to the door.

"What are you and Dad up to, anyway?" I asked Dr. Blake.

"Up to?" He was wearing his most innocent expression. It wouldn't have fooled Timmy.

"Just try to stay out of trouble for a while," I said. "I'm a little tied down with Timmy right now. If you two get arrested, I can't just take off and drive down to North Carolina again in the middle of the night to bail you out."

"That was an unusual situation," Dr. Blake said.

"How were we supposed to know the police were going to stage a raid on the cockfight the very night we were filming it?"

"You could have considered the possibility and had a local lawyer on call," I said. "In fact, here."

I pulled out my notebook, tore out a page, flipped to a page near the front, copied a couple of names and phone numbers, and handed the loose sheet to him.

"What's this?"

"Defense attorneys. Relatives of Mother's. If you get arrested, give one of them a call, mention that you're a Hollingworth cousin, and they'll take care of it."

"Hmph," he said. "So you carry the names and numbers of two criminal defense attorneys around wherever you go?"

"Always," I said. "People I'm related to keep getting into trouble."

"Some family I've found," he said. But he didn't sound too upset, and I noticed that he tucked the slip of paper carefully into one of his dozens of vest pockets as he strode through the lobby.

I went back to the table and found the Driscolls all atwitter with excitement at having met one of their idols.

"You never mentioned that Dr. Blake was your grandfather!" Ambrose Driscoll said.

"We watch all his specials," his wife said.

The subject of Dr. Blake and his exploits got us through the dessert course, and I suspected the Driscolls went home feeling quite happy with their evening. Since it was only a little past eight, and barely dark, my evening would normally have just begun, but I was feeling a lot more tired than I usually would so early. It wasn't all Timmy's fault—some of it was Karen's. But I found myself wondering if Michael had considered the effect parenthood would have on night owls like us.

"I think I overdid it on the wine," Michael said, as we reached the parking lot. "I'll ride with you, and pick up my car tomorrow."

He almost changed his mind when he saw that I was driving Rob's Porsche, but after a brief sigh of regret, he settled into the passenger seat and stared up at the stars as I eased the car down the Inn's driveway.

"This is the life," he said. "If I make tenure, let's celebrate by trading in my old convertible for one of these."

"Another convertible? Not a sturdy minivan for the planned family?"

He frowned.

"We can get one of those, too," he said, after a moment. "Tenure's worth celebrating in every possible way. I don't suppose you want to park down by Caerphilly Creek, for old time's sake? Put in a downpayment on the celebrating?"

I had to smile.

"I'm tempted," I said. "But at the moment, I'm a little anxious about Timmy. You realize he's about to spend his second night with us. That's scary."

"Inconvenient, perhaps, on a night like this, but hardly scary."

"What's scary is that either Karen isn't the person I thought she was, to abandon him for so long, or she's in some pretty serious trouble. And when you come right down to it, it's pretty scary that she left him with me in the first place. When people have kids, they start doing responsible things like buying insurance and minivans, not handing off their kids to near strangers. Karen and I have hardly seen each other in the last two years, and she had no idea whether I had any experience with small children, and Timmy didn't know me."

"He seems to be holding up well," Michael said. "He's a pretty adaptable little kid. And maybe Karen has good instincts about who she can trust."

"I still don't like it."

"I gather you struck out trying to find her today."

"Worse than that. I'm starting to think maybe she had good reasons to disappear."

As we drove along—well under the speed limit, which must have been a first for the Porsche—I brought him up to date on what I'd learned during the day.

"Not encouraging," he murmured, when I'd finished.

"Any theories about what's going on?" I asked.

"None that you probably haven't already thought of," he said. "Frankly, if I were Chief Blake and had to make sense of what you've learned, I'd say she's probably involved in the embezzling scheme, realized that the police were about to close in, and decided to run. And figuring her chances of getting away were a lot better without Timmy, she found a safe place to leave him while she fled."

My stomach clenched.

"I'm sorry," Michael said. "I know she's your friend."

"You're not saying anything I haven't thought," I said. "It just sounds a little worse out loud."

"I can think of some other possible explanations."

"Yeah, but they don't sound too logical, do they?"

We drove on a while in silence.

When we reached the ridge that gave a view of the road, I looked for Mr. Early but it was too dark to see if he was still there or if he'd given up his vigil for the evening.

Then I noticed that our house was dark.

"That's odd," I said, pointing to it. "Do you suppose Rob has gotten Timmy to bed?"

"You never know. He's really rather good with kids. I've seen him in action before, with your nieces and nephews. He really knows how to communicate on their level."

"That's because he still thinks on their level," I said. "It's communicating with adults he can't handle."

"Could be," Michael said, with a chuckle. "At any rate, he has a weak stomach when it comes to diapers, but he's really good at entertaining kids."

I nodded. Good, but not very firm. I'd expected him to leave the hard work of getting Timmy to bed to Michael and me. In fact, I more than half expected to find the two of them asleep in front of the TV. But that was okay, I told myself, determined to keep my mellow, post-dinner mood as long as I could.

I lost the battle when we pulled into the driveway.

"My car's not here," I said. "What's going on?"

Nineteen

As soon as the car came to a stop I jumped out and ran inside.

"Hello," I called. "We're home."

No answer. I saw no one in the living room, the dining room, or the kitchen. And no notes posted anywhere to tell us where Rob had gone with Timmy. Upstairs, I peered into the bedroom where we'd set up Timmy's portable crib. It was empty. So were all the other bedrooms on that floor and the third floor— empty of Rob and Timmy, at any rate. I found the room on the third floor in which Rob was setting up his little home away from home, and in a room at the other end of the hall was an object covered with a tarp. It turned out to be a cage containing six brightly colored birds, all fast asleep. They stirred slightly when I lifted one edge of the tarp, and one of them uttered a faint squawk before settling back into slumber.

I ran downstairs again. Michael was just emerging from the basement. He looked a little pale.

"What's wrong?" I asked.

"We have snakes again," he said. "I think I should

have a word with your father. And your grandfather. This is really getting out of hand."

I was astonished. Michael usually enjoyed all of Dad's projects and antics, and for that matter, all of Dr. Blake's.

"Getting out of hand? What do you mean? What kind of snakes?"

"I don't know. Big snakes. The basement's swarming with them."

"They're loose?" My voice went up at least an octave.

"No, thank goodness," he said, with a shudder. "They're all in terrariums. About a dozen of them. But I'm not really that fond of snakes."

"I never knew that," I said. "Don't let Dad know."

"Why not?"

"He'd probably recommend spending a lot of time observing snakes and handling them as a way of overcoming your fear."

"I'm not afraid of them," Michael said, sounding ever so slightly testy. "I'm just not fond of them, and I have no desire to spend any quality time with them. Normally they don't bother me that much, but I'm not used to going into my own basement, turning on the light, and finding a whole collection of them staring back at me."

"I wouldn't like that either," I said.

"I think it's the fact that they never blink," he said. "That kind of creeps me out."

"It's not their fault," I said. "They have no eyelids."

"I didn't say it was their fault. I just don't like it."

"Let me lay down the law to Dad about snakes,

then," I said. "I could pretend that I've developed a sudden irrational but insurmountable fear of having snakes around with children in the house. Manage to imply that it's either snakes or grandchildren, and lay down an ultimatum. Get Mother to help."

"Good idea," he said. "Meanwhile, I gather you didn't find Rob and Timmy upstairs."

"Not unless an evil magician has transformed them along with Dad and Dr. Blake into brightly colored birds," I said.

"Brightly colored birds?"

"There's a cage of them in one of the third floor bedrooms. I definitely need to speak to Dad."

And possibly rekey the house locks.

"Let's call your father," Michael suggested. "Maybe he knows what's up. After all, if there was any kind of emergency, Rob would probably call him."

"Assuming Rob actually has his cell phone with him and turned on, which seems unlikely. But just in case, you call Dad and I'll call Rob."

But there was no answer at the farmhouse or on Rob's cell phone. Mother and Rose Noire were still up in Washington, of course. I called a few of Rob's friends, none of whom had any idea where he was. Most of them hadn't seen much of him lately.

Always a bad sign when Rob started neglecting his friends. It usually pointed to a new girlfriend or a new hobby, and Rob's taste in both was highly dubious.

"Maybe I should call the police," I said.

"Chief Burke would love that," Michael said. "A missing toddler, with the town in the middle of what amounts to a crime wave by Caerphilly's standards."

"This missing toddler could be related to the crime wave," I reminded him.

Though when I called, I couldn't reach Chief Burke. Debbie Anne, the dispatcher, promised to tell all the patrol cars to keep an eye out for my Toyota and to tell Chief Burke as soon as she could reach him, but the minutes ticked into hours without a call back. And without a sign of Rob.

At about eleven-thirty, we finally heard a car pull into the driveway. I ran out to see Rob stepping out of my car.

"Where the hell have you been?" I asked.

Apparently Rob wasn't expecting to find anyone up. He leaped into the air with surprise.

"Sssh," he stage-whispered. "Timmy's asleep in the back seat."

I peered into the back seat of the Toyota. Timmy looked unharmed. He was clutching Kiki in one hand and Blanky in the other and had his head tilted in one of those impossible angles that would give an adult a sore neck for days but never seemed to bother little children.

"He's fine," Rob whispered.

"He'd better be," I said. "Where the hell have you been?"

"Just after you left, I got a call from a friend who was flying into Dulles and needed a ride back here," he said.

"You took Timmy with you to Dulles? It's a four-hour round trip."

"I didn't figure it would be a problem—he's in his

car seat and everything. He slept most of the way back, actually. You should probably just let him sleep."

"We can't leave him out here in the car all night," I said.

"I'll carry the car seat in," Michael offered. "Maybe we can ease him gently into the crib without waking him up."

It almost worked. It would have worked, if Rob hadn't knocked over the trash can just as we were all tiptoeing out of the room.

Twenty

Michael and I were basking on the beach, drinking fruity drinks with parasols stuck in them. The waiter came around and leaned over—I assumed he was going to ask if I wanted a refill. I smiled, and held up my nearly empty glass. The waiter reached out and said,

"KIKI!"

I'm not sure whether I fell out of bed or rolled out, but I found myself on the floor, ears ringing, while up on the bed Timmy continued to bellow "Kiki! Want Kiki! Where Kiki?" at the top of his lungs. Michael, who had apparently abandoned ship on the other side of the bed, growled something and strode out of the room.

I knew I should get up and try to comfort Timmy, but I was still gathering my wits when Michael returned.

"Here's Kiki," he said. "You left him in your crib. Now go back to sleep."

He sounded a little cranky. I didn't blame him. I was very cranky.

"Meg? Are you all right?"

Michael was peering over the side of the bed.

"I'm fine," I said. "I'm just waiting for the homicidal urge to pass."

"Kiki hungry," Timmy said, in a conversational tone.

"I'll go start breakfast," Michael said.

"It's not even light yet," I said.

"Kiki hungry," Michael said. "Come on, Timmy. Let's let Auntie Meg sleep a little longer."

I tried, but the spell was broken. I tossed and turned until I finally realized sleep wasn't happening. So I got up and went over to the window to see what kind of a day it was going to be.

Seth Early was sprawled on the ground behind his hedge, fast asleep, and from the look of it, probably snoring sonorously.

Rob's Porsche was still parked in the driveway, which was not surprising. Doubtless he'd considered that his baby-sitting services had earned him room and board for the night. Perhaps I could browbeat him into helping with Timmy again today, in return for the scare he'd given us last night.

The thermometer we'd hung outside our bedroom window already showed seventy degrees, and it wasn't even light yet. Not a good sign.

Down in the backyard, Rose Noire was bottle-feeding something small, cute, and furry that would probably break her vegetarian heart by growing up to be a carnivore. I spotted Dad and Dr. Blake doing something near one of the sheds. Between the snakes in the basement, the birds on the third floor, and now the furry thing in the backyard, the place was starting to look like a zoo again.

I showered—not that the heat wouldn't undo that the second I walked outdoors—dressed and stumbled downstairs. Michael had fixed his fruit-and-cinnamon-laden oatmeal again, and was feeding it to Timmy and Rob. Better yet, he waited to offer me some until after I'd finished the cup of coffee he'd made me.

"I'm not due at today's meetings until nine," he said. "So I'll keep Timmy out of your hair till I have to leave."

I smiled my thanks. Yes, Michael was trying. If he hadn't been in the middle of what we privately called Hell Week, with the back-to-back meetings and training sessions the administration thought necessary to prepare the faculty for the new year, he'd probably do more than his share of Timmy-sitting. He'd be a great father—patient, caring, fully involved. Why was I in such a panic about the idea of having kids?

The responsibility, I decided. Even when someone else was temporarily taking care of Timmy, he was always in the back of my mind. Did it get easier if the kids arrived as helpless infants and gradually grew more mobile? Did you gradually stop worrying that every time you turned your back, your child would do something that could get him killed? Or at least get used to the worrying?

Of course, it was hard to tell how much of my anxiety came from having Timmy around and how much from not knowing when—or if—Karen would come back to claim him.

"Oh, I meant to tell you that I started asking around yesterday about babysitters," Michael said. "It's tough this time of year—it'd be much easier if the students were back. But I'm sure we can find someone. Or at least a mother's helper—someone to keep Timmy out from underfoot while you get some work done."

"Great idea," I said. "Of course, I hope by the time you find someone, we don't need a baby-sitter, but . . ."

He nodded.

I turned my attention to Rob.

"So, let me tell you what we're doing today," I said.

"We?" Rob mumbled, through a mouthful of oatmeal.

"The sooner I find Karen or figure out what she's up to, the sooner we can get a certain someone safely back into her hands," I said, nodded toward where Timmy was picking the raisins out of his oatmeal and arranging them in decorative patterns.

"So you're going to be out snooping today."

"Snooping is very difficult with a toddler in tow," I said. "Especially for a person whose nerves were shattered for several hours last night by the inexplicable disappearance of said toddler."

"I already explained—"

"So you have your choice," I went on. "You can stay here and take care of Timmy, or you can ride shotgun with me and lend a hand with Timmy as needed."

"I'm not doing diapers," he said.

"No problem," I said. "But if that's the case, you'd better come along with me."

"We both appreciate how much you're helping," Michael said, as he hoisted Timmy onto his shoulders. "Come on, Timmy. Let's see what kind of animals Dr. Blake has brought this morning."

He sailed out into the yard with Timmy giggling happily.

"I'll be in the yard when you're ready to leave," Rob said, and followed them out.

From the relatively easy time I had talking Rob into accompanying me, I suspected someone else was expecting him to be someplace doing something more challenging, and I'd end up being the fall guy for whatever went wrong. But at the moment, I didn't much care.

When I turned on my car's CD player, planning to treat Timmy to more of his favorite car music, I was nearly jolted out of my seat by a high-decibel blast of Led Zeppelin's "Whole Lotta Love."

"Dammit," I said, punching the off button. "What was that?"

"Led Zeppelin's second album," Rob said, unnecessarily.

"Yes, but what is it doing in my car? Were you playing Led Zeppelin to Timmy? And at that volume?"

"I tried him with Death Cab for Cutie, but I guess the kid's a classic rock fan," Rob said.

Translation: Rob was currently infatuated with playing albums older than he was, so anyone in his vicinity had better get used to it.

After mature consideration, I decided almost anything would be less annoying than Barney the dinosaur and "It's a Small World," so I agreed to play Led Zeppelin during our ride—though at considerably lower volume than seemed reasonable to the boys in the backseat.

"It's not rock if you can't feel the bass," Rob complained.

"Youder," Timmy suggested.

I ignored both of them, and they finally gave up and settled down to listen to Robert Plant's wails at the very modest decibel level that seemed safe for a toddler's hearing.

"So where are we going?" Rob asked.

"Back to where Jasper Walker's been staying," I said. "With you along to watch Timmy, I might have more chance of learning something."

"Are you going to burgle the place?" Rob demanded. "Cool! I charge extra for aiding and abetting felonies."

But as we made our way farther and farther away from town, I noticed that he seemed increasingly uneasy.

"Where are we going?" he finally asked, as we turned off the road and onto the dirt lane.

"Hiram Bass's house," I said. "I'm pretty sure that's where Jasper Walker has been staying."

I glanced in the rearview mirror. Rob was waving a toy at Timmy, but he seemed distracted, looking around as if something made him very nervous. Maybe it was the effect of being in the woods—Rob was never much for roughing it.

He seemed to perk up a bit by the time we pulled up in front of the house—possibly because it presented new, untapped opportunities for sarcasm.

"You have such classy friends," he said, pointing to a discarded toilet that was lying near the front porch. "Unfettered by bourgeois notions of aesthetics and respectability."

"Potty," Timmy said, pointing.

"Timmy, you and Rob stay here in the car where it's cool," I said as I got out. "I'm going to see if I can get in and look around. I'm leaving the keys so you can keep the air conditioning on while you're waiting."

"It's just you and me, kid," Rob said, in a bad Bogart accent. Timmy giggled as if Rob had said something hilarious.

I strolled up onto the cluttered front porch and knocked on the door again.

"Jasper? Mr. Bass?"

No answer. Back in the car, Timmy and Rob were having a tickle fight and giggling nonstop. Apart from that, everything was quiet, except for the window-unit air conditioner at one side of the house, which was still laboring away. Probably on high speed, by the sound of it. That probably meant Jasper wasn't planning to be away too long, didn't it? When I went on vacation, I turned the thermostat way down. Or was Jasper feckless enough to leave the air conditioning running full blast even if he'd left town for a while? Probably. Especially if it was on his uncle's utility bill.

I peered through both of the front windows, then began circling the house, peering into each window in turn. The other rooms—a bedroom and a small kitchen—looked much as the living room had, cluttered and rundown.

When I got to the back door, I pulled out my lock-picking kit. No sense in making Rob a witness to my attempt at breaking and entering, and if I found anything worth reporting to the police, I could always claim that I'd found it open. After all, with Timmy along yesterday, I couldn't easily sneak around to the back of the house to test the windows and doors there. For all I knew, there could be a door open.

Luck was on my side. The back door had an old lock, remarkably similar to the ones I'd learned on during that long-ago summer when Dad's fascination for Lawrence Block's Bernie Rhodenbarr series led him to try learning a few burglar skills. And while Dad had been a hopelessly inept lock-picker, I'd actually gotten fairly good at it. The lock yielded to my fiddling after only a few minutes.

I opened the door and took a deep breath before stepping in.

The deep breath was a big mistake. I gagged, and stepped back several feet, breathing shallowly and trying to calm my stomach.

When I was sure I wasn't going to lose breakfast, I inched closer to the door, still breathing shallowly, and then stepped inside.

The air was frigid—no wonder the poor air conditioner was laboring so hard. And even shallow breaths couldn't keep out the stench of decay. I pulled the bottom of my t-shirt up so I could breathe through that.

Maybe it wasn't anything sinister. Maybe Jasper had run off leaving the remains of dinner on the table. Yeah, right.

I tiptoed through the kitchen and peered into the hall.

A body lay face down on the hall floor. It was male, and tall, with a long, unkempt brown ponytail. I'd remembered Jasper as skinnier, but then maybe the dead guy wasn't plump. It was August, and I suspected he'd been lying there a day or so. Maybe a few days. I heard flies buzzing somewhere, and I realized that there was dried blood pooled beneath one side of the head.

Was that the only body? What if Karen—?

Don't go there, I told myself. If there were other bodies in the house, let the police find them.

I started backing out of the kitchen, reaching for my cell phone as I went.

I noticed, out of the corner of my eye, that about half of the floor looked a lot cleaner than the rest, as if someone had washed it. But they hadn't washed it all that well. I saw a few faint swirling red stains, as if someone had mopped up a lot of blood and hadn't done a perfect job.

But a good enough job to keep anyone who came peering through the windows from noticing the blood. At least I hadn't noticed it when I'd peered in before picking the lock. So maybe Jasper had been killed in the kitchen and dragged into the hall, where he couldn't be seen from the outside. It wouldn't keep him from being found eventually, but it would slow down discovery. Maybe enough to confuse the time of death.

Or enough for someone to unload her toddler on a friend and skip town?

Behind me, I heard a whining noise.

I stepped out into the yard, and suddenly the heavy August heat felt good. Scout, the hound dog, was whimpering slightly, and creeping toward the door.

"No, boy," I said. I grabbed his collar before he could bolt inside, and pulled the door closed.

"Stay here with me," I said, as I flipped open my cell phone to call Chief Burke.

Twenty-One

An hour later, I was leaning against Chief Burke's car, trying to look cool, calm, and collected. At least I'd managed to convince the chief to have one of his officers take Rob and Timmy home—with sirens to gladden both their hearts—but I wasn't sure the chief would let me go anytime soon.

Most of the assembled police were off behind the house. Maybe even in it, some of them, though I had a feeling whoever was in charge of the crime scene probably had less trouble than usual keeping extraneous personnel outside. Some of them were milling around near the chief, talking in low tones, though from time to time I overheard a word or two. I'd heard "gunshot wound" several times, so I deduced someone had shot Jasper. And I'd also overhead that they thought Jasper had been killed two or three days ago.

Off in the distance, I could hear a few of the officers still checking the surrounding area. It was easy to keep track of them, not only by the rustling noises they made in the fallen leaves but also by the fact that they were all exclaiming over how much poison ivy was growing all over everything.

"Whoa!" I heard Sammy shout. "You should see this vine. Thick as your wrist!"

"I've got one to beat it over here," another officer shouted back. "Thick as your ankle!"

"This one's got leaves a foot long," Sammy called. "Where's the camera?"

I checked to make sure my cell phone was still on. I'd talked to Michael, briefly, to tell him about finding Jasper, but he'd been dragged away by his chairman for yet another interminable meeting. He'd call when he could. I focused back on the search team and its poison ivy adventures, hoping that like Timmy and me they'd escape getting the dreaded rash.

I was so focused I started when I heard Chief Burke's voice at my elbow.

"I've got a few more questions for you," the chief said. That was probably a lie. I suspected he had a lot more questions for me. He didn't look happy. Not surprising—between the break-in at Karen's apartment and the embezzlement at the college, he was already in the middle of a crime wave, at least by Caerphilly's standards. And now here I came adding a murder to his workload.

"So what were you doing looking for Jasper Walker?" he asked.

"I wasn't," I said. "Not for his own sake, at least. I just wanted to see if he knew anything about Karen's whereabouts."

"We've been looking for Mr. Walker ourselves," the chief said. "Without any success, I might add, until you called in. Just how did you know to look for him here?"

"One of Karen's friends told me that Jasper was

back, and living at his uncle Hiram's place. And that Hiram was one of the Clayville Basses."

"So you know Mr. Bass?"

"No, but I got a friend to look him up at one of those online phone book sites."

"And it never occurred to you to tell us what you'd found?"

"It never occurred to me that you didn't already know where to find Jasper Walker if you wanted him," I said. I really worked at keeping the exasperation I felt out of my voice. "All your officers are local. If I'd thought about it at all, I'd have assumed that one of them would have told you about the family connection between Jasper and the Basses."

The chief actually growled, so I deduced none of them had. I foresaw a lively discussion about this back at the station.

"Did you notice anything when you came by here yesterday?"

I thought about it for a few seconds.

"It looked the same as today," I said. "Well, the same as it did before you showed up," I added, waving at the dozen law enforcement vehicles enlivening the quiet woods with their flashing lights and squawking radios.

"You didn't see anyone?"

"Only the dog," I said.

We both glanced over to where Scout was sitting in the back of the chief's car. He wagged his tail when he saw we were looking at him.

"What happens to the dog?" I asked. "It's Jasper's dog, you know."

"We'll take care of the dog," the chief said.

"Take care of him how?" I asked, with a frown.

"We'll probably take him to the shelter," the chief said. "Don't worry: it's a no-kill shelter. He'll be fine. Friendly dog like that, someone's bound to adopt him pretty soon."

Scout wagged his tail as if to agree that yes, he was very friendly, and looked anxiously from the chief to me and then back again.

"Let's get back to business," the chief said. "So you had no idea the body was in there?"

"If I'd known there was a body in there, do you think I'd have gone in?" I asked.

Chief Burke looked as if he wouldn't put it past me.

"I was just trying to find Karen," I said. "I figured if Jasper was staying here, even if I couldn't talk to him, maybe I could find something that would give me a clue to where she went. Instead, I found him."

"Would have been nice if you'd found him yesterday," the chief said.

"I know," I said. "But it was just me and Timmy yesterday. I couldn't very well leave him outside while I went into the house—he started crying whenever he lost sight of me. And it's a damned good thing I didn't take him in with me, isn't it?"

I refrained from saying that most people would have given up after finding Jasper not at home the first time, and that the police would probably still be looking for Jasper if I hadn't been nosy enough to come back and poke around some more. If you ask me, he was lucky I'd been the one looking for Jasper, but I suspected he wouldn't quite see it that way.

"So did you find any clues to Ms. Walker's where-abouts?" he asked.

"No," I said. "I just went in far enough to see the body, and then I got right out."

Even though I knew the temperature was in the 90s, I suddenly felt briefly and irrationally chilly.

Chief Burke must have noticed.

"That's all for now," he said. "I guess I know where to find you if I have any more questions."

"Or if you learn anything about Karen's where-abouts," I suggested.

He nodded, rather distractedly.

Or was he only pretending to be distracted? I realized that the chief was acting oddly. More restrained than usual.

Maybe it had something to do with the guys in the plain cars. I suspected they were law enforcement of some sort, though not under the chief's jurisdiction. From the State Bureau of Investigation, perhaps? Whoever they were, I had the feeling that either the chief hadn't invited them or he had come to regret doing so.

I walked back to my car and began the tedious process of getting out of Hiram Bass's yard without running into any other vehicles, living or dead. I did pretty well until I came to the fork in the road. Aubrey Hamilton's red pickup was stopped there, motor still running, while he leaned out, staring at the police activity with visible dismay.

"What's going on?" he asked, craning his neck to see past me.

"There's a reason you haven't seen Jasper Walker for the past few days," I said.

He frowned and looked at me.

"Someone killed him."

"Holy—when?"

"They don't know yet. I bet at least a couple of days ago."

"Damn."

He looked ashen. Did he know Jasper better than he'd admitted? Or was I being overly suspicious—after all, I think I'd be more than a little shook up if someone was killed next door to me. Then he narrowed his eyes.

"How come you know all this?"

"I'm the one who found him."

"Damn," he repeated. "A couple of days?"

"At least. The police are probably going to want to talk to you," I added. "Have fun."

In fact, two officers were already approaching us. Hamilton pulled the truck up a little farther, so I could get by, and cut the ignition. When I glanced back in the rearview mirror, I saw him talking to one of the officers as he stepped out of the cab.

I headed for town. If I were a better person, I'd have hurried home as soon as Chief Burke let me go, to relieve Rob of Timmy-sitting duty. But I was in such a low mood that my mind rebelled at the thought.

"I'll go in and see if Michael wants to do lunch," I said aloud, and felt almost immediately better. To everyone else, I was determined to put on a brave front and pretend that it didn't bother me, finding the days-old dead body of someone I had actually known, however slightly. And in front of the police, I didn't think it was a good idea to show any doubt of Karen's innocence. But I could share it all with Michael.

Of course, when I actually got to his office, it was empty, and the department secretary had no idea where Michael had gone or when he'd be back. When would I learn to use my damned cell phone?

As I was turning to leave, I heard voices behind me.

"Meg!" a male voice called

"Meg, dear!" a female voice added. "How are you?"

Probably symptomatic of my mood that I tensed on hearing my name. But when I turned to see who was calling, I relaxed.

Henry and Phyllis Blanke. Dr. Blanke was one of Michael's colleagues in the drama department, and Phyllis volunteered tirelessly for whatever jobs needed doing backstage at the theater. I'd told Michael not long ago that the Blankes were two of the few sane people in the department.

"I agree," he'd said. "But don't tell them that. In theatrical circles, sane is a bit of a put-down."

I took a deep breath and reminded myself that I wasn't in such a rush that I couldn't stop to chat for a minute with the Blankes. They'd been very nice to me, not to mention vigorous supporters of Michael's quest for tenure. I strolled down the corridor to Henry Blanke's office.

"Come in, come in," he said, while Phyllis hurried to move a pile of books from one of the guest chairs. As I sat down I realized that while it didn't make up for missing Michael, seeing the Blankes did help my mood a little. Phyllis handed me a cup of green tea that she had apparently just brewed on the hot plate on the credenza. I leaned back, sipped my tea, and soaked in the mood of Henry's cluttered but comfortable office, where theatrical memorabilia fought for center stage with relics of the 1960s counterculture.

"How are you?" I asked.

"A little shaken up," Phyllis said. "Meg, what in the world is your grandfather up to?"

"I have no idea," I said, taken aback. "Why? What has he done to upset you?"

"He hasn't upset us," Phyllis said. "The FBI did that."

"DEA," Henry put in.

"They weren't DEA," Phyllis said, in a rather cross tone. "You're just being paranoid."

"I'm sure we're still in their files," Henry said. He was gazing up at a framed vintage "Impeach Nixon Now!" poster.

"And in the FBI's files, too," Phyllis said. "The DEA wouldn't be interested in us now—our normal days were a long time ago."

I blinked in surprise. I'd have called the Blankes eminently normal, at least by drama department standards— though I suspected normal, like sane, wasn't considered praise in theatrical circles.

Phyllis noticed my expression.

"The National Organization for the Reform of Marijuana Laws," she said. "NORML. Henry and I were quite active in our student days."

"And they've got long memories, those Feds," Henry said. "We haven't heard the last of this, you mark my words."

"We really should have insisted they give us names and badge numbers and explain more clearly what agency they were from," Phyllis said.

"We will, when they come back."

"They won't be coming back," Phyllis said. "They weren't interested in us; they were looking for Meg's grandfather."

"So they said," Henry muttered.

"My grandfather? Why?"

"They didn't really say, dear," Phyllis said. "They asked a lot of questions about where we were on various days and times, and didn't sound as if they believed us. And then one of them said, 'Look here, Dr. Blake,' and we realized they had the wrong people. Blake and Blanke, you see."

I nodded. Yes, that was an understandable mistake. But why would the FBI or the DEA or any other federal agency be trying to interrogate my grandfather?

"And they didn't say what it was they were investigating?" I asked.

Henry shook his head.

"It was all very furtive," Phyllis said. "They apologized for the mistake, but they didn't look all that contrite—just annoyed that they'd wasted so much time with us. Anyway, we thought you should know."

"Thanks," I said. Clearly my reputation for being the practical one who should deal with crises had spread to the drama department as well as my own family. "When did this happen?"

"Last night," Henry said. "They showed up just as we were sitting down to dinner."

"Crab soufflé," Phyllis said. "It was ruined; there's no way to reheat a soufflé."

I shook my head in sympathy. Phyllis was legendary for her fabulous gourmet meals, so I could well understand the outrage in Henry's voice.

"You look as if you were on your way somewhere," Henry said. "Sorry to interrupt you."

"No problem," I said. "I just stopped by on the off chance Michael was free for lunch. Let me know if anything else happens. Or if you think of anything else."

As I headed for my car, I realized that I still hadn't eaten. And it was nearing two o'clock. No wonder Michael wasn't around—he was probably back at his meetings. I hadn't felt the least bit hungry during the nearly four hours I'd been waiting for the police or answering their questions—given how my stomach reacted to finding Jasper, I had wondered if I'd ever want food again. But suddenly, I was ravenous. Might as well take care of that while I was here. I changed course, heading for the college cafeteria, and pulled out my cell phone to see if I could kill two birds with one stone. I called Sandie.

"Meg? How are you?" she exclaimed. "How's Timmy? And has Karen turned up yet?"

"Fine, fine, and no," I said.

"You sound down," she said. "What's wrong?"

"Someone killed Jasper Walker a few days ago," I said. "I just found the body today."

"Oh, my God," she said.

"Look, I'm going over to grab a quick bite in the cafeteria. I know Nadine makes it tough for you to get away but—"

"Meet you there in five minutes," she said.

Twenty-Two

Sandie was the perfect person to tell about finding Jasper's body. Well, no—Michael would have been the perfect person, but since he wasn't around, Sandie filled the gap nicely. She ooh'd and ah'd over everything I told her, exclaimed that she would never have had the nerve to do what I'd done, and generally made just the right amount of fuss over the whole thing. She even struck the right balance between concern for me and frank curiosity about the murder scene.

I found myself wondering, briefly, if Sandie might be part of the reason Karen and I had drifted apart. Not in a bad way—but with Karen's marriage breaking up while Michael and I were getting more and more serious, we were definitely at very different stages of our lives. Probably good for both of us if Karen had found a friend nearby with not only a sympathetic ear but also some idea of what she was going through with Jasper.

"Don't be silly," Sandie said, when I tried to apologize for talking her ear off and possibly grossing her out. "You think I mind getting the inside scoop on the hottest story to hit Caerphilly in years? I can't wait to run down to the personnel office and tell everyone there. If they're in today," she said, her face falling a little. "For all I know the police shut them down just like us."

"Shut you down?"

"They took away all our files and computers yesterday," she said. "So it's not like we can do any work to speak of. I thought maybe Ms. Sourpuss would give us the day off, but no—someone has to be in the office to field calls."

"Nadine can't do it herself?"

"Nadine called in this morning to say she'd be in after lunch," Sandie said. "Then she called just before you did to say she probably wouldn't be in at all. And she complains about her staff taking advantage."

"Maybe she can't help it," I suggested. "Maybe she's down at the police station and can't get away."

"You think maybe they locked her up?" Sandie asked. She looked ready to break out the confetti and champagne at the thought.

"I think we'd have heard if they'd arrested her, but maybe they're still questioning her."

"Well, it's a start," Sandie said.

We both sat for a few moments, lost in our thoughts.

"How well did Nadine know Jasper?" I asked finally.

"Jasper?" Sandie said. "I don't know that she did, outside of work. And she wouldn't have known him that well at work—she's big on doing what she calls facilitating lateral communication between decision-makers, which basically means if you're not a vice president or a full professor, she doesn't give you the time of day."

"So she wouldn't know him well enough to have anything against him?"

"You mean you think Nadine had something to do with Jasper's death?" Sandie asked. "How come?"

"What if they were both in on this embezzlement thing the police are investigating?" I said.

"Nadine?"

I could see she was thinking it over.

"That's so hard to believe," she said finally. "She's so dedicated to her job—she's always the first one in every morning and the last to leave. She hardly ever takes a vacation."

"Classic embezzler behavior," I said. "Her best chance of keeping others from finding out is to be around all the time, ready to smooth over any problems."

"I never thought of that," Sandie said. "And the nerve of her, being so strict with us about things like putting it down on our time cards if we leave half an hour early, when she was—"

"It's only a theory," I said. "We shouldn't judge too hastily."

"Sounds like a good theory to me," Sandie said. She smiled, but it was the kind of smile I'd have if I saw something really awful about to happen to my worst enemy.

"We may not know until Karen turns up," I said. "If she succeeded in finding Jasper, she might be the last person who did. And I'm wondering if maybe she found his body, knew people would suspect her of killing him, and decided to disappear until she could figure out how to clear herself."

At least I hoped that's what she was doing.

"What do you figure he came back for?" Sandie asked.

"No idea," I said. "And it's possible he was trying to keep out of sight—his next-door neighbor hadn't seen him."

"Next-door neighbor?" Sandie said. "What neighbor? I mean, from what Karen said, Jasper's uncle's place was in the back of beyond."

"Aubrey Hamilton," I said. "Owner of the bird farm next door."

"Aubrey? I thought she was still summering in Maine."

"No, when I went out there—wait a minute—she? The Aubrey I talked to was a guy. Twenty-something. Silly little goatee."

"I don't know who you talked to, but it sure wasn't Aubrey Hamilton," Sandie said. "She's an older lady—older'n I am, anyway, late forties or maybe fifties. She and her husband used to raise poodles, but after he died, she gave it up. Just keeps a couple as pets. And every Memorial Day, like clockwork, she packs up the poodles and heads off to someplace in Maine, where she grew up."

"Then who the hell did I talk to at her house yesterday?"

"Maybe she hired someone to look after the place while she was gone."

"He didn't correct me when I mistook him for Aubrey."

"Maybe he figured if you didn't know Aubrey any better than that, you didn't have much business knowing she wasn't around."

I bit back a sharp comment. Yes, that was definitely

how some of the natives would react to a nosy outsider asking questions.

And the guy with the silly goatee was definitely a native. He'd had the typical old Caerphilly County accent, blending the round vowels of a Tidewater accent with just a hint of the twang that became more pronounced as you moved west toward the Shenandoah. My own voice, with a hint of Tidewater buried in the rather generic Mid-Atlantic accent I'd picked up from radio and television, instantly signaled to the natives that I was not from around here.

"Does Aubrey Hamilton have family in Caerphilly?" I asked.

"No. Well, maybe some by marriage," Sandie said. "I don't really know her. But I did hear about how she can't take the summers and has to go north every year—everyone knows that."

She sounded rather condescending. I thought Aubrey's plan sounded quite sensible—if you didn't like Virginia's hot, sticky summers, why stay around and whine if you had the means to avoid them?

"So you wouldn't know if she had relatives she let use her house," I said. "The way Hiram Bass let Jasper use his house."

Sandie shrugged.

"Sorry," she said. "I only really know Jasper because of Karen. He was a couple of grades ahead of me in school, you know."

I nodded.

"I should be getting back to the office," Sandie said, picking up her tray. "Just in case Nadine calls or sticks her head in. You can't imagine how nasty she's been. As my gran always said, a person's true character comes out in hard times, and Nadine's true character is just plain mean."

"Good luck," I said. "I'll see you later."

"And you'll let me know if you hear anything from Karen?"

"Of course," I said.

"You're a good friend to her," Sandie said. "You just let me know if there's anything I can do." She gave me a quick hug before dashing out the door.

I went back to puzzling over the identity of the imposter in the goatee.

"A few grades ahead of Sandie," I repeated. "Aha!"

I bussed our table and headed back to my car.

Next stop, the Caerphilly County Library.

Like the rest of the town, the Caerphilly County Library was on a slow, summer schedule. Only a few people lounged over books in the reading section, and they looked as if they were mainly there for the air conditioning. Unfortunately, Ms. Ellie, my favorite librarian, was on a hiking vacation in the Andes and not due back until Labor Day, which meant I was on my own when it came to unearthing local information.

In the reference section, I found what I was looking for—yearbooks from Caerphilly High School, at least fifty volumes lined up neatly on a top shelf.

I'd estimated Mr. Goatee's age at twenty-five, which would mean he'd graduated around seven years ago. If he graduated. Just to be on the safe side, I started with the books from ten years back and moved forward from there.

Sure enough, there he was. Frederick ("Freddy") Hamilton—so he must be a relative of Aubrey's. He'd graduated nine years ago. Apart from the marching band in his freshman year and woodworking club in his senior year, he didn't have any extracurricular activities, which made him a bit of an oddball. He looked a lot younger in his senior photo, and a lot more presentable, too—probably because he hadn't yet grown the unfortunate goatee.

I flipped over a few more pages and found the other name I'd been halfway looking for. Jasper Walker, also looking very young in a coat and tie, and without the scraggly ponytail.

Jasper had a slightly better roster of extracurricular activities—computer club all four years, track and field in his freshman and sophomore years, and the woodworking club for his junior and senior years.

Which meant, in a school as small as Caerphilly High, that Freddy Hamilton must have known Jasper.

Of course, he hadn't denied knowing him. Just hadn't made a big deal about knowing him. Going to high school together, and being in a club together didn't mean they were friends.

And if he was related to Aubrey Hamilton, maybe there wasn't anything sinister about the fact that he was hanging around her house while she was away for the summer.

Still—the fact that he had not corrected my mistake, and had let me go on thinking he was Aubrey—and his clear anxiety when it had looked as if Timmy was about to go into the barn—made me wonder if Freddy had something to hide.

Just then I realized that my purse, which was sitting on the table beside the stack of yearbooks, had begun vibrating. Which meant that someone was calling me on my cell phone.

I closed the yearbook, grabbed my purse, and rummaged around to find the phone while I headed for the library exit. Though I stopped to answer it in the library's vestibule, which still held a little of the air conditioning.

"Meg? Is that you? Meg?"

Rob, sounding panic stricken.

"It's me," I said. "What's wrong?"

"Get back here right away! I don't know what to do about—no!"

Twenty-Three

Rob hung up, leaving me still firing questions at him. And didn't pick up when I tried to call back. Didn't pick up the whole dozen times I tried to call him while breaking every speed limit on the way back to the house.

When I got to the point where I could see the house from the road, I was relieved to see that the house wasn't on fire or surrounded by a SWAT team. In fact, the only thing I could see happening was that Rob was out in the yard, holding the garden hose with the spray nozzle on while a stark naked Timmy ran in and out of the water. Timmy was probably giggling by the look of it. I couldn't tell Rob's mood, though. Had the crisis, whatever it was, passed so soon, or was he pulling a fast one to cut short his stint of childcare?

"Thank God you're here," he exclaimed when he saw me striding across the yard toward him. "Timmy has—no! Get back!"

Timmy had started to run toward us, until Rob spotted him and turned the hose on him, much the way I'd seen police on television turning fire hoses on rioters. Luckily the spray from our garden hose was considerably less forceful and wasn't likely to hurt Timmy, only make him giggle and prance around gleefully.

"Easy with the hose," I said. "You don't want to knock him down or get water up his nose."

"No, I'm just trying to keep him the hell away from me."

"Why? What's wrong?"

"He's covered with poop!"

I glanced at Timmy. He didn't seem to be covered with anything, except maybe drops of water. I could see one or two dabs of what I had supposed was mud, but nothing thirty seconds with a washcloth couldn't fix. Still, given Rob's well-known queasiness . . .

"What happened?" I asked aloud.

"I turned my back on him for a minute, and the next thing I knew, he'd taken his diaper off and was waving it around. What a mess! You should see the kitchen."

I closed my eyes to count to ten. At three I got hit in the face with a blast of water.

"Dammit, enough!" I said, putting my hands on my hips. "Turn the hose off!"

Rob dropped the hose. It landed at an angle and continued to squirt me just below the left knee until he reached the spigot and turned it off.

"More! More!" Timmy called. He ran in to pick up the spray head and shake it, to make it start again. I snagged him.

"Come on Timmy," I said. "Uncle Rob and I are going to give you a bubble bath. Rob, put on your bathing suit."

Timmy didn't actually look particularly dirty, but I shared Rob's squeamishness to the extent of wanting to make sure. And besides, I knew the only way to calm Rob down was to convince him that Timmy was no longer noxious. I hauled Timmy into Michael's and my bathroom and gave him a quick scrubbing in the walk-in shower while Rob, at my orders, prepared the bubble bath and fetched Timmy's bath toys.

"There," I said, plopping Timmy in the tub. "Splash to your heart's content."

"You're so good with kids," Rob said. "I couldn't get him to cooperate."

"I didn't get him to cooperate," I said. "I just picked him up. Where was he running around without his diaper?"

"All over the kitchen," Rob said, wrinkling his nose.

"Keep him entertained while I clean the kitchen, then."

Apart from the diaper dumped in one corner, the kitchen seemed about as clean as it had been when I'd left it. Either Rob had cleaned up the marks left by Timmy's diaper-swinging rampage or he'd exaggerated the whole incident out of proportion. My money was on exaggeration.

I dumped Rob's and Timmy's discarded clothes in the washer. Then I shed my own clothes, trying to ignore the fact that I had a sizeable audience—the snakes that had so disconcerted Michael last night. While in theory I knew they were only responding to light and motion, and not watching me with any kind of menace, it was still rather creepy.

"We need to get you guys back to the zoo," I said to the snakes, and reached for my cell phone—at least, I reached for where my cell phone would be if I hadn't just dumped my jeans, cell phone and all, into the washer. I fished out the phone, started the machine, and called Dad.

As the phone rang, I rummaged through the piles of clean clothes on the folding table. I could tell how busy Michael and I were by how full the table was. Right now, it contained over half of our wardrobe.

I got Dad's voice mail.

"Dad," I said. "When you get this, I need you to get the snakes out of our basement ASAP. I want everything to go smoothly when Mother comes over tonight, and you know how she feels about snakes. And don't just stash them somewhere else over here—if she starts measuring one room, there's no telling where she'll go."

Okay, it wasn't quite a lie—odds were Mother would find some reason to drop by tonight, if only for a few moments; and it had been at least a week since she'd dragged me off to some corner of the house to propose a decorating scheme, so we were probably overdue for that, too. I threw on some clothes, waved at the snakes for what I hoped would be the last time, and went up to clean the kitchen—which could use a good scrub, even if Rob had seriously exaggerated the damage done by Timmy's diaper-slinging.

As I scrubbed, I kept an ear open to make sure the splashing and squeals of laughter from upstairs still sounded as if both boys were happy. After Timmy's bath, it would be time for his supper, followed by watching some of his favorite videos and then getting him into pajamas and reading him a few stories.

I supposed I could have delegated more of it to Rob, or to the various other family members who had begun drifting in. But I was feeling irrationally guilty for dragging Timmy to a murder scene and then abandoning him to Rob's care. And I also found it a lot easier to forget about finding Jasper's body with Timmy around.

Although having Timmy around didn't ease my anxiety about Karen. Quite the contrary.

I continued to brood and fret, unnoticed by the rest of the family—possibly because I spent a lot of my time in the kitchen, cleaning up, or in the basement, catching up on the laundry. At least until Michael came home.

"What's wrong?" he asked about two seconds after he clattered down the stairs to find me.

"Apart from the fact that we still have too many snakes?"

"One is too many," he said. "What else is wrong? You look worried."

"Nothing's wrong," I said. "At least nothing that hasn't been wrong for the last several days."

"But it's starting to get to you," he said. He pulled a stack of clean but tangled laundry toward him and began sorting it out.

"How can she just leave him here like this?" I said.

"I know it feels like a big imposition," Michael began.

"Screw the imposition," I said. "I'm not talking about the effect on us. Clearly Timmy needs a safe place to stay for whatever reason—no problem. He can absolutely stay here as long as he needs to. But what kind of a mother could leave her kid somewhere for three days with people she doesn't know that well, on no notice, and not even call to see if he's okay?"

"A pretty lousy mother," Michael said. "Which Karen isn't, as far as I can see."

"You've only met her a couple of times," I said. "How can you possibly know what kind of a mother she is?"

"From Timmy. He's a pretty good kid. Rambunctious and headstrong—I suspect she's a little more indulgent than I would be—kids need limits. But then again, we don't know what he's like at home, under normal, unstressed conditions. I suspect she does a decent job of parenting, so dumping him here on no notice and disappearing for days isn't in character. Which means there must be something else going on. I have no idea what."

"I have a whole lot of ideas," I said. "None of them reassuring."

"Such as?"

"Maybe she only planned to leave Timmy here a little while but hasn't come back or called because she was physically unable. She could be dead, seriously ill, kidnapped, in jail, in a looney bin, or traveling on a spaceship to the third moon of Jupiter with a malfunctioning deep space radio."

"Plausible," he said. "Well, except for the spaceship theory. No one goes to the moons of Jupiter anymore. So twentieth century! Alpha Centauri, maybe."

I smiled to show that I appreciated his attempt to lighten my mood, not because anything was going to strike me as funny under the circumstances. Michael shoved his hand into a sock, waggled two fingers at me through a hole in the toe, and then pulled it off and tossed it into the rag bin. Okay, I chuckled slightly at that.

"Second possibility." I went on. "She is physically able to come back or communicate with us if she wanted to, but has some reason not to. Which would pretty much boil down to bad guys after her, and she's afraid to lead them here, or even to communicate with us. Afraid of involving us—and Timmy—in whatever danger she thinks is after her."

Michael paused with a half-folded towel in his hands to ponder that.

"Problem with that theory is that Timmy's whereabouts aren't exactly secret," he said. "Anyone who really wanted to find him could, anytime."

"So maybe she's only afraid that something will happen to her and doesn't want it to happen with Timmy nearby," I said.

"Or maybe she was—and is—too stressed out to think it through and realize that someone trying to find her could use Timmy as leverage. As a hostage."

"Which would mean Timmy's in danger."

We both involuntarily glanced up at the ceiling. We could hear Timmy squealing with delight at something.

"I'll kill anyone who tries it," I said. "Maybe I should take him away someplace. Hide him until this blows over."

"I'd feel better if you were both here, with lots of friends and family around," Michael said. "I think that's safer in the long run than trying to go it alone. And frankly, Karen on the run from bad guys doesn't seem to me the most likely option. I can think of at least one you haven't mentioned yet."

"Such as?"

"She's dodging the police. Not necessarily because she's done anything wrong," he added, seeing my face. "But what if she's afraid they'll arrest her—for Jasper's murder, or for the embezzlement—and thinks she needs to be free to clear herself?"

"Seems unlikely," I said, shaking my head.

"Are you the only person who thinks maybe she could do a better job of finding the bad guys than the police?"

"I don't think I can do a better job," I protested. "Chief Burke has the skills and the resources. But he's got other things on his plate, and you can't expect him to drop them all to focus on looking for Karen and—"

"And you can," Michael said. "What if Karen feels the same way and is off doing what she thinks is the best thing for her and Timmy's future?"

"So we trust Karen?" I said, after a bit.

"We keep our minds open," Michael said. "And how about if I drop by the station tomorrow and make Chief Burke aware of our concerns about Timmy's safety?"

"You think he won't listen to me?"

"I think maybe he'll be more inclined to listen to me when I do my concerned, overprotective husband routine. And did I mention that I offered to give Dr. Driscoll a ride tomorrow? I'm sure he won't mind coming into the station for a few minutes to look stern and disapproving if the chief doesn't take me seriously enough."

"And since Dr. Driscoll is Karen's department head," I said, nodding.

"More important, Dr. Driscoll's department ultimately oversees the Camcops, with whom Chief Burke is working so hard to build a more congenial relationship. . . ."

"Oh, excellent," I said.

"Normally I like to avoid all this town versus college political stuff," Michael said, shaking his head. "But this is serious."

"Thanks," I said. We folded and hung in amicable silence for a few minutes, until I came across a t-shirt I'd never seen before.

"This isn't yours, is it?" I asked, holding it up.

"No," he said. "What's 'Death Cab for Cutie'?"

"A band Rob likes," I said. "I don't mind him using the washer and dryer, but I draw the line at doing his laundry for him."

"It could be the t-shirt Timmy puked on," Michael said.

"Puked? When? Why didn't anyone tell me?"

"Relax," Michael said. "This morning, before you got up. It was only a little bit, and it only happened because Rob was tossing him in the air too soon after breakfast. He's fine."

Okay, Timmy was fine. But if taking care of kids was going to turn me into a nervous wreck . . .

I'd worry about that later. We finished folding all the laundry and Michael offered to put it all away. The laundry room was empty—well, except for the snakes. I stuck out my tongue at them—after all, they'd been flicking theirs at me for hours now. They didn't seem to notice.

Twenty-Four

Up in the kitchen, Rose Noire was fixing dinner—for the rest of us as well as Timmy. Mother, of course, was supervising. I heard a lively game of tag going on in the hallway and went out to see. I found Dr. Blake sitting on the hall bench, watching as Dad, Rob, and Timmy raced up the stairs.

"So," he said, when the giggling had retreated to the second floor. "I understand you had quite an exciting day!"

I blinked in surprise, and glanced quickly over my shoulder to make sure he was talking to me.

"That's one word for it," I said. "I actually think 'lousy' is a better adjective for any day that includes finding a dead body."

He beamed.

"Tell me about it," he said. He leaned back and folded his hands, gazing at me expectantly. It was rather like the way Timmy looked when I'd agreed that yes, yes, I'd read him another story.

"Why?" I asked. "I didn't see a single endangered species all day."

"There's more to life than endangered species."

Who was this—the pod Dr. Blake?

"Yes," I said. "There are also animal welfare and the responsible stewardship of the earth's resources, but I don't think I did anything today to further those causes, either. Or hinder them," I added hastily.

"Well, what the hell did you do, then?" he asked.

Okay, that was closer to the real Dr. Blake.

"I went looking for my friend Karen again," I said. "And found her estranged husband's dead body."

"Yes, that Jason somebody."

"Jasper," I said. "Jasper Walker. And then I had lunch with a friend and did some research in the library."

A pause.

"That's it?" he said.

I nodded.

"Then elaborate. Give me a little local color. You found a body. That must have been exciting. Did you check his pulse? Attempt CPR? Or just assume he was dead?"

"He'd been dead several days," I said. "So no, exciting wasn't exactly the word I'd use, and you couldn't pay me enough to check his pulse, and as for CPR, let's not even go there."

"Several days? Did you check to see if he had any pets that might need rescuing?"

I knew there had to be an animal angle to this.

"I called the police," I said. "And they took custody of his dog."

Blake frowned.

"I fed the dog some cheese crackers," I offered, just so he wouldn't think I was completely stone-hearted.

"Cheese crackers," he repeated.

"I didn't have any nutritionally sound dog food with me," I said. "And he wasn't starving, and at the time I didn't know the poor thing had been orphaned."

He continued to gaze at me for a few moments, as if hoping I'd offer something more interesting.

"What kind of dog?" he asked, finally, though it sounded as if he was only asking to be polite.

"Big dog," I said. "Maybe seventy-five or eighty pounds. Some kind of mixed hound. Very friendly."

He nodded, then got up and strode off with a preoccupied look on his face. Just then Michael came out of the kitchen door and strolled over.

"He's up to something," I said.

"Your grandfather? Why do you think that?"

"He's been asking me to tell him what I did today."

"Egad," he said. "I've been guilty of that a time or two myself, haven't I?"

"Yes, but you're actually interested in what I've been doing, or at least have a vested interest in pretending to be. Dr. Blake tends to ignore anything that doesn't have an animal angle."

"And your day didn't?"

"Well, there was a dog. He seemed mildly interested in the dog."

Michael nodded.

"If I go back there again, I'll drop by and check out the canary farm," I said. "Just so I can give him the lowdown. Though I can't imagine why I'd want to go back. And odds are canaries are too mundane to intrigue him."

"Dog fighting," Michael said.

"What?"

"Maybe he's investigating dog fighting. He's got that show he's working on about cock fighting—maybe he's expanding it to include dog fighting. Illegal animal fighting in general. Was the dog a pit bull or a bulldog or something?"

I shook my head.

"Big, friendly hound dog," I said. "The kind that just looks puzzled when Spike runs up and tries to pick a fight."

"Still, if Blake is showing an interest in ordinary domestic dogs, you can bet it's some kind of animal welfare issue," Michael said. "And the show on cock fighting hasn't aired yet, so maybe they're still doing some filming."

"That would make sense," I said. "Of course, there's another explanation."

Michael cocked one eyebrow.

"He could just be trying to take an interest in what I'm doing," I said. "Trying to build a relationship. You know what he's like—brilliant as hell, but with absolutely no social graces. Maybe it's not his fault that he does the whole relationship-building thing so oddly that I react with suspicion. Maybe I'm just too hard on him."

"Maybe you are," he said. "But much as I like the old guy, he has pulled some crazy stunts. Like that whole cock-fighting raid that landed him and your father in jail. Here's a deal for you—you keep an open mind on whether Blake's got an ulterior motive when he interrogates you. And I'll see if I can use my irresistible charm to find out what he and your dad are up to."

"Deal," I said. "And if he is investigating dog fighting, or more cock fighting, see if you can get him to at least consider working within the system this time."

"Definitely. Meanwhile, I'm supposed to tell everyone that dinner will be on the table in five minutes."

"While you're at it, remind Dad and Dr. Blake about the snakes."

Since we were eating rather late, I took Timmy up to bed as soon as he'd finished dessert. We only had one difficult moment, when I had successfully wrestled him into pajamas and picked up the toothbrush to begin the battle over brushing. He suddenly stopped fighting and just looked at me.

"Mommy not coming back?" he asked.

"Of course Mommy's coming back," I said. "Soon. Just not tonight."

He nodded, and didn't put up much of a fight about brushing his teeth. Was he really reassured? Or had he given up on his mommy? Surely kids didn't give up that easily? If this went on much longer, maybe I should find a child psychologist to help Timmy cope with it all. For that matter, if this went on much longer, I might need a shrink myself.

I shoved the thought away to concentrate on Timmy. I read him a story. Handed him a sippy cup of milk. Maybe I was starting to get the hang of this parenting thing after all. I tucked him in, turned the night-light on and the main light off, tiptoed toward the door, and was just stepping into the hall when he sat bolt upright again.

"Want Kiki," he said.

I returned to the crib and checked. No, Kiki wasn't

there. And Timmy hadn't thrown her on the floor beside the crib.

"Here's Blanky," I said, plucking the green blanket from the rest of the covers and toys. "You lie down and try to sleep, and I'll go look for Kiki. I'm sure he's just downstairs. I'll be back in—"

"Want Kiki!" Timmy threw Blanky overboard and howled with such volume that everyone in the house came running to see what was wrong. Dad even brought his medical bag. Once I'd convinced everybody that Timmy was unhurt, I formed them all into a posse to search the house and yard for Kiki.

Who was nowhere to be found.

In between bouts of searching, various members of the family pitched in on the effort to calm Timmy down and lull him to sleep. Rob and Michael gave him endless horsie-horsie rides, all ending up in the crib where Timmy still refused to lie down. Dad brought in an awesome assortment of living creatures for Timmy to inspect and pet—snakes, prairie dogs, iguanas, ducks, small monkeys, bats, and a half-grown skunk that he swore had been de-scented. Rose Noire dabbed lavender and chamomile essential oils on the light bulbs, put Mozart on the portable CD player, and tried to demonstrate yoga breathing exercises. Seth Early—who had heard Timmy's wails from his lurking post across the street and come running—even offered to bring in some sheep to help calm him down. I wasn't sure whether Timmy was supposed to count them or cuddle them, but since even the smallest of them weighed at least 150 pounds and none of them had been washed in weeks, we passed.

"In my day, we'd just give the little brat a slug of bourbon in his milk," Dr. Blake said.

"I think not," Mother said, in such an icy tone that even Dr. Blake got the message.

I began to suspect that our efforts to calm Timmy were having the opposite effect, so I shooed everyone downstairs to see if he would eventually calm down if left alone.

As an experiment, it was a failure.

"There he goes again," Michael said, after yet another shriek. By this time, we were all clustered at the foot of the stairs, wincing at every noise from above— except for Mother, who was sitting nearby in the living room, reading one of her decorating magazines and frowning.

"KIKI!" Timmy shrieked. It was a heart-rending wail, slightly hoarse and quivering with pathos. We all flinched when we heard it. Well, all but Mother.

"Oh, for heaven's sakes," she exclaimed. She slapped her magazine down on the coffee table and began marching up the stairs.

"I thought we were testing Michael's theory," I whispered, as I hurried to keep up with her.

"Theory's a bust," Michael murmured, from the bottom of the stairs.

"I could try a massage," Rose Noire suggested. "A drop or two of lavender in some baby oil—it works wonders with Seth's sheep."

"I've got a baby wombat we could show him," Dad said. "Just let me run out and get it."

"This is no time for wombats," Mother said. "Or aromatherapy."

She reached the top of the stairs and strode down the hall.

"Mother, what are you going to do?" I scurried into Timmy's room behind her.

Timmy was standing in his crib, holding onto the bars and shaking them like a prisoner, and howling with more determination than energy. I could swear I saw a look of satisfaction cross his face when we entered. He had an audience again. Then again, the poor kid was tired and cranky and no doubt getting more and more upset by his mother's absence. He still had a long way to go before we cast him in a remake of *The Omen*. And I was pretty sure the fuss wasn't really over Kiki.

"Timothy," Mother said. "This Will Not Do."

Timmy paused for a moment and cocked his head to one side in puzzlement.

"You will go to sleep now," she said. "And while you are sleeping, Meg will find Kiki and bring him back, so he'll be here when you wake."

She gave him her gracious smile, with a little hint of the don't-push-it glance.

Timmy considered for a moment.

"Promise?" he said.

"I promise," Mother said. "Now lie down and go to sleep. I will wait here with you for news of Kiki."

She sat down in the rocking chair, turned on the reading lamp, and picked up several books from the floor. After inspecting them, she opened a Dr. Seuss book and began reading it. Silently. She was rocking very slowly and waving one graceful hand to the soft strains of Mozart.

Timmy stood in his crib, watching for a few moments, then lay down, pulled a blanket over his head, and fell silent. After a minute or so, I heard his soft, slow breathing, and then a soft snore.

Mother looked up from her book.

"Well?" she said.

"Are you going to help me hunt?" I asked. "Since you promised results that I have no confidence we can deliver."

"I will supervise from here. And keep an eye on Timothy." She lowered her eyes to her book and turned a page.

Downstairs, muted celebrations were taking place.

"Your mother is a wonder," Dad said.

"I could use a nap myself," Rob said, with a yawn.

"I think I'm going to try some of that lavender," Rose Noire said. "It's also very good for headaches."

"We still have to find Kiki before he wakes up," I said, to muted groans. Everyone scattered and resumed the search, though most of them were so tired and frazzled they were searching places they'd already searched two or three times. I'd have tried to convince them to go home and get some sleep, but I was too tired to think straight.

"Maybe Kiki isn't even in the house," Michael said. "I can go search some of the places you and he went today."

"Some of the places will be closed," I said.

"I'll find night watchmen. Or break in."

Something in me cracked, seeing the look of grim determination on his face. I burst out in tears.

"I'm sorry," I said, as Michael swept me in a

comforting embrace. "You're being so great about this—everyone is. And it's my fault he's here and I should have been keeping a better eye out for Kiki and—I can't believe I'm having hysterics, too, over a stupid stuffed cat."

My tears mutated into giggles.

"It's important to Timmy," Michael said. "And the poor kid has been through a lot. If we can't bring his mother back, at least we can find Kiki."

"If you're game to go driving around the county in search of a stuffed cat, I'm not going to argue with you," I said. "Let me get my notebook—I left it in the car. Jasper Walker's address is there."

"I'll change into something more likely to inspire confidence in a night watchman," Michael said.

On my way to the car, I passed by the outdoor section of Spike's pen. Damn! In our distraction over Kiki, we had left Spike out, which was dangerous. No matter how fierce Spike thought he was, to a fox or a large owl, he'd be easy pickings. We always made a point to take him inside before dark.

"Come here, Spike," I said. "Time to come inside for dinner."

Normally the D-word got his attention, but he was off in the far corner of the pen chewing on something.

Something black and fuzzy that was leaking cotton stuffing.

Twenty-Five

"Kiki!" I exclaimed. "Spike, drop it!"

Spike stubbornly refused to drop Kiki. Maybe it was just because I wanted the stuffed toy, or maybe Timmy had spilled enough food on Kiki over the years to make him downright tasty, but Spike had no intention of surrendering his prey. It finally took me, Rob, and Dad to pry the two apart.

"Come on, Rob," Dad said. "Let's go put antiseptic on these bites. Meg, did he get you?"

"No," I said. "But he really did a number on Kiki."

Back inside, things were still quiet upstairs. I fetched my sewing kit and sat down at the kitchen table to mend Kiki. Rob, Michael, Dad, and Rose Noire gathered around, looking as anxious as the family of a human patient. And after my preliminary examination, I realized that the patient needed more than surgery.

"There's a good chunk of stuffing missing."

"I could go out and look for it," Rob offered.

"No, Spike will have eaten a lot of it, and the rest will be muddy. For that matter, half of what's still here is pretty nasty. And so's Kiki—she needs a bath, and then she needs a stuffing donor. Find me a stuffed animal, pronto!"

They all looked at each other and then scattered.

I spread some old newspapers on the kitchen table and began removing the remaining stuffing. The bits that were clean—very few of them—I put in a pile for reuse. The bits that were stained with mud and possibly dog poop went into the trash. Once I had emptied Kiki, I could throw her into the wash and—

Suddenly the finger I was using to pull out bits of stuffing hit something hard, stuffed into Kiki's left hind leg. It took me a couple of minutes to tease it free. Michael came back into the kitchen while I was working on it.

"I checked all the stuff Karen left with Timmy, but there weren't any other stuffed animals," he said. "Your mother and father have gone back to the farmhouse and will let us know if your nieces and nephews have left any stuffed animals behind."

"Unlikely," I said. "Most of them had outgrown stuffed animals by the time Mother and Dad bought the farmhouse."

"And I stopped Rob from taking the sofa apart for its stuffing. Rose Noire is driving back to her apartment—she thinks she might have a stuffed animal there. Do we—what's that?"

I was holding my find up to the light to inspect it.

"I think it's a thumb drive—you know, one of those tiny little computer storage things you can hang on your keychain."

"Where'd you get it?"

I gestured at the disemboweled Kiki.

"Remember how Timmy kept saying that Kiki had a boo-boo?" I asked. "Maybe he wasn't just doing it for attention. Maybe he was trying to tell us about this."

"This could be important," Michael said.

"Yes," I said. "Why don't you put Kiki in the washer—delicate cycle. I'm going to the office to see if I can figure out what's on this thing."

"Shouldn't we turn it over to the police?" Michael asked, as he picked up Kiki. "A data storage device that could be directly connected to a murder and an embezzlement case?"

"We will," I said. "But not before I've checked it out. After all, if the only thing it contains is a backup copy of Timmy's favorite musical selections, there's no sense running to Chief Burke with it, is there?"

He shook his head as if he didn't quite buy it, but didn't argue with me.

In the office, I booted up my laptop and attached the thumb drive to it. I was able to see the files on the thumb drive, but I could tell figuring out the contents wasn't going to be easy. The file names were cryptic and apparently random strings of numbers and letters, and my computer stubbornly refused to open any of them.

I had just finished copying the contents of the thumb drive into a directory on my laptop when Michael joined me.

"Any luck?" he asked.

"Clearly, this wasn't intended to contain a top-secret message from Karen to us," I said. "Because if it was, she'd have made at least some of the files in a format normal human beings could read."

"Chief Burke can probably call on forensic computer analysts to unravel it."

"No doubt," I said. I could tell he was relieved when I picked up the phone and dialed the police station.

To my surprise, Chief Burke was still there. Caerphilly's crime wave must still be going strong. And also to my surprise, he actually seemed interested in the thumb drive.

"Can you bring it down to the station?" he asked.

"Sure," I said. "Now?"

"First thing tomorrow will do," he said. "Good-bye."

Rats! I was hoping he'd say that no, he wanted it now. Not that I was very keen on driving into Caerphilly just now, but I wanted to know that the chief felt a sense of urgency about it.

"I can drop it off on my way to the college," Michael said.

I handed over the thumb drive to Michael.

"Don't trust me to do it?" I asked.

"You'll be busy with Timmy," he said. "And I'm going that way anyway, remember. You coming up?"

"As soon as I finish fixing Kiki," I said.

Though after he left the office, I found myself frowning at the directory in which I'd copied the files from the thumb drive. No doubt the police would figure out how to open them, but fat chance they'd tell us anything. I opened my e-mail program and sent the entire file collection to Jack Ransom, with a message to call me if he could figure out what the files were.

Down in the laundry room, I moved Kiki from the washer into the dryer, and had a sudden inspiration. We had several old socks in the rag bag, and if that wasn't enough, a shelf over the washer and dryer contained, among other things, the Lonely Socks Club, a basket where we stowed all the unmatched socks on the off chance their mates would eventually turn up. I fetched my scissors and began shredding some of the nicest, softest cotton socks. By the time Kiki emerged from the dryer, I was all prepared to restuff her and sew her back up.

Timmy looked deceptively angelic when I slipped Kiki in beside him. And he would be up early tomorrow, I told myself, so I should probably get to bed. It was already . . . ten o'clock.

Michael had already fallen asleep. I wasn't sure I liked what having children was going to do to our love life. But I had no energy to stay awake and worry about it.

Twenty-Six

Apparently I slept through Timmy's early morning incursion into our bed. When I woke up, I was alone, except for Blanky, who had no doubt been left behind in the excitement of Timmy's reunion with Kiki.

Blanky could use a trip through the washer, I decided, so I threw him on top of the contents of the hamper, added the discarded clothing from Timmy's room, and dragged the pile downstairs.

The kitchen was empty—of people, at least; there was a pot of reasonably fresh coffee on the counter and a still-warm bowl of oatmeal on the table. I took the hamper down into the basement and nodded with approval to see that I once more had the laundry area to myself. The snakes were gone.

Back up in the kitchen, I could see Dad's truck in the driveway, its bed loaded with glass terrariums containing the snakes. Michael and Timmy were standing near the truck. Timmy was trying to climb into the truck bed with the snakes. Michael was holding him back while talking to Rose Noire, and he looked as if his patience was wearing rather thin. I grabbed my oatmeal and a spoon and strolled out to join them.

"It's important to acknowledge and work through our fears," Rose Noire was saying. "Because children are so sensitive and impressionable, and if they realize you're afraid of something, they could pick up your fears—"

"I'm not afraid of snakes." Michael said. "I just really dislike them. And I doubt if Timmy's going to be scarred for life if he realizes that I don't like snakes as much as he does. Are you, Timmy?"

"No," Timmy said. "Can I have 'nake now?"

"No," I said, coming up to join them. "The snakes have to go back to the zoo. If you're good, we'll take you to see the snakes later, at their house."

"Do you want to say good morning to the sheep?" Rose Noire asked. A couple of stray sheep—escapees from Seth Early's pastures, no doubt—were grazing nearby.

Timmy frowned at first. Clearly sheep were no competition for the snakes in his mind. Then he smiled.

"Sheep play horsie-horsie," he said, and dashed off toward the unsuspecting ewes, with Rose Noire in hot pursuit.

"Well, that will keep them both busy," Michael said. "It would help if your father would hurry up and haul the snakes away while Timmy's torturing the sheep. Which reminds me—I have some good news."

"You've located Karen and she's coming to pick up Timmy in half an hour?"

"No, but I seem to have convinced your father and grandfather to let me help with whatever they're doing. I'm supposed to meet them in our barn at seven tonight, wearing dark clothes that are easy to run in."

"Oh, great," I said. "As if Dr. Blake should be running at all, much less after dark. Or Dad. You couldn't talk them out of doing whatever it is they're doing?"

"I couldn't even talk them into telling me what we're doing, even after volunteering to help and promising to keep their secret. But don't worry; I'll be with them, and I'll look after them. And I'll have my cell phone along. I'll give you a call as soon as I know what we're doing. Meanwhile, it's time I left for work."

He gave me a quick good-bye kiss and strode toward his car, draining the last of his coffee as he went.

I spotted Dad and Dr. Blake in the backyard, near one of the sheds. They seemed to be looking for something. They were scuffling along with their eyes glued to the ground, stooping to peer under the shrubbery from time to time. I strolled over nearer to them.

"Lost something?" I asked.

"Oh, no," Dad said.

"Just one of the snakes," Dr. Blake said.

"But not here," Dad said quickly. "Back at the zoo."

"And you're only looking here because the light is better," I said. "I see. What kind of snake? Is it poisonous?"

"No, it's not poisonous," Dr. Blake said.

"And we didn't lose it in your yard," Dad added, his tone desperate. "Did we, Dad?"

"Eh? Oh, no, of course not," Dr. Blake said, finally catching on. "Left her over at the zoo, I'm sure."

"We're just making absolutely sure before we go back there to get him," Dad said.

"Her," Dr. Blake said.

"Okay," I said. "Just out of curiosity, what kind of

snake did you not lose in my yard? In case I happen to run across any spare snakes in my travels."

"Six feet long, bright green," Dr. Blake said.

"It's Jade," Dad said. "The Emerald Tree Boa."

"I thought she was going back to the zoo after she finished her shed," I said.

"Yes, but she's still retaining her eye caps," Dr. Blake said. "The part of the skin over the eye. Dangerous for the snake, because when it thickens and becomes opaque during a shed, it impairs the vision. Snakes get irritable and unpredictable when they can't see properly. But it's treatable, and of course a fairly common form of dys-ecdysis."

"Dysecdysis means a bad shed," Dad explained.

"I was going to remove them today," Dr. Blake said. "I will as soon as we find her—"

"Over at the zoo," Dad put in.

"She'll turn up when she's hungry enough," Dr. Blake said. "Very soon, I should think. She's got a healthy appetite, Jade does."

"So we have a half-blind boa constrictor wandering around somewhere feeling peckish and irritable," I said. "Should I make sure Spike and the ducks are safely locked up somewhere snakeproof?"

They looked at each other.

"Probably a good idea," Dad said. "Just as a precau-tion, you understand. In case we're wrong about her being at the zoo."

They shuffled off, searching the grass as they went. I realized that I'd completely forgotten to ask them if they'd also removed the birds they'd hidden on the third floor. Not that I'd get a straight answer out of them if I did.

I peered into the shed. Empty, except for a terrarium—presumably the one Jade was supposed to be occupying.

Spike wasn't in his pen, though.

I hurried over to where Rose Noire was standing. Timmy was mounted on one of the sheep yelling "Giddyap!" and "Go horsie!" while Rose Noire wrung her hands anxiously. The sheep seemed unperturbed.

"Have you seen Spike?" I asked.

"Rob took him someplace," she said. "Oh, dear. Do you think Timmy is upsetting that poor sheep?"

"I don't even think he's got its attention yet," I said.

I hurried back out to the barn. Yes, Spike's carrier and leash were gone. Of course, I found myself wondering where Rob had taken Spike, but at least he was safe.

Just then my cell phone rang. It was Jack Ransom.

"So you're still sleuthing," he said. "Any idea what these files are?"

"I was hoping you could tell me," I said.

"I can probably figure out eventually," he said. "But some of them are encrypted, and the rest are in some kind of proprietary format. Possibly some kind of accounting data. Any information you have could save me some time."

"Sorry," I said. "All I know is that Karen put them on a thumb drive and hid them inside her son's stuffed cat. I'm assuming they might be related to her disappearance."

"This is your friend from the college financial department," Jack said. "Are these files from her office, do you think?"

"Probably," I said. "It occurred to me that they

might have something to do with the embezzlement scheme."

"Could be," he said. "I'll get Ashok to look at them, too—if they're related to the college financial system, he might recognize the formats. There is one thing I can tell you. If you look in the properties, you can see that Nadine Hanrahan's the owner of some of these files."

I was surprised at what a fierce sense of relief I felt at hearing Nadine's name.

"Not Karen?"

"No. Of course, all that means is that they were created on Nadine's computer," he said. "And that's just some of the files."

Still, I wasn't sorry at the possibility that the chief might be seeing something to implicate Nadine.

"Anything else I can help you with?" Jack asked.

I thought about it for a moment. It occurred to me to check on how accurate some of Sandie's local scoop was.

"Okay, maybe this is a weird question," I began.

"Weirder than usual, or just Meg weird?"

"If that's an insult, I'm ignoring it."

"Actually, it's a compliment. What's the question?"

"I need some information about an Aubrey Hamilton. That's Aubrey, with a B."

Keys rattled.

"I can find several of them," he said. "What else do you know about him?"

"Well, that's the question. Is he a him, or a her? The one that lives in Caerphilly County, that is, and has something to do with the Belle Glade Bird Farm."

I heard keys rattling again.

"You're right. Her. Ms. Aubrey Hamilton. Owns the property next to Hiram Bass's—I see you've been meeting the neighbors. Widowed or divorced about five years ago—at least that's when the property changed from joint ownership with a Martin Hamilton to sole ownership by her. Yes, obit for Mr. Hamilton around the same time. I'm not finding anything about a bird farm, though. Not anything current, anyway."

"That's odd. Then again, maybe she wouldn't be inclined to advertise her business around here."

"Like maybe she doesn't have a business license?"

"You have such a devious mind. I was only thinking that maybe there isn't a big market locally for canaries and cockatiels. Maybe she sells them wholesale to pet stores, or something. What would you do if you wanted to sell birds?"

"I'd put up a Web site, of course," he said. "Which she hasn't done."

"But if you're not very computer-oriented, maybe you go where the bird fanciers are. They must have shows and magazines and such. I can start there."

"At a bird show?"

"At the bookstore. I'll buy a few bird magazines. See what I can learn about canary farms and cockatiel breeders."

"Sounds like a plan. Anything else I can do?"

"I'll give you a call if I think of anything."

Of course, as soon as I hung up, I thought of something else he could have done. But at least this computer chore was something I knew very well how to do. I went into the home office, turned on my computer, and logged into the real estate listing service Michael and I had used so much when we were trying to find a place to buy. I couldn't help feeling a brief sense of relief that at least we weren't back in the tiny basement apartment where Michael had lived during his bachelor days, struggling to find anything for sale in town that we could even hope to afford.

As usual, listings in Caerphilly were few, and mostly in the pricier sections of town. Aha! I found one—no, two—in Westlake, where Nadine lived. I printed them out and tucked them in my purse. And while I was at it, I shuffled through the recycling stack until I found the real estate section from Sunday's copy of the *Caerphilly Clarion* and circled the two Westlake listings.

I had a plan for the day.

Twenty-Seven

Okay, it wasn't much of a plan, but I was running out of places to look for Karen. So first I'd head over to the campus and drop by Renfrew's bookstore, which was famous for its large periodical selection, to get some magazines about pet birds. Then check out Nadine's neighborhood—under the guise of house hunting for Rob.

Of course, since Rob had disappeared, taking Spike with him, I couldn't enlist him to ride shotgun with me. Maybe Spike was just camouflage, and avoiding me—and Timmy—was the real reason for Rob's disappearance.

Well, never mind. I could enlist Rose Noire instead. We could always say that we were doing the first round of house-hunting for Rob. If we ran into anyone who actually knew him, that would sound a lot more plausible anyway.

I went back outside to talk her into it. To my relief, the snake truck was gone, and Dad and Dr. Blake with it. Rose Noire looked happier, too, probably because Timmy had given up trying to go sheepback riding and was writhing in the grass, doing a pretty fair imitation of a snake.

"Oh, that's such a good idea," Rose Noire said, when I explained my plan. "I have a lot of ideas about how to help you! Just wait a minute while I gather a few things."

Actually, it took her closer to half an hour, and apparently her ideas were mostly aimed at Timmy's well-being rather than my quest to find Karen or figure out what had happened to her.

She immediately took charge of improving Timmy's environment—replacing Led Zeppelin with some kind of New Age CD, full of flutes and chimes.

"Are you sure that's a good idea?" I said. "What if I fall asleep at the wheel?"

"Oh, no," she said. "This isn't relaxation music. It's supposed to stimulate your mental and physical acuity."

It sounded the same as the relaxing, sleep-inducing CDs she'd given me a few months before, but she was the expert.

"I thought that might be helpful if you're doing some kind of sleuthing," she added. "And of course, it's so important to make sure a child's brain receives proper stimulation, don't you think? Especially during those all-important, formative preschool years."

"Want Zeppewin," Timmy said.

On the way into town, Rose Noire attempted additional brain stimulation with a set of flash cards about colors and shapes. Timmy was having none of it.

"Timmy, what shape is this?" she asked, holding up a green square.

"Horsie," Timmy said.

"No, Timmy, it's a square," she said. "Square. And what color is the square?"

"Poopy," Timmy said. "Yuck!"

"No, it's green," Rose Noire said, in a deliberately upbeat, patient voice.

A dozen flash cards made absolutely no dent in Timmy's cheerful refusal to play. But I could tell he was getting to Rose Noire. Worse, even Timmy could tell.

"Why don't you give the flash cards a rest for the time being?" I suggested. "Sometimes, with kids, it's not necessary to do anything with them—just be present for them."

"Oh, that's so wise!" she exclaimed.

I didn't tell her it was a line straight out of one of the child care manuals she'd brought over on Timmy's first day with us. I'd been boning up.

Rose Noire's method of just being present was to smile encouragingly at Timmy every few minutes, and occasionally pat his shoulder. The first time she did this, Timmy earned a time-out by spitting some of his juice on her. Even after I made him apologize, she was clearly upset by this.

"I'm just no good with children," she kept moaning.

She cheered up a bit after I suggested that Timmy, like Dad's pet llamas, used spitting as a form of pack bonding behavior.

Rose Noire must not have been listening when Dad explained the llamas' spitting. Llamas spit to establish dominance. Timmy was succeeding beautifully.

Of course, the only way I had thought of to impose a time-out in the car, where Timmy was already strapped into his car seat, was to interrupt the musical entertainment. A few minutes after his time-out ended, Timmy asked if he could have another one. I deduced that he wasn't all that fond of Rose Noire's New Age music. So by the time we made our stop at the bookstore, I'd insisted on a return to Led Zeppelin, and we cruised into the ritzy suburb of Westlake to the dulcet strains of "Ramble On."

One nice thing about Rose Noire was that she bounced back from defeat as cheerful as ever. And our arrival in Westlake sent her mood soaring.

"Oh, this is such a nice neighborhood!" Rose Noire exclaimed. "Look at that house! It looks just like a castle! And there's a Spanish hacienda!"

Faux gothic and faux Spanish colonial, actually, but I let her enthuse while I concentrated on peering at the mailboxes for the house numbers. We were getting close to Nadine's address.

"Look at all the open green spaces!" she exclaimed. "Isn't it lovely? What a beautiful neighborhood! Why didn't you and Michael move here?"

"Because there isn't a house on this street that goes for less than a million and a half," I said. "The farmhouse was a bargain in comparison."

"Oh, I can't believe that," she said. "Look at that quaint little cottage there—you can't tell me that's a million-dollar house."

"No," I said, following her pointing finger. "It's the gatehouse. The big house is up there!"

I saw Rose Noire's jaw drop as her eyes traveled up the hill behind the cottage and saw the huge faux Georgian mansion looming overhead. You half expected

Mr. Rochester to come striding out in pursuit of Jane Eyre.

"Oh, my," she said. "It's . . . it's . . ."

"A grotesque example of conspicuous consumption, aesthetic bankruptcy, and ecological insensitivity?" I suggested. "An absolute travesty?"

"Well, yes," she said. "But at least it's a pretty travesty. Oh, look—that one looks like something out of *Gone with the Wind*."

"Yes," I said. "It looks like what you'd get if you took a bicycle pump and inflated Tara to three times its original size."

"Oh, Meg," she said. "You can be so negative."

"We're chasing a killer, remember?" I said. "It brings out the cynical side of my personality."

"Playground! Playground!" Timmy exclaimed. He had begun bouncing up and down in his seat with excitement.

"Look, there's Nadine's house," I said, a few hundred feet farther on.

Timmy and Rose Noire both stared with me as I drove slowly past. Nadine's house was a two story in faux Tudor style.

"Aren't you going to stop?" Rose Noire asked.

"Not right out in front, no," I said. "Look, it's a cul-de-sac."

I turned around in the circle at the end of the road and we cruised past Nadine's house again. Rose Noire and I were still fascinated, but not Timmy.

"Want playground!" he pleaded. He managed to sound as if being prevented from going to the playground was causing actual pain.

"Oh, Timmy, I'm so sorry," Rose Noire began. "We don't have time to go to the playground right now—"

"Yes, we do," I said, as I began pulling over to park the car.

"Not that I object to giving Timmy some recreation," Rose Noire said. "But I thought the whole purpose of this trip was to pursue leads to the disappearance of his . . . um . . ."

"The playground gives us an excellent reason for being in the neighborhood," I said. "We came over from the low-rent district to take insidious advantage of the rich people's playground."

"And it's only two houses down from the house you want to spy on," Rose Noire said. "How convenient."

"Yes," I said, as I went around the car to unfasten Timmy. "You can keep an eye on Timmy while I rove the neighborhood, conspicuously carrying the real estate section from Sunday's paper to make me look harmless."

"You're not going to break in, are you?" she asked, in an anxious tone. "Having intruders does such horrible things to the energy of a house—the occupants usually need a cleansing ceremony afterward, and they so rarely realize that. Of course, I suppose it helps that you're breaking in for a good cause rather than to commit a crime, but still—it can be the start of a whole downward spiral in the lives of its occupants."

"No, I probably won't break in, because getting caught would start a whole downward spiral in my own life. I expect most jails have even worse energy than burgled houses. I just plan to look in the windows."

Actually, I wouldn't hesitate to sneak in if I thought

I could, but most houses this fancy tended to have working burglar alarms. I didn't think Rose Noire needed to know my reasoning.

"Still, even looking in the windows is a kind of violation," she said. "Ask the house's permission first."

"Um . . . right," I said. "Let's get Timmy down to the playground before we worry about that."

It was an awesome playground, with at least a dozen pieces of equipment of various degrees of size and complexity. Timmy made a beeline for a structure like several small log cabins on stilts, with stairs and ladders leading up to them, slides coming out of them, and a variety of rope and board bridges connecting them. The whole area around the cabins was paved with some sort of rubbery substance that bounced underfoot, which probably did a lot to cut down on broken bones.

And the whole playground was empty. A pity, really, to build such a nice playground and have no one use it.

"Watch me! Watch me!" Timmy shouted, as he began scrambling up a ladder to the tallest cabin.

"Oh, dear," Rose Noire said, sprinting after him.

"I'll be back," I said.

When I got back to the street again, I glanced back and saw Rose Nore, with her ankle-length India-print skirt tucked up to a more practical level, waving her hands frantically as Timmy leaned backward out of one of the cabin windows.

With Timmy safely occupied—well, at least occupied—I strolled back toward Nadine's house.

Holding my folded newspaper like a totem, I scanned the street. It didn't look as if my acting efforts were particularly necessary. Not a creature in sight. Perhaps the residents of Westlake were all double-income couples who worked long hours to pay for their mansions.

As I crossed the street and slogged up the sidewalk toward Nadine's house, I thought of another possibility—most of the residents were probably wealthy enough to summer someplace else. Days like this, I could understand why. Though if everyone had gone away for the summer, why had they all left their air conditioning on high—the only sound I heard was the hum of several dozen huge compressors laboring away up and down the street.

Nadine's house was small, compared to some of the others, but still impressive. Like all her neighbors, she had a lawn manicured to velvety smoothness and lined with neat pruned shrubs in beds of perfectly mounded mulch.

As I trudged up her walk, I found myself thinking about what Timmy and Spike could do to all that uncanny perfection if you turned them loose on it for five minutes.

I pressed the doorbell, producing not a single note or even a chime, but several bars of vaguely familiar music. As I stood there waiting for an answer, I tried to hum it and figure out what it was.

When I thought enough time had passed, I pressed the doorbell again. This time I listened more closely and recognized the notes—the college anthem.

Most people at Caerphilly College tried to forget about the anthem whenever possible. The tune was twittery and unmusical, while the original words were embarrassingly flowery and sentimental—no doubt be-

cause they had been written by Mrs. Ginevra Braken-
ridge Pruitt, a late nineteenth-century poet of dubious
talent. The administration would have replaced the
song long ago except that Mrs. Pruitt and her family
were among the college's biggest donors—nearly every
third building on campus was named after one or another of the Pruitts. The students had succeeded in getting the administration to agree that the anthem needed
new words, but since the commission to write them
was now in its fourth decade of existence without coming any closer to agreement, I had no doubt that if Michael achieved tenure, we'd be humming the damned
song at college gatherings until his retirement.

The tune didn't sound any better when played on
doorbell chimes, I decided, as I pressed the button for
a third time. The doorbell had to be an expensive cus-
tom order. What kind of lunatic—apart from the
Pruitts—would even want it?

I allowed plenty of time for Nadine to answer the
door—after all this was the sort of house where you
probably needed roller skates to be sure of getting to
the door in under ten minutes, and I couldn't see Nadine doing that. I concentrated on listening for any
sound inside the house, and from time to time I looked
at my watch and tried to look impatient, so anyone
watching me would think I actually had an appointment with Nadine.

Clearly she wasn't home. I looked around to see if
anyone was in sight. No one. And there were only a
couple of houses within view anyway, and their sight-
lines would be largely obstructed by all the ornamental
trees and shrubbery.

"Hope you don't mind, house," I said. "I'd like to see your insides."

I stepped into a flowerbed and peered into the foyer window.

It was empty. No furniture, no rugs, no pictures—nothing.

I stepped back to the walk and pondered. I'd heard of people who overextended themselves by buying more house than they could afford and were too house-poor to afford furniture. In fact, Michael and I had been in that boat ourselves initially. But we did have some furniture and junk left over from our single lives, not to mention family members who would gladly have donated enough furniture and tchotchkes to fill the house from top to bottom if we let them. Our house was still a little minimal, but by choice. Nowhere near empty.

I walked around to the next window, pretending I belonged there. I pulled out my notebook and a pen and tried to look preoccupied and professional, like someone who'd been asked to give an estimate on taking over the landscape service.

"Lovely glass panes," I said to the house. "Mind if I use them?"

Hearing no objection, I peered in again. This window offered a view of the living room. Also completely empty.

I continued around the perimeter of the house, peering into each window as I went and exclaiming enthusiastically about what I saw, to avoid hurting the house's feelings. Though despite what I said to the house, I wasn't very impressed. It was big and immaculately clean, but rather cold and formal. Though maybe the poor house would look better if it had some furniture to add a bit of warmth. I contemplated the other end of the vacant living room, an empty dining room, a kitchen stripped of everything but the appliances, and several more bare rooms that were probably intended to serve as family room, home office, guest room, or who knows what else. Curious how hard it was to put a name to a room when it was completely devoid of any contents.

I did find a stepladder at the back of the house—it was leaning up against the wall behind some bushes, and looked as if it might have been forgotten. Or maybe the house, grateful that I'd asked permission before snooping, had provided the ladder to help me snoop more efficiently.

Yeah, or maybe it was holding out the ladder to tempt me into getting into even deeper trouble.

Still, I couldn't resist. I used the ladder to climb from the rear terrace onto a deck that ran across much of the back of the house on the second story. I tiptoed over to the windows and peeked in, seeing only several empty bedrooms.

Nadine didn't have any stickers warning me that she was protected by one of the several local alarm services, so I was pondering the wisdom of trying some of the windows and doors, to see if I could sneak inside, when I heard the garage door opening.

Damn! Nadine was returning at the worst possible moment. I ran back to the ladder, scrambled down, and began dragging it behind the bushes where I'd found it.

I succeeded in hiding the ladder but not in fleeing

the scene of the crime. I spotted a huge boulder near the side of the house, so I ducked behind that. While scrambling behind the boulder, I whacked my knee into it, and was surprised to realize it didn't hurt much. And that the impact had jarred the boulder out of place. I looked closer and realized that the boulder was actually made of plastic, put in place to cover up the water meter. I settled it back in place just as Nadine strode out onto the terrace.

I flinched, but she wasn't looking for me. She had a highball glass in her hand, filled with ice and something liquid.

I suddenly realized how hot and thirsty I was. And my throat was dry and dusty.

Nadine sat on the stone wall that separated the terrace from the lawn and shook her ice.

I could feel a cough trying to burst free. I took deep breaths.

Nadine lifted her glass—there were little drops of condensation running down the side—and took a long swallow.

The urge to cough was growing. Was there any way I could sneak out of the shrubbery without her noticing?

She pulled out a cell phone, punched a few numbers into it, and then held it to her ear, with an irritable scowl on her face.

"Hello, I'd like to put my mail on hold. . . ."

Where was Nadine going? My urge to cough vanished as I listened to her giving her zip code, then her name and address.

"Beginning tomorrow. . . . Yes. Indefinitely. . . . I don't know precisely when . . . well, then put it down for thirty days—I can change that if I'm back sooner, right?"

She scribbled something in a pocket notebook—the confirmation number, I assumed—said "thank you," and hung up.

Where was Nadine going tomorrow for an indefinite stay? Was she skipping town? It certainly looked as if she'd already packed up and moved all her stuff.

She stared out across her flawless back lawn as she took another chug from the glass. Then she punched more numbers into the cell phone.

"Hello? . . . yes, I'd like to arrange for a car to the airport tonight. Six p.m. . . . Just one."

She rattled off her address and her home and cell phones. I took notes on the phone numbers—you never know.

She hung up again, and dialed another number.

"Hello, is Duke in? . . . Do you know when he'll be back?"

Evidently the answer was not to her liking. Her tone became so frosty it made the ice cubes rattling in her glass sound warm.

"Tell him to call Nadine Hanrahan ASAP. I want an update on the job he's doing for me."

She pressed a button and snapped the cell phone closed. I got the idea she'd have found a land line, where you could slam down the receiver, much more satisfactory at that moment.

After another sip, she pressed a couple of buttons.

One of her speed dial numbers, apparently. She waited with the cell phone to her ear, tapping her foot in triple time, and finally spoke.

"Sandra? I was expecting to find you, at least, in the office today. Call me as soon as you get this."

She stared at the phone for a few moments as if peeved with it. Then she pulled out her notebook again and began flipping through the pages, occasionally crossing something out or scribbling something in. It looked for all the world like me spending some quality time with my notebook-that-tells-me-when-to-breathe. I wasn't sure I liked finding any resemblance between me and Nadine.

The resemblance was there, though. Like me, she seemed to find communing with her notebook soothing. That or the icy beverage she kept sipping. At first, her forehead was creased with a frown and she tapped her pen impatiently against the pages. But as time wore on, she stopped tapping and the frown began smoothing out, to be replaced by a faint smile.

Problem was, time was wearing on down at the playground, too. And given the innate contrariness of toddlers, if I tried to hurry Timmy away from the playground, odds were he'd cry and clutch one of the support poles with a death grip, begging to stay, but since I was hoping he would stay happily amused until I got back, odds were he was getting bored with it. How much longer was Nadine going to commune with her to-do list?

She finally drained the glass and went inside. I waited a few minutes before extricating myself from the bushes and creeping along the side of the house to the front, and then walking down the driveway. Act as if you belong, I reminded myself. Pretend you're someone who lives here.

What I really wanted to do was pretend I was someone who jogged here, but I wasn't dressed for it, so I forced myself to stay down to a walking pace. As soon as I was out of her yard and across the street, I pulled out my cell phone and dialed Chief Burke.

Twenty-Eight

"What can I do for you?" he asked. He sounded tired. Was he really tired, or just trying to discourage me from bothering him?

"I was just over at Nadine Hanrahan's," I said. "Did you know she's leaving town?"

"No," he said. Rather guardedly. "Should I be concerned about that?"

"Did you also know that her two-million-dollar mansion, which she certainly did not purchase on her college salary, is completely empty? No furniture, no pictures, not even any boxes?"

A pause.

"That's interesting," he said. "And you know this because . . . ?"

"I peeked in all her windows while waiting for her to come home."

"And then when she came home, she told you she was leaving."

"No, I decided I didn't want to talk with her after all, so I hid, and I overheard her arranging to stop her mail indefinitely and have a car pick her up at six p.m. tonight to take her to the airport."

Silence on the other end, and then a sigh.

"Thank you," he said. "I think. Why don't you try to stay out of trouble for the rest of the day, and let us take care of Ms. Hanrahan?"

"Roger," I said. He hung up.

I wondered if I should have mentioned the last phone call. To someone named Duke. There was nothing innately wrong with the name Duke, was there? So why did I keep picturing a hulking thug Nadine had hired to do something sinister and unspeakable?

My overactive imagination plus my dislike of Nadine, I decided. So even though the call raised my hackles, probably just as well I hadn't mentioned it. No sense letting Chief Burke think I was totally irrational and paranoid.

I hurried back to the playground, and was relieved to see that Timmy was still happily climbing up the ladder into the tallest cabin and then sliding down one of the slides.

Rose Noire looked a little the worse for wear, though. She was sitting on a platform near the top of the log cabin structure with her feet over the side and her head and arms leaning over the railing. I'd have thought she was unconscious, except that her head moved slightly to follow Timmy as he ran across her field of vision.

"Auntie Meg!" Timmy shouted, when he saw me. He swooped down the slide and ran toward me, arms outstretched. When he reached me, he grabbed onto my legs, with both hands, almost knocking me down.

"Come watch me slide, Auntie Meg!" he pleaded.

"There you are," Rose Noire said. "We were just going to look for you."

We stayed at the playground for a little while, letting Timmy wear himself out on all the slides and swings and climbs. I let Rose Noire do the running around at ground level while I perched at the top of one of the playground structures, in a sort of lookout post, shouting encouragement to Timmy as needed and flipping through the classified sections of the bird and pet magazines I'd picked up at the bookstore on our way.

The pet magazines had virtually nothing about birds at all, though they had some interesting articles on dog care and training. I put them aside for Rob, who seemed to be taking an increasing interest in Spike's welfare. Two of the three bird magazines appeared to deal exclusively with bird watching, so I put them aside for Dad. But *Bird Talk*, with a brightly colored close-up of a parrot on the cover, looked like the ticket. They had eighteen or twenty pages of ads from places selling birds—mostly parrots, macaws, and other exotics, but a few places offered canaries, parakeets, and cockatiels.

The Belle Glade Bird Farm wasn't among them, though. No other aviaries anywhere near Caerphilly, so they weren't advertising under an alternate name. And they weren't listed among the several hundred vendors providing specialized bird merchandise, from cages and perches to food and toys. There were even people selling bird car seats and little bird harnesses, similar to what I was still considering buying for Timmy.

I couldn't find Belle Glade in the classified section of the *Clarion*, either. They weren't even in the *Caerphilly Shopper*, the free weekly advertising rag. In fact—

I hopped out of my perch, dashed back to the car and rummaged under the seat, where I kept a spare copy of the local phone book. Aubrey Hamilton was listed, but Belle Glade Bird Farm didn't appear in the white or yellow pages.

So Belle Glade wasn't an established bird breeder. In fact, it looked as if someone—Aubrey Hamilton or her reclusive nephew—was just breeding a few birds in the barn.

I'd also seen an article in *Bird Talk* about all the ghastly things that could be wrong with your birds if you bought them from anyone but a responsible breeder. Could Belle Glade be one of those irresponsible, fly-by-night breeders the article condemned so roundly?

Perhaps I'd mention the bird farm to Dad and Dr. Blake. No doubt they'd go dashing off to check the place out, and I could stop worrying about it.

"Auntie Meg! Take me, too!"

Timmy came running up and launched himself at my leg. Rose Noire came puffing along behind.

"He got very upset when he saw you go up to the car," she said. "He seemed to think you were leaving him behind."

"No, I'm not leaving him anywhere," I said, putting my arm around Timmy. "Who wants some ice cream?"

"Ice cream! Ice cream!" Timmy scrambled into his car seat and sat completely still waiting for me to buckle him in. I found myself wishing I'd resorted to bribery much earlier.

After ice cream, we went home, and Rose Noire retired to one of the guest rooms to lie down with a lavender-scented compress over her eyes while Timmy and I played, had lunch, napped, and played some more. I didn't get much done, but then I couldn't think of much else that needed doing.

Well, with one exception. I wanted to find someone to babysit Timmy this evening. I had several expeditions I wanted to make. Probably a lost cause, finding someone in time to follow Nadine to see what I could learn about her travel plans, but perhaps a return visit to her house after six might be fruitful. Or some snooping around the Belle Glade Bird Farm. Maybe even a little stroll around the college campus, to see if I could find an excuse to go back to Karen's office. The financial administration building wasn't that far from the drama department—if I ran into anyone, I could always pretend I was on my way to see Michael. But all of these were expeditions I'd rather make under the cover of darkness, and without a toddler underfoot. And baby sitters were proving strangely hard to find.

Michael was out, of course, because he was tagging along with Dad and Dr. Blake, who were similarly unavailable. Rose Noire managed to sound genuinely sorry when she informed me that she was driving Mother somewhere. When Rob finally showed up, he turned me down with a convoluted and implausible excuse. I felt more sure than ever that he'd once again found true love with someone he suspected would not pass muster with the family. And none of the other relatives were answering my phone calls.

But late in the afternoon, when I was beginning to think I'd have to give up my plans, I got a call from Sandie.

"What's new?" she asked.

"Not much," I said. "Timmy has several new boo-boos, and the sheep are getting very tired of playing horsie-horsie."

"Oh," she said. "I thought you were, like, investigating. Trying to find Karen and all."

"There's a limit to how much investigating you can do with a toddler underfoot," I said. "And for some reason, everyone I ask to baby-sit Timmy seems to have other plans this evening."

"Oh, dear," she said. "If you really, really need someone, I suppose I could help out. Of course, I don't have that much experience with kids."

"Neither do I," I said. "And if you're serious . . ."

"Sure," she said. "Just let me know when you need me. After all, if you can do anything to help wrap this up and get bloody Nadine off my back, it's worth it."

We agreed that she would come over around eight and I returned to playing tag with Timmy with a lighter heart.

Dad tried to join in the game, but while trying to hide, he found several vigorous new poison ivy shoots behind the barn and took it very personally.

"It's my fault," he kept saying the whole time we were putting on our plastic gloves, pulling the vine out by the roots, and shoving it safely into a trash bag. "It's all my fault."

"Why, did you plant it?" I asked. "Some notion of Dr. Blake's perhaps? Does one of the animals from the zoo need freshly picked poison ivy to thrive?"

"No, of course not. I just haven't done a poison ivy hunt in weeks."

"Probably because Dr. Blake has been keeping you too busy with his projects."

Dad looked pained.

"Yes," he said. "But they're such worthwhile projects. And I think it's important to spend time with him. You understand that, don't you?"

Yes, I understood—Dr. Blake was over ninety, and since he and Dad had only found each other a few months ago, they had a lot of catching up to do.

But I could also see that Dad felt incredibly guilty about falling down in his self-appointed mission to keep his family safe from poison ivy. As a young man, while on a bird-watching trip to the Dismal Swamp, Dad had volunteered to climb into the water and untangle some vines that were keeping the boat from moving. The water had been up to his neck and the vines turned out to be poison ivy, resulting in the worst case of poison ivy anyone in the county had ever seen. The experience had made Dad passionate about exterminating any poison ivy that dared to grow near his family or friends. Discovering that the enemy had infiltrated our yard while his back was turned definitely depressed him.

"You've been spending a lot of time helping Dr. Blake with his projects," I said. "Maybe it's time to let him learn about some of your interests. He'd probably enjoy it."

"You think so?"

"Definitely," I said. Actually, I cared a lot less about whether Dr. Blake would enjoy poison ivy wrangling than whether Dad would. As I watched a smile growing on Dad's face, I realized that one reason I'd rather resented Dr. Blake was that he seemed to be monopolizing all of Dad's time for his own projects. Dad's garden, his poison ivy extermination efforts, and many of his pet projects had languished all summer—it felt as if Dad himself had been partially eclipsed.

To Dr. Blake's credit, when he showed up a little while later he joined in the poison ivy hunt with reasonably good humor, and Dad and I spent a happy afternoon teaching him and Timmy how to recognize and safely remove the ubiquitous three-leaved menace. He even seemed entertained by Dad's vast store of poison ivy lore and trivia. Maybe I was being too hard on him.

When Michael got home, he took over Timmy-wrangling while I fixed dinner. Then he slipped off with Dad and Dr. Blake on their still-secret mission while I put Timmy to bed. I was in luck—I'd managed to wear him out enough during the day that he barely made it through two Dr. Seuss books.

Or maybe my newfound resolution to be gentle but firm with him was paying off.

I was already in my skulking clothes—jeans and a dark t-shirt—when Sandie arrived.

"So where's the little cherub?" she said.

"You're in luck," I said. "He's already safely in bed. And if your luck continues, he'll sleep through, and all you'll have to do is entertain yourself while he sleeps. Still—just in case."

I introduced her to the mysteries of Timmy's now well-organized instruction manual. Showed her the stash of juice, milk, and fruit all ready if Timmy woke up and wanted something to eat or drink. Demonstrated how to secure the car seat, and then brought it in so it would be handy in case of emergencies. Made sure all the emergency numbers were right by the phone.

I was beginning to understand why Karen had lost touch with me after Timmy's birth—why some new parents ceased to have a social life at all.

About the time I was finishing up my demonstration, I heard a knock on the door. I opened it to see Mother and Rose Noire standing on the front porch.

"What's up?" I asked.

"Meg," Mother said. "You're not dressed."

I looked down at my jeans and t-shirt.

"Actually, I think I am," I said. "Unless you're trying to tell me I'm having an 'emperor's new clothes' moment."

"You're not dressed for the garden party," Mother said.

"That's because I'm not going to a garden party."

"It's the garden club summer outing," Mother said. "I know I told you."

"If you did, I didn't remember it," I said. "Sorry. No can do. Unless it's okay to bring Timmy."

"Perhaps next time," Mother said. "Unless perhaps your friend . . ."

She looked at Sandie, who glanced over at me.

"This is Sandie, a friend of Karen's," I said. "And I'm sure if she could, she'd love to take care of Timmy while I go with you to the garden party. But she has to leave pretty soon."

Sandie looked puzzled, and then caught on.

"Yes, darn it all," Sandie said. "Maybe some other time."

Mother sighed as if deeply disappointed in both of us and floated out.

"Isn't it a little late in the day for garden parties?" I asked Rose Noire.

"They're illuminating Mrs. Wexford's garden with hundreds and hundreds of those little fairy lights," Rose Noire said. "It's going to be so magical—are you sure you can't come?"

"Duty calls," I said. Rose Noire sighed, and followed Mother.

"Was I supposed to say that?" Sandie asked, after I shut the door. "I mean, I thought you did need a baby sitter."

"Yes, but not to go to a garden party," I said. "I'm going to snoop and see if I can find anything incriminating about Nadine."

"Good," Sandie said. "I suppose it's wicked of me, but I do hope you find something. In fact—wait a sec."

She rummaged in her purse and came out with a college key card.

"You can get into the building and our department with this. You're on your own when it comes to getting into Nadine's office, but at least I can get you that far."

"That's great," I said. "Thanks!"

"Now you just go on," she said. "And don't worry about me. I brought my book. I'll just sit here and keep an ear open for Timmy."

She sat down in the living room. I peered out the front windows, to make sure Mother and Rose Noire weren't still out there. No, I saw Rose Noire's car chugging off.

I also noticed that Seth Early was already on guard,

lurking behind the hedge at a low spot in the road. Still watching for the swarthy man? Another mystery I was still no closer to solving—who was the swarthy man, and was he watching our house, and if so, why? And could I figure out something to call him other than the swarthy man, which sounded more melodramatic every time I thought it?

Of course, I could see why Mr. Early hadn't had much luck accosting the so-called swarthy man. Unfortunately, it still hadn't occurred to him that while his hiding place was concealed from our side of the street, anyone coming out from town could clearly spot him from the ridge. If anyone had been watching our house, he had probably already seen Mr. Early and chosen his hiding place accordingly. I wasn't going to make the same mistake.

"I'll see you later," I told Sandie. "I'm going to check something in the yard and then I'll take off."

"I'll be here," she said, holding up the thick paperback she was reading.

Twenty-Nine

I went out the kitchen door and set out across the back-yard then down the hill as if planning to walk across the fields to Mother and Dad's farm. I ambled along as if on a pleasure outing—Meg enjoying the scenery, and maybe relishing a break from childcare. Not that I expected anyone to be watching, but you never knew.

Once I reached the woods, I picked up the pace and circled around, heading for a place where the woods came right up to the road. I figured that would be the perfect place to cross the road. I could skulk through the woods on Mr. Early's side of the road, climb up the back of one of the hills that overlooked our house, and keep an eye on him and our house at the same time.

But as I approached the road, I realized that some-one had anticipated me. A dark blue Honda Accord was parked by the side of the road, just out of sight of our house.

I watched it for a while, until I was sure it was empty. Then I carefully approached it and peered in the windows. Neat and clean inside, and almost empty, except for a couple of books on the front seat. Books very familiar to the daughter of an avid bird-watcher: *The*

Sibley Field Guide to Birds of Eastern North America and *Hawks and Owls of Eastern North America.*

So did this mean that the owner of the empty car was an innocent bird-watcher, out prowling the countryside in search of owls and other nocturnal birds to add to his life list? Or was that only the impression the bird books were supposed to make on a suspicious passerby? When Dad went bird-watching, he usually took his guides with him, along with a small pocket flashlight so he could consult them in case he ran into an uncommon species. Perhaps leaving your guides in the car was an act of bravado—the bird-watching equivalent of doing crossword puzzles in pen. Then again, I didn't see any of the other detritus that usually accompanied Dad's birdwatching forays—the water bottles, the snacks, the compass, the Tecnu in case he had to wade through poison ivy, the tripod and telescope, the dry clothes in case he fell in a swamp. Perhaps Dad went overboard on the paraphernalia, but still, the more I stared at those two books, placed with such artful carelessness in the front seat of the Honda, the more suspicious I found them.

Of course, since I'd been looking for a missing friend for several days, had discovered a dead body along the way, and was suffering from a slight case of sleep deprivation, maybe I was more paranoid than usual.

Not a puzzle I could solve by continuing to inspect the car. I wrote down the license plate number, then I crept along the edge of the woods for a way, until I came to a nice, climbable tree that gave me a good view of the Honda, the road in front of our house, and

Seth Early. I found a comfortable perch and settled back to watch all three.

I realized that I could have kept tabs on Mr. Early even without seeing him, since the sheep flock tended to hover near him, and there was a constant trickle of sheep coming to him to be petted and then returning to the main flock to resume grazing. Must have made the wait more amusing. From a distance, though, the sheep were less amusing. Did they really have some kind of sleep-inducing qualities? Or could I blame Timmy for the fact that I kept almost nodding off and then jerking awake just as I was about to slide off my perch. I positioned myself so the stump of a dead branch would poke me in the chest if I started nodding off and resolutely avoided looking at the sheep.

After fifteen minutes, I began to think better of my surveillance. After half an hour, I had decided it was a waste of time. But it was too early for the next item on my agenda, and when I thought of climbing down and going home, I reminded myself that at least it was quiet and peaceful up in my tree. Odds were I'd have an even harder time finding a babysitter the next time I wanted a Timmy-free evening. And the later the better for most of the other places I planned to prowl.

I settled back and concentrated on enjoying the unaccustomed solitude. I did my yoga breathing exercises— the ones that were supposed to bring clarity and energy, not the relaxing and falling asleep ones. Clarity and energy were proving elusive.

Then I spotted something at the house that woke me up a little. Rob, coming out the front door.

Rob, who refused to baby-sit because he was going

to be out all evening? Rob, who I thought had already left for his rendezvous with Ms. Wrong?

Well, maybe he was going out after all. He was dressed in jeans and a t-shirt, but he had a garment bag thrown over his shoulder. He was carrying something in his other hand, but I couldn't quite see what.

He set the something down to stuff the garment bag into the Porsche's almost nonexistent trunk, and I recognized the other piece of luggage—Spike's carrier. Just then the carrier rocked back and forth slightly, which meant Spike was in there, hurling himself from side to side as he usually did to protest his imprisonment.

Rob squatted down beside the carrier, and leaned toward the screen in the door, as if speaking to Spike. Then he laughed and patted the top of the carrier— safer, most of the time, than patting Spike directly. He buckled the carrier into the passenger seat, got into the car, and drove off.

Where on earth was Rob taking Spike at this time of night?

While I was still pondering that dilemma, I heard a car engine off to my right. The Honda had started up. I couldn't see its driver, but I watched in astonishment as it gently glided down the road, following Rob.

I might have assumed it was a coincidence if the Honda hadn't been driving with its headlights off.

As soon as the Honda passed him, Seth Early leaped into action, running across the fields. I hadn't seen that he had his truck stashed nearby, but I saw it join the spread-out caravan.

Aha! Apparently my fake bird-watcher in the Honda was also Seth Early's swarthy man.

What the hell. I climbed down the tree again, ran back to the house the shortest way possible—along the now deserted road—and jumped into my car. Rob hadn't been going that fast, so if they were following him, I should be able to catch up with them before they got too far.

After a couple of miles, I spotted Seth Early's truck and slowed down to keep a safe distance behind it. When we came to a long, gentle curve, I got a chance to check out the others. Rob in the lead, cruising along a mere five miles above the speed limit. The Honda, its lights now on, following about ten car lengths behind him. Seth Early, about ten car lengths behind him. Since ten car lengths seemed to be the generally approved standard distance for tailing people, I made sure I was in sync with the rest of the caravan and tried to think ahead to any places where they could do something clever and lose me.

I don't know why I bothered. Rob and Seth Early were clearly oblivious to the possibility that someone might be following them, and even if the Honda's driver realized he was part of a parade, he probably couldn't do anything about it.

Near town, Rob signaled way in advance before turning left onto the Clay Hill Road, and then again before his right turn onto Whitetail Lane. Did Rob's errand have anything to do with Jasper Walker?

Seth Early and the Honda fell back a little on the small country lane, and I followed suit. I breathed a slight sigh of relief when we cruised past the Belle Glade Bird Farm sign without turning in. Still odd that Rob happened to be going out in this direction, but at least it wasn't likely to be anything connected with Jasper's murder and Karen's disappearance.

Then a few miles farther, we hit another long curve through open fields, and I realized that Seth Early must have fallen too far back. He was now lead car in a truncated caravan.

He cruised on, apparently oblivious. Or maybe he was speeding up slightly, assuming the others had merely gotten a little too far ahead of him and trying to catch up.

I turned around in the next driveway and hightailed it back to Hiram Bass's house and the bird farm.

I parked my car on one of the vestigial side lanes, near the ruins of a cement truck, and made my way on foot.

The Bass place was deserted. No sign of Rob's car or the Honda. I took the lane toward the bird farm. I was halfway there when I heard some faint ticking noises in the shrubbery. I wasn't sure what caused them, but my car made those same sounds when it had recently stopped and the engine was cooling.

I followed the noises, trying very hard to avoid touching any vegetation, since it was too dark to tell harmless vines from the ubiquitous poison ivy. Sure enough, I found the blue Honda parked at the side of the road, the bird books still lying on the front seat.

I stood listening for several minutes, trying to discover where its occupant had gone.

Then I heard voices farther along. Up at Aubrey Hamilton's house. I left the Honda and walked cautiously along the road, expecting the fake bird-watcher to leap out of the bushes at any second.

At the end of the lane, I saw that both the house and barn were illuminated. Rob's car was parked at the side of the lane, near the barn. The voices seemed to be coming from the barn, so I headed that way.

As I drew closer, I heard Rob's voice.

Thirty

"Okay, I'm not sure it's ready for prime time," he was saying.

"Well, I told you this was harder than it looks," a woman's voice said. "And frankly, you couldn't have picked a less promising subject."

I felt incredibly exposed as I walked across the barn-yard, and sighed with relief when I reached the shadows beside the barn.

"It hasn't been easy," Rob said. "But I like a challenge."

"You could have fooled me," I muttered. Maybe this wasn't my slacker brother, but his long-lost industrious identical twin. I crept to one of the barn windows and peeked in.

Rob was wearing jeans, a black t-shirt, and a leather jacket. He had somehow managed to tie a red bandanna around Spike's neck. Not the first time he'd done it either, to judge by the relatively calm way Spike reacted—he only turned around from time to time and growled over his shoulder at the offending fabric.

Rob took up a position beside Spike. Spike looked up at him and curled his lip. Somehow, with the bandanna, it almost looked cute. Probably did look cute if you didn't know Spike.

"Okay," Rob said. "Hit it."

Music blasted out—evidently the woman had turned on a tape or CD player. I recognized the crashing opening chords of George Thorogood and the Destroyers' "Bad to the Bone."

Rob immediately assumed a pose of utterly theatrical menace, narrowing his eyes, slouching with his left hand hooked into his belt loops while he snapped the fingers of the right occasionally to punctuate the opening bars. Then, he extended one finger dramatically down, pointing straight at Spike.

Spike leaped up toward the finger, jaws snapping shut with less than an inch to spare. Rob and Spike then proceeded to execute nearly five minutes of the most demented dance routine I'd ever seen. At least Rob was dancing—a skill I'd never seen him display before. Dancing and acting; if I hadn't seen the transformation, I'd have had a hard time recognizing my brother Rob as the cool leather-clad troublemaker strutting around the barn floor. Spike wasn't acting or dancing, though—he was out for the kill, leaping up and snapping whenever Rob extended a finger down toward him. And by keeping one finger or the other just out of reach the whole time, Rob deftly managed to lead Spike through some fairly intricate choreography. Spike wound around and through Rob's legs, eyes always fixed on that elusive, teasing finger, occasionally twirling in a circle or leaping over an extended ankle.

I was amazed at how well Rob took Spike's monomaniacal urge to bite and channeled it into a really cute routine. Cute even to me, and I knew all too well how close Rob was to losing those fingers Spike found so irresistible. As the music built to its final crescendo of guitars and drums, Rob even went down briefly on one knee, leading me to cover my eyes and hope he was smart enough to be wearing a hockey protector.

"Bravo!" came a voice. A spry-looking older woman with a mop of unruly salt-and-pepper curls came into view, applauding vigorously. "You've worked wonders with him! You're definitely ready for the contest."

Rob grinned, and Spike stood graciously accepting her praise, as if he'd done something really clever instead of spending the last five minutes attempting mayhem.

I actually had to remind myself that I was spying and probably shouldn't join in the ovation. Their performance was a tour de force. Rob must have been working on it all summer. No wonder Jack Ransom and the guys at the office had been so undisturbed.

But why all the secrecy? And why was the fake bird-watcher tailing Rob? And speaking of the fake bird-watcher—where was he?

I stepped away from the window and circled around a bit. Toward the back of the barn I heard smothered laughter.

The fake bird-watcher was standing outside another of the windows, with one hand over his mouth and the other clutched to his stomach, shaking with suppressed laughter.

"Bit off the beaten path for bird-watching," I said.

He stopped laughing, and I suddenly found myself staring down the barrel of a gun.

"Don't make a sound," he said, suddenly serious. "And put your hands in the air. What are you doing here?"

I put my hands in the air. Inside the barn, the opening bars of Bruce Springsteen's "Dancing in the Dark" began playing.

"I asked, what you were doing here," he repeated.

"You also said don't make a sound," I said. "I was trying to figure out if you expected me to mime my answer. I'll need to put my hands down to do that."

He didn't look amused. Over his shoulder, in the barn, I could see that the gray-haired woman was doing a spirited dance routine with two enormous gray poodles.

"I followed you to see why you were following my brother," I said. "What are you, a rival canine choreographer?"

"Hmph." He glanced over his shoulder at the canine acrobatics inside, shook his head slightly, and focused back on me. "You'll have to come with me."

"I don't think so," a voice said from behind me. "Drop the gun."

I turned slightly to find Freddy Hamilton holding a gun of his own.

"I said drop it," Freddy repeated. "And put your hands in the air."

The fake bird-watcher dropped the gun and raised his hands. I wasn't sure whether I'd been rescued or had only gone from frying pan to fire. I kept my hands up, just in case.

"Now move, both of you," Freddy said. "Inside the barn."

We marched inside, holding our hands up. Rob and
the woman turned in surprise when we entered. The
poodles stopped dancing and raced over to lick our
faces—well, my face and the other prisoner's. They
didn't seem all that keen on licking Freddy's face. From
the portable CD player in the corner, Bruce Springsteen sang on unheeded.

In one corner of the barn, I saw a giant bird cage,
about six feet square and eight feet tall, with several
dozen brightly colored canaries and cockatiels roosting
in it. Or trying to roost—about half the birds had their
heads under their wings while the rest were fluffing
their feathers and looking around rather irritably, as if
loud rock and roll wasn't their idea of a bedtime sere-
nade. And one wall of the barn was lined to a height of
six feet with rough shelves containing several dozen
smaller cages, with or without brightly colored birds in
them.

"Over there," Freddy said, pointing with his gun to
where Rob and the woman were standing.

"Freddy, what are you doing?" the woman asked.

"My business," Freddy said.

"You're doing it in my barn," she said.

"I'm sorry," Freddy said. "But why'd you have to
come back so early? You usually stay up in Maine till
Labor Day. Everything would have been straightened
out by Labor Day. Will you shut that damned thing
off?"

Evidently Freddy wasn't a fan of the Boss. The CD
had segued from "Dancing in the Dark" to "My Hometown." The woman—whom I deduced must be Aubrey
Hamilton—walked over and cut the power.

"Great," Freddy said. "Now put the dogs in one of the stalls. I don't want them drooling all over me."

"Poodles don't drool," Aubrey said. But she opened the door of one of the stalls and called to the poodles, who obediently followed.

"Him, too," Freddy added, gesturing at Spike, who was fixing him with a stern look and growling slightly.

"What's going on?" Rob asked, as he dragged Spike into the stall with the poodles.

"Shut up," Freddy said. He tossed a roll of duct tape at Aubrey. "Here, take this and tape their hands together."

"Freddy!" she exclaimed. "I can't believe you're doing this!"

"Start with him," Freddy said, pointing to the fake bird-watcher.

"This isn't helping your case," the man began.

"Shut up," Freddy said, waving the gun a little wildly. "That means all of you."

Aubrey sighed, but she didn't try to talk him out of tying us up, which probably said a lot about Freddy's character. That, and the fact that even though he let her use a utility knife to cut the duct tape, she made no attempt to escape—she just obediently taped the fake bird-watcher's wrists together, then mine, and finally Rob's. Freddy then ordered her to secure us to the vertical posts that supported the hay loft—perhaps he'd caught me measuring the distance between us. And when she'd trussed the three of us up to Freddy's satisfaction, he secured her to a fourth post. Took him long enough, since he was still holding the gun in his right hand and had to do all the taping with his left.

When he'd finished tying up Aubrey, he came around and checked the rest of us. He must have been satisfied with Aubrey's handiwork—he looked a little more relaxed and stuck his gun in his belt.

Not having the gun pointed at anyone made me feel a little bolder.

"So, did you kill Jasper Walker?" I asked.

"Hell, no," Freddy said. "Him and me were friends."

"He and I were friends, Freddy," Aubrey said.

"You were not," Freddy said. "You never could stand Jasper. But he was working with me in the bird business. He was the one who figured out where to get the cash so we could expand our operations—why would I kill him?"

"Thieves fall out," I said. "Where did he get the cash?"

"The jerk never told me," Freddy said. "And he never showed up with the rest of the cash he promised. He's left me in the lurch, owing a hell of a lot of money to some really impatient guys."

He shook his head as if disappointed with Jasper's inconsiderateness.

"So you weren't involved with the embezzlement?" I asked.

"The what?" Freddy said. He looked genuinely puzzled. As if he not only hadn't been involved in embezzlement but didn't even know what the word meant.

"Jasper was using the computer system he designed to steal money from the college," I said. And apparently investing the proceeds in illegal finches.

"Don't look at me," Freddy said. "Computers are Jasper's thing, not mine. And I had nothing to do with his death." His voice sounded a little shrill, and I winced when he pulled the gun out of his belt again. "Look at that crazy wife of his. I was coming home a couple of nights ago, and she came tearing out of Jasper's driveway like a bat out of hell. Almost sideswiped my truck. I just figured they'd had a fight until I heard he was dead. Then I realized she must have been running away after killing him."

After killing him, or perhaps after finding his body?

"Did you tell the police about seeing Karen?" I asked aloud.

"No," he said. "I figured, why cause her any trouble?"

"More like you didn't want to talk to the police," the fake bird-watcher said.

"Whatever," Freddy said, with a shrug. He stuck the gun back in his belt. "You can tell them for me. I'm getting out of here."

He picked up a small bird cage, strolled over to the aviary, and opened the door. He reached in, grabbed a bird, and put it in the cage. Then he peered around as if looking for a particular bird.

"What the hell?" he muttered.

He closed the door to the aviary and scanned the cages lining the far wall. He went over to pull the covers off the few that had them. Then he whirled and strode back to Aubrey.

"What the hell have you done with my birds?" he shouted, waving his gun at her.

Thirty-One

Was Freddy crazy? Two walls of the barn were lined with cages full of birds—some sleeping and others twittering softly. It looked like plenty of birds to me, but I try not to argue with people carrying guns.

Apparently Aubrey agreed with me.

"Done with your birds?" she repeated. "The place is full of those messy canaries and cockatiels of yours."

She pointed with her chin to the aviary and the cage-lined walls.

"Not those," he said. "The finches."

He held up the cage with the single bird he'd grabbed from the aviary. A rather dramatically colored bird, with an orange head, green body, purple and yellow breast, and stripes of blue and black around the face.

I'd seen birds like that before—in the cage that had mysteriously appeared on the third floor of our house.

"A Gouldian finch," the fake bird-watcher said, causing me to wonder if I'd been wrong in thinking of him as a fake. He wasn't particularly swarthy, either. "They're endangered in Australia. And illegal to import. Of course, I'm sure you bred those, right?"

"Yeah," Freddy said. "You didn't let them go, did you," he asked, turning back to Aubrey.

"I just got here last night," she said.

"And the day after you get here, my finches disappear. They were here yesterday."

"I had nothing to do with it," she said. "I didn't even know you had finches here."

"Maybe Dad and Grandpa took them," Rob put in.

Freddy's eyes narrowed.

"Why would they do that?" he asked.

"Just give up," the bird-watcher said. "We're not after you—we're after the big guys."

"We?" I asked. "Who is we?" The man glanced at me and ignored my question.

"If you give us information on them—" he went on.

"Look, dude," Freddy began.

"Arroyo," the man said. "Carlos Arroyo, with the—"

"Whatever," Freddy said. "Do I look that stupid? Like turning stool pigeon on them is going to be good for my health. No thanks."

"No one's going to hurt you over a bunch of birds," Aubrey said.

"Yes, except it isn't just about birds, is it?" I said. "Because the same guys who smuggle in birds are also smuggling drugs, right?"

Freddy and Arroyo both looked at me with surprise.

"Montgomery Blake is my grandfather," I said, with as much of a shrug as I could manage in my trussed-up condition. "He's always going on about the connection between wildlife smuggling and drug smuggling and for that matter, arms smuggling. So what are the odds that birds are the only thing Freddy's smuggling? He's probably dealing a little cocaine, too, or is it heroin?"

"Oh, Freddy," Aubrey said. "How could you?"

"You can't get away with it, you know," Arroyo said. "They'll be watching for your car. Just give up."

Freddy stared at him for a moment, then went over and began rummaging in Arroyo's pockets.

"What are you doing?" Arroyo said.

Freddy emerged with a set of car keys.

"But they won't be watching for your car, will they?" he said. "By the time you get loose, I can be long gone."

He turned on his heel and headed for the door. As he walked, he pulled out his cell phone and punched a couple of keys.

"Trey?" he said. "Change of plans. I've just got a few things up at the house to load and then—No, I've got them tied up."

Who was he talking with, I wondered. And then I remembered that Trey was one of the names on the message slips on Karen's desk.

Of course, so was Jasper. And the slips were dated Monday or Tuesday, when Jasper was already dead, which meant someone had been trying to reach Karen and pretending to be Jasper. Why?

"Dude," Freddy was saying on the phone, "that's way over the top. We can just leave them tied up here, no problem. And if—"

That's all I caught before he slammed the door behind him.

We all looked at each other.

"What's he up to?" Aubrey asked.

From outside, I heard the sound of a car door slamming.

"This is what Dad and Dr. Blake have been investigating lately, isn't it?" I asked, looking at Rob.

"Probably," he said. "I haven't been involved in it for months."

"But you were involved?"

"They sent me out to find out whatever I could about the Belle Glade Bird Farm," he said. "That's how I got started doing the doggie dancing. Sorry," he added, turning to Aubrey.

"And I thought you were interested in learning," she said.

"I was—I am!" Rob protested. "When they sent me, I didn't realize how cool it was going to be. They were annoyed when you went to Maine and there was no reason for me to come out here for the rest of the summer, but I was relieved. I figured by the time you came back, they'd have finished their raid, and it would be okay again, and I could keep working on the dancing without them expecting me to spy on anyone. I mean, I felt pretty guilty, spying on Aubrey's cousin."

"Why should you feel guilty about spying on a major drug and wildlife smuggler?" I asked.

"Major?" Arroyo said, with a laugh. "That's rich. Freddy isn't a major anything. Except maybe a major idiot."

"How do you know?" I asked. "And for that matter, who are you, Mr. Arroyo, and what are you doing here, anyway?"

"Carlos Arroyo," he said. "U.S. Fish and Wildlife Service. I'd show you my ID, but . . ."

"You can do that when we get loose," I said. "Are you one of the guys who interrogated Henry and Phyllis Blanke?"

"Blanke? Who are they?"

"Never mind," I said. He sounded puzzled, so maybe Fish and Wildlife wasn't the only federal or state agency snooping around Caerphilly. "So you don't think Freddy's a major player in the smuggling game."

"He's chum," Arroyo said. "We were hoping to follow him to the big sharks."

"The drug suppliers," Rob said, nodding wisely.

"Well, I'm sure the DEA would be interested in them," Arroyo said. "We'd bring them in once we had enough evidence to make our move. But we mainly want the guys who've been doing the finch laundering."

"Finch laundering," Rob repeated. He and Aubrey burst into laughter. Okay, I admit I chuckled a bit myself.

"Why am I imagining a clothesline filled with brightly colored birds fluttering in the breeze?" I asked.

"Because you're way old-fashioned," Rob said. "Me, I see a passel of them tumbling round and round in the dryer."

"Ouch!" Aubrey exclaimed. "They wouldn't like that."

"I always use the delicate cycle," Rob said.

"Very funny," Arroyo said, as if he didn't really think it was the least bit amusing. "Finch launderers are the people who provide phony provenance to prove the birds are legal—that they were bred in captivity, either in this country or in a country where it's legal to export them to the U.S. That way the smugglers have an easier time selling them. In the wild, Gouldian finches are endangered, and I'd bet anything those finches weren't bred in captivity."

"Endangered species," I said. "Yeah, that's probably what got Dr. Blake interested."

"His heart's in the right place," Arroyo said. "I just wish he'd cooperate with us a little more. Do you think he stole Hamilton's finches?"

"Seized, not stole," I said. "At least that's how Dr. Blake would see it. But yes, I'm pretty sure he did. Let's concentrate on practical matters, shall we? Like getting ourselves untied and trying to catch Freddy? Preferably before whoever Freddy was talking to has time to get over here, because it sounded to me as if he was talking someone out of doing something a lot more drastic than tying us up."

They all looked at me as if awaiting further instructions.

"That was an invitation to throw out some suggestions," I said. "Anyone have an idea?"

"I can move my hands up and down," Rob said. "I'll start working on sawing through the tape with the corner of the post I'm tied to."

His shoulders began twitching rhythmically.

"Well, this might help," Aubrey said. "Paris! Julie!"

I heard a scuffling noise as the two poodles snapped to attention, and one of them barked gruffly.

"Come here!" Aubrey coaxed. "Here, Paris! Here Julie!"

More scuffling from the stall, and a little whining.

"Come here! Treats!"

The door to the stall swung open, bringing one of the dogs with it—it looked as if he had jumped up and used his paw to open the latch. Or her paw; I couldn't exactly tell the two shaggy beasts apart. They trotted over and began licking Aubrey's face.

"Good girl! Good boy!" she said, her voice a little muffled by all the fur around her.

"Well, that's a start," I said. "Now what can they do? Gnaw the duct tape off? Maybe go fetch Chief Burke?"

"I don't know yet," Aubrey said. "Down girl! Settle down."

Just then Spike came trotting out of the stall and looked around expectantly.

"Oh, great," I said. "Spike's loose."

"Do they fetch?" Arroyo asked. "Hamilton left his duct tape and utility knife over there in the corner."

We all craned to see. Yes, the utility knife was lying in plain sight. If Hamilton hadn't taped us to the posts, any of us could have crawled over to get it.

"Go get it, Julie! Fetch, Paris!"

Aubrey began jerking her head toward the utility knife and staring at them. The dogs watched her with great interest, but they didn't seem to be grasping the notion.

Spike trotted over to the cages along the wall and began growling at the birds. The birds weren't too thrilled by this—they began fluttering and squawking.

"Am I making any progress?" Rob asked.

"A little," I said, glancing over at his hands. Of course, at the rate he was going, we wouldn't be free for weeks, but I didn't want to discourage him.

"Fetch! Fetch!" Aubrey repeated.

One of the dogs began to get the idea, and walked over a little in the direction of the utility knife.

"Good boy! Fetch!"

The other dog—Julie, presumably—rose up on her hind legs and began dancing around in a circle.

"Good girl!" Aubrey said.

"How is that helping us?" I asked.

"Well, it isn't," she said. "But I've been trying to get her to do that for weeks."

Arroyo began giggling.

"Now fetch!" Aubrey repeated.

Paris got the idea. He picked up the roll of duct tape, trotted over to Aubrey, dropped it beside her, and began licking her face.

"Good boy!"

"He got the wrong thing," Rob said.

"Yes, but he's getting the idea. Good boy! Now fetch again."

Paris dashed away a few feet, then rose up on his hind feet and began dancing beside Julie.

"Oh, brother," Arroyo groaned, through his giggles. "They're never going to believe this back in Richmond."

About that time, Spike got tired of torturing the cockatiels and looked around to see what other mischief he could get into.

"Fetch! Fetch!" Aubrey repeated.

Spike seemed to notice where all our eyes were glued. He trotted over and picked up the utility knife.

"Good boy!" Aubrey exclaimed.

"Oh, great," I muttered.

Having taken possession of the utility knife, Spike began trotting around the barn floor, as if deliberately taunting us with it. For a few minutes, we were all calling "Here, Spike! Here, boy!" but the more we called, the happier he was to prance around out of reach.

"Everyone shut up!" I said. "And don't look at him."

I turned my head so I could pretend to be looking away while keeping tabs on Spike in my peripheral vision. Almost as soon as we stopped paying attention, he stopped prancing and stood looking irritably around.

"Spike," I said softly.

He turned and looked at me.

"Here, Spike," I said.

"It won't work," Rob muttered.

"Quiet," I said. "Here, Spike."

This time I wiggled my fingers. Spike lifted his lip slightly. I wiggled the fingers again. He began slowly stalking toward me. Every time he slowed down, I wiggled my fingers tantalizingly. He finally fell for it, and ran forward to lunge at my fingers, dropping the utility knife at the last second.

"Yow!" I yelled, as he sank in his teeth. "Here, Paris! Here, Julie!"

The two poodles romped over, tails wagging, and began licking my face. As I'd hoped, Spike felt threatened by the proximity of two much larger dogs, and let go of my mangled fingers to bark furiously at them. Julie stuck her nose down to sniff Spike and had to jerk it back quickly when he lunged at her. Paris growled, and lowered his head to stare at Spike in what any sane dog would recognize as a stern warning. Julie barked at Spike, who snapped at her again.

"Oh, great, a dogfight," Rob said.

"Call them over so I'm not in the middle of it," I said. "If I can just have a minute or two of peace and quiet, I think I can cut myself loose.

"Paris! Julie!" Aubrey called. "Treat!"

"Here, Spike!" Rob called. "Fingers! Fingers!"

The dogs couldn't decide whether to come when called or fight, but at least they milled a little farther from me. After a couple of false starts, I managed to slice through the duct tape around my wrist—not without giving myself a few minor lacerations.

"Good job!" Arroyo said. "Now cut me loose."

I did as he asked, and then moved on to Aubrey and finally Rob.

"I was getting there," Rob said, as I lowered the box cutter to his tape.

"I can leave you to get on with it if you like," I said, pausing. Perhaps he didn't realize his escape efforts had only produced a barely visible dimple in the duct tape.

"No, that's okay," Rob said. "I'd better rescue Spike."

Arroyo had pulled out a cell phone and retreated to a corner to talk to someone. Aubrey and Rob waded into the fur tangle and hauled away their respective dancing partners.

I heard a car start outside.

Thirty-Two

Freddy was still here? What was taking him so long? Not that I liked the idea of his getting away, but it shook me up a bit, knowing he could have walked in at any moment during our dog-enabled escape. I ran over to flatten myself against the wall beside the barn door, ready to jump him if he came in. But after a few seconds, I heard the car begin to bump and rattle over the rutted dirt driveway. Maybe he hadn't heard the dogs, or assumed their barking came from the stall. And he had said something about loading something up at the house. After all, if Dr. Blake was right, he probably was smuggling a few things other than birds.

Whatever had delayed him, it was a break for the good guys. I glanced over to see if Arroyo had noticed. He was still on his cell phone.

"He's driving off," I said.

"Good." Arroyo didn't even look up.

"He's getting away," I said. "Aren't you going after him?"

"He has my gun," Arroyo said. "I'm calling for backup."

"We're in the middle of nowhere," I said. "Backup will take forever."

"I'm working on it," he said.

"I'm going after him," I said. I grabbed my purse and sprang for the door, fishing out my car keys and my cell phone as I ran.

"Wait!" he shouted.

"Tell your backup I'm following Freddy," I called over my shoulder. "I'll try to reach Chief Burke and tell him where we're going."

Outside, I saw taillights disappearing rapidly down the dirt lane. I scrambled into my car and pulled out. I didn't turn the headlights on—I figured that could wait until I was on the road and Freddy wouldn't know for sure it was someone following him.

I got to the end of the lane and glanced up and down, to see which way Freddy had gone. Taillights disappearing to the right—that figured. Away from town.

Just then another set of headlights appeared across the road from me. A pickup truck pulled out of a small side lane and took off after Freddy's taillights.

I couldn't be sure with the brief glimpse I got as it passed—but it looked like Seth Early. Apparently he'd eventually figured out where he'd lost his prey and backtracked to the last place he'd seen it. Our caravan was reassembled—well, minus Rob's car.

It took Mr. Early a little while to figure out that the new caravan was going at a much higher speed, but once he caught on, he fell into the same comfortable trailing distance he had before. I turned on my headlights after a couple of turns and followed suit.

After a couple of miles, I realized that another car

was following me. Was it Arroyo, perhaps, in a borrowed car? Or his backup? I hoped so. The only other people I could think of who might be motivated to keep pace with our breakneck crew would be some criminal ally of Freddy's, and that would definitely be bad news.

When we reached the Clay Hill Road, Freddy turned left—away from Caerphilly. I fished out my cell phone and managed to dial 911 without landing in a ditch.

"Hello, Meg, how are you?" Debbie Anne, the dispatcher, said.

"I've been better," I said. "I'm on the Clay Hill Road, heading toward the county line at sixty-five miles an hour, chasing an illegal bird smuggler who may also be Jasper Walker's murderer."

"Oh, my!" Debbie Anne said. "You don't mean Freddy Hamilton, do you?"

"The very same," I said. "He's not driving his own truck—he stole a car. Dark blue Honda Accord. I have the license number—oh, damn!"

"What's wrong?"

"I'm bleeding all over my notebook."

"Bleeding! What happened?"

"Just another Spike bite."

I managed to find the page where I'd written down the Honda's tag number, used the map light to read it to Debbie Anne, and then held on while she issued an all-points bulletin. We were going seventy-five now, and I was getting a little nervous about how close behind me the unknown car was following. And, for that matter, even more nervous about who was in the unknown car.

"So you already knew about Freddy?" I asked, when Debbie Anne came back on the line.

"Oh, yes," she said. "The chief and the DEA have been watching him for days. I have to tell you, the chief's a mite peeved at the way you kept showing up over there."

"He could have told me what was going on. Warned me off."

"Those DEA men wouldn't have liked that, now, would they?"

So there were DEA men in town. I made a note to tell Henry Blanke he'd been right after all.

"I mean, the chief knows you and your family wouldn't be mixed up in drugs or murder," Debbie Anne was saying. "But it's different with the Feds. I can tell you, the chief is going to be that relieved when we've finally got them out of our hair. Oh, good, the chief's heading your way, and one of our patrol cars, and they've got a couple of state troopers coming from the Clay County direction. You should hear the sirens pretty soon."

"Can't be soon enough for me," I said, as we rounded a rather sharp curve. It occurred to me that it would be wiser to hang up and drive with both hands, but if Debbie Anne was giving out information, I didn't want to miss my chance. "You don't already have a car on the scene, do you? There's someone I don't know tagging along behind me—is that one of your people?"

"I'll check," she said, putting me on hold.

Was that a siren in the distance, or was I only imagining it?

"If it's one of ours, it's not anyone who's checking in," Debbie Anne said. "You be careful now."

"Call me if there's anything I should know," I said, and cut the connection.

I definitely heard a siren now—it was still faint, but getting closer. Coming from ahead of us.

Suddenly, I heard squealing tires ahead and hit my own brakes. I stopped without too much trouble, but in front of me, Seth Early's truck skidded and landed with the truck bed on the road and the front end in the right-hand ditch. The car behind me nicked my right rear fender before coming to a halt about ten feet past me. Beyond it, I could see the blue Honda backing out of a driveway. Evidently Freddy had heard the sirens and decided to turn around.

The unknown fourth car—a beat up old sedan that looked vaguely familiar—moved again. At first I thought it was going to turn around to follow Freddy, but then instead the driver pulled it to block the left-hand lane. Seth Early's car was blocking part of the right-hand lane. I said a few words Mother probably didn't think I knew and pulled my car into the remaining gap, passenger side toward Freddy, of course, and I immediately cut the engine and leaped out, cell phone in hand.

The sedan's driver wasn't as quick, and I think Freddy accelerated as much as he could before plowing broadside into the sedan, knocking it partly out of his way. He backed up, shedding bits of his car and the sedan, and I suspected he was going to ram the sedan again.

Probably not the smartest thing to do, but I ran over to see if I could pull the sedan's driver out.

I heard a familiar sound—someone racking a shotgun.

"Stop the car or I'll shoot!" Seth Early shouted.

He strode out into the roadway with his shotgun pointed at the Honda. The shotgun that according to Chief Burke he wasn't supposed to be carrying anymore, though at the moment, I wasn't complaining.

I looked into the sedan and my jaw dropped.

"Karen!"

No wonder the sedan had looked so familiar—it was the same one Karen had driven off in. Though that seemed a century ago now.

Karen was lying across the front seat—evidently she'd unhooked her seat belt and had been moving to jump out the passenger side when Freddy rammed her car.

Her eyes fluttered open.

"He's the one who did it, isn't he?" she said. "Don't let him get away."

I heard an engine rev, and then the blast of the shotgun, followed by screeching brakes. The sedan shook as Freddy clipped the rear end before landing in the left-hand ditch with one of his tires in shreds.

"I've got another barrel," Mr. Early said. "Next one goes right into your thieving head!"

"I think Mr. Early's stopped him," I said. "Are you all right?"

I reached over to check her pulse, as Dad would have ordered. A little rapid, but not bad.

"Where's Timmy?" she asked.

"Safe at home," I said. "You don't think I'd bring him along when I was chasing murderers and driving like a maniac?"

"No," she said, closing her eyes. "I knew you'd take care of him. And when I saw you come to Uncle Hiram's house, I knew you'd find the killer."

"You saw me? Where were you?"

"I hid in the old Airstream trailer in the woods near Uncle Hiram's," she said. "When I found Jasper's body, I was afraid whoever killed him would think I knew something and come after me. Jasper's been involved with some very dangerous people. So I packed up all Timmy's stuff and left him with you, for safekeeping, and then I realized I didn't have anyplace safe to go. I just went back to Uncle Hiram's place and hid my car with all the other old wrecks, and holed up in the trailer. I figured it was the last place anyone would look for me."

"Yeah," I said. "The poison ivy alone was better than a ten-foot wall topped with razor wire." Though I suspected Chief Burke would have a few sharp words to say to his officers when he learned that they'd let poison ivy keep them from doing a thorough search. "You fed the dog, too, didn't you?"

"Scout? Yes, poor old thing," she said. "It's not his fault I'm allergic to him. Anyway, I thought maybe the killer might come back. They do that sometimes, don't they? To make sure they haven't left any clues? But the only person who kept showing up was you. They'll know Freddy's guilty, though, now that he's made a run for it, won't they? And they'll lock him up."

"You bet," I said. I didn't feel as confident as I tried

to sound—after all, Freddy hadn't yet admitted his guilt, and for all I knew, whoever he'd been calling on his cell phone might be the actual killer. And there was still the whole college embezzlement issue—how did that fit into the picture? But Freddy wasn't going anywhere, and I had every confidence that Chief Burke and the DEA would get the truth out of him. And Karen was alive, if a little battered.

"What was with those files on the thumb drive, anyway?" I asked, as I checked her pulse again.

"They were embezzling from the college," Karen said. "I saved the files in case Jasper could get in to cover it up, but then after I found his body—can you take them to the police?"

"Already did," I said. Her pulse was better, and her color and breathing were good. Not that I was a doctor, but over the years, Dad had drummed a few basics of first aid into most of the family.

"Do you hurt anywhere?" I asked.

"I think my leg's broken," she said. "Or at least sprained. I'd get out if it wasn't for that."

The police would be here soon, though they seemed to be taking forever. And once they got here, no doubt it would take forever to answer all their questions.

And that bothered me, I realized. Because even though Freddy wasn't going anywhere, he had known that Dad and Dr. Blake had taken his birds. What if he'd told that to whomever I'd heard him calling, back at the barn? I'd assured Karen that Timmy was safe, but I wasn't sure Sandie would be a very effective guardian if some truly desperate finch launderer showed up at the house looking for his birds.

I dialed 911 again.

"Debbie Anne?" I said. "We've had—"

"Hang on," she said. "The Chief wants to talk to you."

And then the chief's voice broke in.

"What the dickens is going on? Are you still chasing Freddy Hamilton?"

"No," I said. "He heard sirens ahead of him and tried to turn around, but Karen and Mr. Early and I stopped him."

"Stopped him how? Did you—Karen? Karen Walker? I thought you hadn't seen her in days?"

"I hadn't, but it turned out she was the third car I told Debbie Anne about. She was hiding in Hiram Bass's Airstream out in the poison ivy jungle. She was injured when Freddy rammed her car—can you send an ambulance?"

"Make that two," Seth Early said, from out in the road. "I think Freddy banged his head, too—he's not looking too lively."

I could hear the chief barking out orders on the other end of the phone.

"Look, chief," I said. "I need to get home. Timmy—"

"You stay there till I get there!" he snapped, and hung up.

"But what if—"

I stopped myself. I'd just assured Karen that Timmy was safe. I didn't want to upset her.

Seth Early circled around so he could look in on Karen while still keeping his shotgun pointed at Freddy.

"I can handle things here," he said. "If you want to take off and check back home."

"The cops are coming from both directions," I said. "They won't let me pass."

"There's a dirt road about a quarter mile back," he said, nodding his head toward Caerphilly. "An old logging road from Civil War days. It's not on the maps. I doubt if most of the cops even know it exists. You take that till it dead-ends at Route 313, then turn right. Should get you home in no time."

"Thanks," I said. "Karen, Mr. Early is going to look after you."

"That's right," he said. Then he paused for a moment, and added. "And that's Seth. Now go along before those state troopers get here."

I would have liked to take the time to savor this sudden small gesture of acceptance from our reserved and rather formal neighbor, but I could see the flashing lights in the distance now. I scrambled into my car, backed it out of the roadblock, and raced along until I found the dirt road. Then I turned my headlights off, so my escape wouldn't be as easy to spot, and didn't turn them on again until I was several miles down the dirt road.

I took it slow, but even at twenty miles an hour, it was a rough ride. And it didn't help my anxiety that as I drove along, I called both Michael and Dad without getting an answer.

"Damn it, what are they doing?" I muttered.

Just then, my phone rang. I glanced at the caller ID. Chief Burke. I let the phone ring. I could pretend I still had the phone on vibrate and hadn't heard it. In fact, I flipped it over onto vibrate, just for good measure.

I'd call him back as soon as I got home and saw that everything was okay. Or got home and dealt with whatever wasn't okay. I was probably being hyper, I told myself.

But I had a bad feeling about what could be going on at home. I kept trying to remember exactly what Freddy had said on his cell phone call and wondering who he'd been calling. Trey—that was the name he'd used. One of his confederates? Surely there had to be confederates—I had a hard time imagining Freddy and Jasper running even a moderately successful criminal enterprise without some kind of competent help. Maybe even a boss who would want to tie up loose ends. Why did Rob have to mention that Dad and Dr. Blake might have taken the finches? What if this Trey knew who they were and where they might have gone?

I slowed down when I reached the ridge that gave me a view of our house. Only the one car, Sandie's, parked there. But that didn't mean Dad and Dr. Blake weren't there—they could have hidden their car. Or they might not have turned up yet.

I kept on till I reached Seth Early's driveway, where I turned in and parked. I locked the car, made sure I had my flashlight and that my cell phone was still on vibrate, and set out walking along the road toward the house.

Thirty-Three

When I reached our yard, I watched from behind the hedge. All was quiet. I crept along the edge of the yard to the barn and slipped inside. No contraband birds or vengeful thugs there or in any of the various outbuildings. The only birds I found were the ducks, roosting in their shed. Another shed still contained a couple of terrariums of snakes, which meant that Dad and Dr. Blake hadn't taken my diatribe on our need for a reptile-free environment as seriously as I'd have liked. The rest of the sheds were unoccupied.

I heard a noise from the house. A noise that sounded like a bunch of birds squawking. I glanced up and saw that light had come on in one of the third floor bedrooms. The squawking seemed to be coming from there. Then the light blinked out and the squawking subsided.

Aha! Had I caught Dad and Dr. Blake in the act of smuggling more birds into our house?

I was creeping up to peek in the back door when I heard a shriek inside.

"Want Kiki!"

I hurried the rest of the way up the steps and peered

in. Timmy's car seat was on the floor. He was strapped into it, flailing as hard as he could with hands and feet. His face was streaked with tears and snot.

Kiki was on the floor nearby. What was left of Kiki. She lay, limp and empty, with little piles of stuffing all around her. All my careful repair work had been undone, and she looked worse than she had after Spike had finished with her.

"*Kiki!*"

I controlled the impulse to rush in without thinking— that might not be the best thing for Timmy, or for me, either. Why had someone been eviscerating Kiki? To find the thumb drive, of course. Which probably meant that the person who'd ripped open Kiki was looking for evidence connected with the embezzlement. But only someone who knew Karen and Timmy reasonably well would think to look inside the stuffed cat.

Sandie. I backed away from the window, reaching for my cell phone, I'd call the police and—

"Don't move."

Sandie was standing at the foot of the steps, holding a gun.

"I'm afraid I can't let you make that call," she said. "Drop the phone, now."

I stared at her, pretending to be stunned into immobility. Actually, I was fairly stunned, but my brain was racing, making and discarding plans to rescue myself.

"Now," she said, gesturing with the gun. Then she giggled. "Wow, that sounded so dramatic. Like something out of the movies."

"Sandie—"

"It's too bad shooting people's not at all like in the movies. They don't get blown half across the room or spurt blood everywhere. They just die."

I dropped the phone.

"Now go inside."

She followed me up the steps. Timmy redoubled his efforts to get out of the car seat when he saw me.

"Auntie Meg!" he shrieked. "Want Auntie Meg!"

"It's okay, Timmy," I said. I went over to the car seat and hugged him.

"Out! Out!"

"Don't let the miserable little brat out," Sandie said. "I had a hard enough time getting him tied up in that thing."

"I'm sorry, Timmy," I said. "Sandie won't let me let you out. If I try, she might hurt me."

"Don't like Sandie," Timmy muttered.

"I don't either," I said.

"Well, pooh," Sandie said. "I'm just so broken up about that."

Bad enough that she was holding a gun on us, but did she have to be so . . . perky about it?

I swallowed my irritation. The thing to do was stall her. If Dad, Dr. Blake, and Michael were not here, they'd show up sooner or later. And surely Chief Burke would be mad enough to come looking for me before long. If I could just stall her.

I handed Timmy the limp shell of Kiki. He clutched the tattered bit of fur eagerly and began talking to Kiki in a low tone.

"Good thinking," she said. "Keep the brat quiet."

I turned to face her.

"You shot Jasper, didn't you?" I said. "Was it because of the finch-laundering?"

"The what?" she asked. She sounded puzzled.

"No, I didn't think so," I said. "Then it was because of—" I stopped myself. Probably not a good idea to admit that I knew Jasper's inside person in the embezzlement scheme wasn't Karen or Nadine but Sandie. And that she'd probably killed Jasper when he got greedy and hit her up for a bigger share of the cash. And set up Karen to find the body so she'd look guilty.

I saw, very fleetingly, a smug smile cross her face. Then she frowned, and steadied the gun.

"Knock it off," she said. "You think I'm going to stand around bragging about how clever I am until some of your family show up? I want the thumb drive. I know Karen hid it in the brat's stuffed toy—that's where she always used to hide stuff from Jasper. And now it's gone, so I know you took it. Where is it?"

"With the cops," I said.

"Yeah, right," she said. "You spent the last couple of days running around playing Nancy Drew, and when you find a hot piece of evidence, you turn it over to the cops."

"I didn't just turn it over to the cops," I said. "I made a copy and then turned it over to the cops."

Her face fell a little.

"Honest," I said.

"Where'd you copy it?"

Great. Now she'd try to trash my laptop.

"And then I e-mailed it to a friend who's a cyber expert," I said. "To see if he could decipher it. So there's no sense trying to find the thumb drive and collect all the copies, because they're not even all in the state by now."

Actually, they probably all were, unless Chief Burke had sent a copy to someone in Washington, but no sense getting her fired up to hunt down my cyber expert.

"How could you do something like that to me?" Sandie asked. Clearly she was a few ants short of a picnic.

"I wasn't trying to do it to you," I said. "I thought I was doing it to Nadine. In fact, with Jasper dead, there's no one else who knows you were in on it. Blame Nadine."

She shook her head. Ah, well; it was worth a try.

"I haven't got much time here," she said. "I want you to—"

We heard a knock on the door.

"Don't answer it," Sandie said.

"Fine," I said, with a shrug. "That'll look real normal, all the lights on and no one answering the door."

She thought about it for a moment.

"Okay, answer it, but if you try anything—remember, I've got the kid."

And if you do anything to him, I'll kill you, I thought. Even if I have to come back as a ghost to do it.

"Timmy—we should hide Timmy," I said aloud. Sandie glanced at Timmy's car seat and realized that I was right—Timmy was directly in the line of sight if I opened the door.

"I can just put him down here," I suggested, opening the basement door.

"Don't close the door all the way," she said. She inched around until she was in a spot where she was out of sight from the front door but had a good view of the basement door.

I picked up Timmy's car seat, pretending to find it harder than it was, and huffed as I carted it across the kitchen. Though thanks to my blacksmith work, I wasn't really having any trouble. And my back was to Sandie, so I hoped she didn't notice that while pretending that I could barely lift the car seat, I was actually holding it with one hand while undoing the buckles with the other.

"Sssh," I said to Timmy. "Don't move." He looked a little puzzled, and I was relieved to see that he didn't immediately leap out. I pushed the door almost closed so Sandie couldn't see him.

The knock came again. Sandie waved with the gun. I walked over to the door and opened it.

It was Rose Noire.

"Meg, what's going on?" she asked, stepping inside. "I just dropped your mother off from the garden party, and your dad wasn't home, and he's not answering his cell phone and then we called to see if he was over here and you didn't answer, so I came over to see what was going on."

"Relax," I said. "I have no idea where Dad and Dr. Blake are, but Michael talked them into letting him go along, so I'm sure they'll be fine. And the reason I didn't answer is that after I finally got Timmy to sleep, I must have conked out myself while watching TV." I pretended to stifle a yawn. "Thanks for waking me, though—I always get a crick in my neck when I sleep on the couch. I'm going to bed."

"Are you sure you're all right?" Rose Noire said. "Your aura is very strange tonight."

"My aura's probably tired," I said. "I know the rest of me is. Busy day. I'll tell you about it later, though. Hey, why don't we meet for a burger tomorrow at the grill? You can bring Sammy."

Since Rose Noire was a passionate vegetarian, I was hoping this suggestion would strike her as odd. And since Sammy, in addition to being one of her beaux, was also one of Chief Burke's deputies, I was hoping maybe she'd get the message and call the cops.

She blinked.

"Okay," she said, after a few seconds. "That sounds nice."

She was turning to leave when a brightly colored bird suddenly flew down the stairs and began fluttering around the chandelier.

"What's that?" Rose Noire asked.

"A Gouldian finch," I said, trying to sound nonchalant. "Dad and Dr. Blake are keeping a few upstairs in one of the bedrooms."

"Oh, dear," she said. "Look what he's doing to your rug."

Yes, the Gouldian finch was doing what most birds do when stressed or excited. Assuming I figured out a way to survive whatever unpleasantness Sandie had planned, I'd worry about the rug tomorrow.

"Do you want me to help you catch him?" she asked.

"No, you go on home," I said.

The finch tired of circling the lamp and flew into the kitchen.

"Birdie!" Timmy exclaimed from the kitchen.

"Stop!" Sandie yelled.

"Get out and get help!" I said, giving Rose Noire a shove out the door and slamming it behind her.

In the kitchen, Sandie shrieked, and then a shot rang out.

"Oh, my God," I muttered and headed for the kitchen.

The finch flew out, leaving another white streak along the hallway floor, and I almost collided with Timmy.

"Run away!" I said, and ran to open the front door for him.

"Stop right there!" Sandie said.

Instead of running outside, Timmy continued up the stairs after the finch.

I followed Timmy.

When we reached the second floor hallway, we met a flock of Gouldian finches coming down from the third floor. To judge by the number of droppings they were producing, none of them were too happy about the situation.

"Birdie! Birdie!" Timmy called, and jumped up and down, trying to reach the brightly colored finches.

"Keep running," I said.

Our arrival spooked the finches, and they wheeled and headed back up toward the third floor. Timmy gave chase and I followed.

"Stop!" Sandie called. She fired another random shot, and I heard breaking glass.

It occurred to me, halfway up the stairs to the third floor, that I should have stayed on the second. The second floor was more completely furnished, which meant I'd have had a better chance of finding something to use as a weapon. On the third floor, the only two rooms that contained anything were the bedroom at one end of the hall, where Rob had been stashing his stuff, and the bedroom at the other end, where I'd seen the cage of tropical birds.

When they reached the third floor, the finches swooped in a circle around the light fixture a couple of times and headed for the room they'd presumably come from. Timmy followed, thus narrowing down my choices.

The first thing I saw after bursting into the room was a cloud of brightly colored birds whirling in front of my eyes. Some were Gouldian finches, but there must have been several other species as well.

Then I spotted Michael, Dad, and Dr. Blake. They were all three trussed up, hand and foot. But apparently Sandie was less experienced in bondage than Freddy, and hadn't thought to anchor them to anything. Michael was hopping from birdcage to birdcage, opening the cage doors with his teeth. Dr. Blake was hunched over by the window, trying to dial a cell phone with his nose. Dad was in one corner, and appeared to be attempting to stuff himself into the dumbwaiter, in preparation for a Houdini-like escape.

They all three greeted my arrival with glad cries. At least I assumed, from the expressions on their faces, that it was glad cries they were trying to utter through the neckties Sandie had used to gag them.

She had also used neckties to tie them up. I felt a twinge of irritation at her lack of consideration. Totally irrational, but I knew how much Michael's ties cost, and for that matter, how pricey it was to clean them. I spotted Michael's tie rack on the floor nearby—apparently she'd wrenched it off the wall and brought it in here. It only had a couple of ties left. Couldn't she have used something else? Because clearly I was going to have to slice the ties off to free everyone and, assuming we all survived this, replacing Michael's entire tie wardrobe was going to be expensive and troublesome.

I'd worry about that later, I thought. I realized that I still had the utility knife stuck in my pocket and reached for it.

Timmy seemed to think the hopping was a wonderful game, and was hopping around madly. Bad enough that I was thinking of waylaying a gun-toting criminal when the only weapon I had was a utility knife. Doing it with Timmy in harm's way—

"Dad!" I said. "Let's send Timmy down in the dumbwaiter. Rose Noire's calling for help."

Dad wriggled out of the way and, to my immense relief, Timmy was charmed with the dumbwaiter and crawled in without even being asked. I quickly sent him down ten or fifteen feet and was pulling out the utility knife to begin slashing ties when—

"Stop that! Hands up!"

We turned to see Sandie standing in the doorway, pointing the gun at us. Well, waving the gun all around in her attempt to cover all four of us.

"Drop the knife!" she snapped at me.

I followed orders.

"Get over there," she said to Michael, waving him in our direction. "You too," she added to Dr. Blake.

Michael hopped over to my side. Dr. Blake used more of a slow shuffle.

"Sometime today," Sandie said.

"He's over ninety," I said. "That's as fast as he goes."

Dr. Blake gave Sandie a look that ought to have felled her, and growled something through his gag.

"Where's the kid?" Sandie asked.

We all looked innocent. I shrugged. Sandie looked around. We might have gotten away with it if Timmy hadn't chosen that moment to giggle.

"What's that—a secret tunnel? Get away from there!"

We all obediently hopped, walked, or shuffled away from the dumbwaiter door. I tensed to jump her—surely while she examined the dumbwaiter and figured out how to raise the platform Timmy was on, she'd have to take her eyes off us for a few seconds.

"Uppie!" Timmy shouted from the shaft. "Want uppie!"

Sandie began shuffling around the perimeter of the room toward the dumbwaiter door. She didn't take her eyes off us. Nor did I take mine off her. Sooner or later—

Suddenly she screamed, and leaped into the air. This sounded more like panic than anger. I looked down and realized that the missing Emerald Tree Boa had reappeared, and had slithered over Sandie's foot on the way to the birdcage.

"Snake!" she shouted. She leaped back, fired a wild

shot at the snake, and knocked over one of the bird-cages in her flight. Panicked birds fluttered around the ceiling and fled the room. Michael, Dad, Dr. Blake, and I all hit the floor as she continued whirling about and firing wildly.

It could only have been a few shots—she'd already fired several at the finches and the snake—but it seemed to go on forever. When I finally heard the click that meant she was out of ammo, I leaped over, tackled her, and sat on her.

"Is everyone okay" I asked.

I heard the distorted sound of Michael, Dad, and Dr. Blake trying to talk through their gags. I glanced over. Dad and Michael were nodding vigorously. Dr. Blake was scowling, and appeared to be scanning the room for something.

Holding Sandie's arm in a hammerlock, I dragged her with me over to where the tie rack was and used two of the remaining ties to bind her hands and feet.

Then I raced over and managed to pull the gag out of Dr. Blake's mouth.

"What's wrong?" I asked. "Where are you hurt?"

"I'm fine," he said. "But it'll be a miracle if she didn't hit any of the birds. Is the boa all right? Untie me so I can check."

"The boa's fine," I said. "I'm going to—"

"Put the gun down!" I turned to see Rose Noire, hair wildly askew, standing in the doorway holding a pitch-fork.

"Relax," I said. "She's tied up. Are the police on their way?"

She nodded, eyes still darting left and right for enemies.

"Great," I said. "Start untying everyone, will you? I'm going to put the snake back in the hall bath, before he eats any of the birds. Then I'll come back and help you."

"Uppie! Uppie!" came Timmy's voice from the dumb-waiter.

"Oops," I said. I draped the snake over my shoulders, the way I'd seen Dr. Blake do it, so I'd have both hands free to haul the ropes. When Timmy's head appeared in the dumbwaiter doorway, his eyes lit up.

"'Nake!" he said. "Want 'nake!"

"This is Dr. Blake's snake," I said. "If you behave yourself until we get everyone untied, I'll find you a snake of your very own."

Timmy sat down in a display of ostentatious good behavior. He stayed that way for a good ten seconds. Then he popped over to look out of the window.

"'Leese cars!" he exclaimed.

Thirty-Four

Two hours later, we were all still answering questions from Chief Burke, the DEA, the USF&WS, the state troopers, and even a few stray Clay County sheriff's deputies who'd followed the state troopers over to our house and hadn't quite given up hope that some of the excitement might have strayed over onto their turf. But I could tell that the end was in sight. Not that anyone was running out of questions, but I could see that Chief Burke was running out of patience with the various interlopers.

And also running out of patience with my questions.

"Yes, we've got Freddy's accomplice in custody," he finally said, the fourth or fifth time I asked. "It was another one of his cousins. Trey Hamilton. You didn't really need to skedaddle back here in such a hurry. Trey's no killer. We picked him up halfway to Richmond with a flat tire and a van full of foul-mouthed parrots. And if he and Freddy give us a whole lot of information about the higher-ups in the smuggling business, they might get out of prison in time to collect social security."

He also got a little irritated when I asked if Sandie's gun was the same one that had killed Jasper.

"We can't just eyeball it and tell, you know," he said. "We have to send the darned thing down to the crime lab in Richmond, and overworked and backed up as they are it could be weeks before—"

"I understand," I said. "But is it at least the same caliber?"

"Yes," he said, as if he begrudged even that one syllable.

The proverbial last straw landed when a grim-faced woman from the county social services department showed up to take charge of Timmy.

"Ms. Walker is refusing to talk any more until she can see for herself that her son is safe and sound," the social worker said. "I'm supposed to take him down to see her."

I glanced down at Timmy, who was sprawled across my lap. He was fast asleep. So was my left leg.

The social worker looked at her watch.

"They told me to hurry," she said.

I shook Timmy awake as gently as I could.

"Wake up," I said. "You're going to see Mommy!"

"Mommy?" he said, sleepily. He slipped off my lap to stand on the floor and look blearily from side to side, but he kept one hand on my leg while the other held Kiki in a death grip. Kiki was overdue for another round of major repairs, but thanks to the safety pins, cotton wads, gauze, and adhesive tape from my traveling first aid kit she probably wouldn't fall apart until things quieted down enough that I could get to work with the sewing kit.

Or would it be Karen wielding her sewing kit? She hadn't looked all that seriously injured at the accident scene, so maybe she'd be able to go home and take Timmy with her.

"Yes," the social worker said, cheerfully. "I'm going to take you to see your mommy!"

She came closer and bent down to pick him up.

"No!" he shrieked. He scrambled back into my lap and threw both arms around me.

"But I'm taking you to see your mommy," the social worker said.

"No!" Timmy wailed. "Want Auntie Meg!"

I stared at him in astonishment. Okay, so over the last few days, Timmy had no doubt gotten used to me, but I assumed he'd drop me like the proverbial hot potato the minute Karen turned up again.

"We see that sometimes," the social worker said. "They feel abandoned by their parent and cling to the caregiver. He'll get over it."

I found myself frowning. Cling to the caregiver? Get over it? Wasn't it possible that Timmy had become just a little fond of Auntie Meg? And for that matter, wasn't it even more probable that Timmy was objecting not to the idea of seeing Mommy but to the prospect of some stranger tearing him away from the place and people who had become familiar over the past few days? Not even a very friendly looking stranger, though I suppose I should make allowances for the fact that she'd been awakened well past midnight to come and get him.

And she was trying to reunite Timmy with Karen— the same thing I'd been working on so hard over the last several days. And it wasn't as if I'd never see him again. Odds were he'd need a place to stay for another night or two. After all, even if they didn't detain Karen for some reason, she couldn't very well go home to her trashed apartment at the ghastly College Arms. She could come to stay with us—plenty of room—and let me and Dad and the rest of the tribe look after her and Timmy for a bit.

"Come on, Timmy," I said. I pried his arms loose and then took a firm grip on the hand that wasn't holding Kiki. "We'll go down together to see your mommy."

"But we're not finished with her," the DEA agent and the USF&WS agent said in unison.

Chief Burke exploded.

"Not finished!" he roared. "Damn it, these are honest, God-fearing, law-abiding citizens of my county. They've been answering your questions for three hours, and if you want the continued cooperation of the Caerphilly Police Department, you treat them properly, you hear?"

"Don't worry, Chief," my grandfather said, popping out of the dining room where another set of agents had been interrogating him. "A little persecution from misguided authorities will make for a much better story when I'm editing my special on the finch-smuggling ring."

The chief scowled at him.

"And the excellent cooperation from the Caerphilly police will make such a wonderful, enlightened contrast," Michael added, popping in from wherever they'd been interrogating him.

"Definitely," Dr. Blake said.

"Sammy," the chief shouted. The young deputy also

popped in, as if he'd been waiting for his cue. "You take Ms. Langslow and Master Timothy down to the station to see his momma. The rest of us will be coming along as soon as we can."

"But Chief—" one of the Feds began.

"And anyone who has an objection is welcome to leave now, and file a complaint with his or her agency head and the Caerphilly Town Council in the morning."

Nobody cared to voice an objection, so the various interrogators and suspects began shuffling out to the cars. Scout, the hound dog, came over and thrust his head at the chief to be petted. Scout had arrived with the police and followed the chief from room to room for the past couple of hours. From the calmer look that came over the chief's face as he was petting Scout, I had a feeling the dog had already found a new home.

"I'll need to pack some things for Timmy," I said to the chief. "Everything's upstairs in his room."

I picked up Timmy and headed for the stairs.

"I hope you're not expecting to offload your little charge immediately," he said, following me. "I don't think Ms. Walker did anything wrong—well, nothing criminal, anyway. Stupid, yes, all that running around and sneaking and making it harder for us to figure out what was going on, but if stupid was a crime, the town would be out of jail space. But it might take a few days for all these Feds to figure that out. Of course, the contents of that thumb drive you gave me should do the trick. Apparently Ms. Walker got some pretty conclusive evidence that this Sandie person was the embezzler."

"I thought the thumb drive files incriminated Nadine," I said "Did I just interpret that wrong or—"

I suddenly realized that I was confessing to something the chief might consider tampering with evidence.

"I should have expected you'd be messing with that thing," the chief growled.

"I made a copy," I said. "In case something happened to the original before I got it into your hands."

The chief snorted.

"But what about Nadine?" I asked again. "If she's not in on the embezzling scheme, what was she running away from?"

"Dust," the chief said. "Her house was empty because she'd put all her furniture in storage so Duke Borden's decorating shop could come in and redo the floors. Which, as you probably know from all that construction you did on this place, kicks up a heck of a lot of dust. She was going on a Caribbean cruise till the floors were done and Duke's crew had given the whole place a white-glove cleaning from attic to cellar."

"Does that sound reasonable to you?" I asked. "That she would have someone doing that much work without being there to see that it was done right?"

"Doesn't sound reasonable to me, no," he said. "But she's a Pruitt by birth and you know how those Pruitts are."

"She's a Pruitt?" I exclaimed. "Why didn't you tell me? It explains how she can afford a two-million-dollar house in Westlake. Though not why she's working at the college."

"No idea," the chief said. "Except those Pruitts always think they know best when it comes to running the college. Incidentally, I didn't mention that you had anything to do with making her miss her boat."

"Thanks," I said. "I can just see her sabotaging Michael's paycheck for the next decade out of spite."

"She is spiteful," the chief agreed. "Keeps threatening to sue the department. Well, she has the right."

"Talk to Dr. Driscoll," I suggested. "Nadine's boss. I'm sure he could convince her that if she sues the department, it will all come out about how she never noticed the embezzlement going on right underneath her nose. I suspect that will cool her urge to sue."

"Now that's a right smart idea," the chief said. "Thank you."

"You're welcome," I said. "Getting back to Karen—"

"As I said, I don't think she had anything to do with the murder or the embezzlement, but she's got a lot of explaining to do. Why didn't she just turn in that thumb drive herself? And why did she hide from us?"

"She was going to turn it over to you—she asked me to at the accident scene," I said. "But when she found Jasper's body, she panicked. Knew he was in with some bad people, and she was afraid they'd come after her and her son. So she brought him to me for safekeeping. And she was probably afraid you'd suspect her of the murder, at least to begin with, so she hid until you'd have time to find the real culprit."

"More likely she was expecting you to figure it out," he grumbled. "If more people would talk to the police, we'd have a lot easier time solving crime around here. And you have no idea how much trouble you've been the last few days, popping in and out of that damned cockatiel farm every five minutes. Been a full-time job convincing the damned Feds that you're not a drug smuggler, just a meddling busybody."

"Sorry," I said. "If I'd known you were taking Karen's disappearance seriously and making the hunt for her a priority, maybe I'd have stayed out of it. I thought you suspected her of the murder. Now that I know what was going on that I didn't see—well, I'm sorry I added to your stress."

The chief snorted.

"Which is a good ways still short of promising you'll never do it again," he said. "Well, it all worked out in the end." And then, as if annoyed with himself for unbending that far, he stomped off. Dad and Dr. Blake came in.

"Meg, what's wrong?" Dad asked. "You look pale."

"I think Chief Burke understands that Karen wasn't involved in the embezzlement or the murder," I said. "But I'm not sure about some of the other agencies."

"I'm sure the chief will bring them around," Dad said. Did he really think that, or was he just being optimistic?

"Don't worry," Dr. Blake said. "I've already called both those lawyers whose names you gave me. They're on their way down to the station, and I'll make sure they have Karen on the list of people they're supposed to represent, if need be. Between the two of them, I'm sure they'll sort all this out."

"Speaking of sorting all this out," I asked, "where did all those finches come from? There were only six here yesterday."

"Well," Dad said. "Last night we were right in the middle of stealing them—"

"Confiscating them," Dr. Blake corrected.

"When a car drove up, and we thought it was Freddy coming home," Dad went on. "It turned out to be Rob, bringing Ms. Hamilton home from the airport, but it still meant we had to cancel the mission for the evening. We thought we'd have to call it off entirely—it was heavy work, carrying those cages, more than we could handle at our ages."

"Speak for yourself," Blake said, with a sniff.

"But when Michael volunteered to help us—well, that was perfect!"

"Unless they put all three of you in jail for burglary," I said.

"I'm sure it will turn out all right," Dad said. "But we should be getting down to the station to make our statements. Wish us luck."

"Good luck, Dad," I said, giving him a quick hug.

Dr. Blake looked rather wistful. What the hell.

"And you, too, Grandpa," I said, giving him a hug of his own.

He stiffened, as if he wasn't quite expecting my hug, but he looked pleased.

"Don't worry," he said. "If they try to railroad your friend, we'll stir up a hornet's nest!"

Something he was all too good at, I thought with a sigh. But strange to say, I found it nice to think that he was on our side.

They strode out, passing Michael on the way in.

"Here, let me help you," he said. "Timmy, want a horsie ride downstairs?"

Timmy thought about it a moment, then held out one arm as if to agree to the transfer. Clearly he was very tired. He merely slumped over Michael's head as if about to fall asleep.

"He should be in bed," I said, hoisting the bulging diaper bag to my shoulder and heading for the stairs again.

"Well, it's been an unusual night," Michael said. "He'll love having another ride in the police car, and we can get him back into his normal schedule tomorrow."

"Not really," I said. "After all, his normal schedule would involve being with Karen. I don't think Karen is guilty of anything except panicking, but what if they convict her of something anyway? I can see Karen pleading with me to take care of Timmy, just until she gets parole. And me dutifully mailing off pictures of his first day at school, his lead role in the class play, his prom date, his wedding. . . ."

"Well, if it comes to that, we'll cope," Michael said. "He's a good kid. Make a good consolation prize if I can't convince you we need a couple of our own."

"Or a nice big brother to those couple of our own," I said. "But let's hope in a few days' time he'll be back with his mother and we can discuss the whole kid issue in peace and quiet."

Michael looked happy at that, and there was a bounce in his step as he carried Timmy out to Sammy's patrol car and set him down. Timmy reflexively grabbed onto my pants leg.

"Okay, Timmy," I said. "We're going to take a ride

in the police car, and then we're going to see your mommy!"

Timmy perked up slightly. He wiped his nose, partly on my pants leg and partly on Kiki, and nodded.

"Come on, Kiki," he said. "Go see Mommy."

Read on for an excerpt from

Swan for the Money

the next Meg Langslow tale from Donna Andrews—
available soon in hardcover from Minotaur Books!

"Dreadful news!" Dad said.

He collapsed into a chair at the foot of the breakfast table, as if no longer able to bear the weight of his dire tidings, and wiped his balding head with a pocket handkerchief. The head, the handkerchief, the hand holding it, and nearly every stitch of his clothing were so encrusted with mud and garden dirt that Mother would probably have ordered him off to take a shower immediately if she weren't so visibly curious to hear his news.

"Yes?" she said, one hand clutching her throat in a gesture that would have looked artificial and old-fashioned on anyone else. On her it merely looked elegant.

"We've lost Matilda," Dad said.

"Oh, no!" she exclaimed. From her expression, I could tell that she found this news genuinely heartbreaking.

Faint murmurs of sympathy arose from the dozen assorted friends and relatives seated around the table, but I could tell from their uniformly puzzled faces that they were all mentally asking the same question I was: who the heck was Matilda?

We used to have a Matilda in the clan, my Great Aunt Matilda. But she'd been dead for years, and I couldn't recall anyone else gracing a recent arrival to the family with such an unusual name. Nor could I remember any friends or neighbors named Matilda. There was a time when I would have assumed Matilda was one of Dad's patients, but he was semi-retired now, and his medical practice consisted mostly of those same family, friends, and neighbors, whose names I would recognize. Not a Matilda in the bunch.

"And what's more," Dad went on, sitting up and frowning fiercely, "it was foul play. No question. I only suspected it with Adelaide, but I'm sure of it now."

"It's the Pruitts," Mother said. "I've suspected them all along." Not surprising. The Pruitts were an old local family who used to own most of Caerphilly County and often behaved as if they still did. Most locals were quick to blame the Pruitts whenever anything sneaky or underhanded took place. Mother and Dad only spent weekends here in Caerphilly, in the old farmhouse they'd dubbed their summer cottage, but they were quickly picking up many local attitudes.

"You suspect the Pruitts of two murders?" my brother, Rob, asked. "Have you told the police?"

"Murders?" Dad echoed. "What murders?"

"This Matilda and Adelaide you're talking about," Rob said.

Dad burst into laughter. I suddenly realized what he'd been talking about.

"It's not murder," I said. "Because Matilda and Adelaide aren't people, are they? They're roses."

"Meg's right, of course," Mother said, sounding slightly cross, as if baffled at how long it took us to figure this out.

"Sheesh." Rob returned to his food. "Roses. That's all we talk about these days."

"Now you know how I feel," I muttered, though not loud enough for anyone but Michael to hear. For the last two months, ever since Mother had recruited me to organize the Caerphilly Garden Club's annual rose show, roses had taken over my life. Normally I'd be asleep at this hour, not trekking to my parents' farm to collect boxes of rose show equipment and hauling them to the farm whose owner, Mrs. Winkleson, was hosting tomorrow's show. And normally the gala breakfast might have made up for the early hour, but today my stomach was wound too tightly to enjoy it.

"Can't we talk about something else for a change?" Rob was saying.

"Peonies, for example," my husband, Michael, said. "Much more practical for our yard. They don't require a lot of cosseting, like roses, and the deer don't seem to eat them."

I could tell from Rob's face that he didn't consider peonies a conversational improvement over roses, and Mother and Dad ignored the interruption.

"Meg," Mother said to me, "your father needs coffee." She managed to give the impression that only with an instant infusion of caffeine could Dad possibly survive this new horticultural tragedy.

"I could use some, too," Michael said, and shot out to the kitchen before I could even push my chair back.

"Matilda and Adelaide were two of my most promising black roses," Dad said to the rest of the table.

"And two of our best chances for winning the Winkleson Trophy," Mother said. "Which will be given out this weekend at the Caerphilly Rose Show to the darkest rose," she added, on the off-chance that any of the assembled relatives had managed to escape hearing about the Langslow household's new hobby of breeding and showing roses.

"Is there a big prize?" Rob asked.

"No money involved," I said. "Just the thrill of winning."

"Big thrill," Rob said, through a mouthful of scrambled eggs.

"And a trophy," Mother added. "Quite possibly a lovely engraved Waterford bowl. That's what I suggested." Yes, that sounded like Mother's kind of suggestion. She was a confirmed human magpie, easily seduced by anything that glittered, and a sucker for anything that had ever come out of the Waterford factory.

"Well, if the winning rose is bred by the exhibitor, there's always a remote possibility that a commercial rose company might want to buy it," Dad said. "Of course, that would only happen if it were a significant advance toward the creation of a truly black rose. All the big commercial breeders have their own black rose breeding programs."

"And ridiculous programs to begin with," put in my grandfather. "A genuinely black rose is a scientific impossibility."

"Oh, I hope not," put in my cousin Rose Noire, *aka* Rosemary Keenan, to those who had known her before she'd become a purveyor of all-natural cosmetics and perfumes and adopted a name to match. "I do hope one day to greet one of my namesakes!"

She probably would. Talking to plants wasn't even unusual in my family. Although Rose Noire was one of the few who expected the plants to answer.

"Useless things, roses," my grandfather said. "Had all the vitality bred out of them, so the poor things can barely survive without massive applications of chemicals all the time. Environmentally unsound." A typical reaction from my grandfather, Dr. Montgomery Blake, the world-famous zoologist and environmental activist. Of course, he could merely be vexed that Dad's rose-growing was preventing him from working full-time on the Blake Foundation's latest animal welfare campaigns, whatever they were.

"Getting back to Matilda and Deirdre—" I said.

"Adelaide," Dad corrected.

"Sorry," I said. "It's no wonder I didn't recognize the names—last time I got an update on your rose breeding program, you were just referring to them by numbers."

"But that's so dehumanizing!" Rose Noire exclaimed.

"Don't you mean deflowering?" Rob asked, with a snigger.

"How can you expect a living creature to thrive when all it has is a number, not a name?" Rose Noire went on.

"That's why we decided to name them," Mother said.

"Unofficially, of course," Dad added. "I haven't yet

registered them with the ARS. Officially, Matilda is L2005-0013."

"But we're going to name them all after family members," Mother said.

"No shortage of names there," Dr. Blake muttered. He was still getting used to the fact that when he claimed Dad as his long-lost son, he'd found himself allied by marriage with Mother's family, the Hollingsworths, whose numbers exceeded the population of some small countries.

"I hope you stick to dead relatives," Michael said, as he emerged from the kitchen with a pot of coffee. "Otherwise we'll have no end of confusion. And imagine if it got around the county that Rose Noire was suffering from black spot disease, or that Rob had thrips."

"What are thrips?" Rob asked, looking alarmed.

"Getting back to Matilda and Adelaide," I repeated. "What happened to them, and what makes you think it was foul play?"

"They were eaten," Dad said. "Undoubtedly by marauding deer. And I found this in some bushes nearby."

He held up a small brown glass bottle with a neatly printed label proclaiming that it contained "100% Doe Urine."

"James!" Mother said. "At the breakfast table?"

"Someone obviously sprinkled this near Matilda," Dad said. He tried to pocket the bottle discreetly, out of deference to Mother's sensibilities, but Dr. Blake held out his hand for it. "In fact, they probably sprinkled the stuff in a path leading from the woods straight to Matilda."

"Yuck," Rob said, making a face. "If I was a deer,

I'd steer clear of roses some other deer had already peed on."

"But you're not a deer," my grandfather said. "To a deer, especially a male, doe urine would be an irresistible lure. Hunters have used deer urine for centuries to cover up their human scent and attract deer to their hunting areas. It's particularly effective if the urine is—"

"Dr. Blake!" Mother exclaimed. I wasn't sure whether she was objecting to his words or to the fact that he had opened the bottle and was sniffing it curiously.

"So hunters use the stuff," I said. "You're sure that bottle wasn't just discarded by some passing hunters?"

"We hadn't given anyone permission to hunt our land," Mother said.

It took a few seconds for the grammatical implications to sink in—the fact that she said "hadn't" rather than "haven't." Did her use of the pluperfect tense mean that now, after Matilda's demise, they *had* given hunting rights to someone? But by the time that thought struck me, Mother and Dad were deep in a discussion of which surviving black roses were likely to produce a prizeworthy bloom by Saturday's contest. Everybody else appeared to be listening attentively, or as attentively as possible while consuming vast quantities of bacon, sausage, country ham, French toast, waffles, pancakes, cinnamon toast, croissants, and fresh fruit. Were the rest of the family really that interested in rose culture, or did they just figure they'd better come up to speed on the subject in self-defense?

"Meg," Dad said, "I'm leaving this in your hands."

He gestured to my grandfather, who ceremoniously handed me the empty doe urine bottle.

"Yuck," I said, dropping the thing on the table. I wasn't normally squeamish, but my stomach rose at the thought of the little bottle's former contents. "What in the world do you expect me to do with it?"

"Find out who used it on Matilda," Dad said. "And help me figure out how to stop it. I'm counting on you!"